DOWN

with the

SHINE

Also by Kate Karyus Quinn

Another Little Piece

(Don't You) Forget About Me

DOWN

with the

SHINE

Kate Karyus Quinn

HARPER TEEN
An Imprint of HarperCollinsPublishers

HarperTeen is an imprint of HarperCollins Publishers.

Down with the Shine
www.epicreads.com

Library of Congress Control Number: 2015947488
ISBN 978-0-06-235604-8 (trade bdg.)

Typography by Brad Mead
16 17 18 19 20 CG/RRDH 10 9 8 7 6 5 4 3 2 1
❖
First Edition

To my mom and dad

DOWN

with the

SHINE

PROLOGUE

"I gave you my name for a reason, Lennie. It might not be worth much now, but someday, someday real soon, I'm gonna make it so Cash is a name nobody ever forgets. I'm serious, Lennie. People are gonna remember us."

When I was a little kid, I didn't get tucked into bed with a story or a song. Instead, I listened to the ravings of my father. The nightly routine ended on my sixth birthday. That was the day he made the nightly news for the first time and they rechristened Leonard Cash the Bad Daddy Bandit.

Over the next two months, Daddy and I crisscrossed the country on a hold-'em-up, shoot-'em-down crime spree. With me in tow, he took down six banks and three toy stores, killing two people who got in the way. He was finally pinned down at a Chuck E. Cheese's, but managed to escape by taking the guy dressed in the mouse costume as a hostage. They found me hours later, burrowed deep in the ball pit, still waiting for Daddy's all-clear whistle.

The only place I've seen him since then is on the FBI's Ten Most Wanted webpage.

That all happened eleven years ago, but it's not the sort of story people forget. Maybe if I'd become a super-smart honor-student nerd or a chipper rah-rah leadership council type, they'd dwell on it a little less often. But I'm not either of those things, and most people think it's just a matter of time before my daddy comes back for me and the two of us pick up where we left off at Chuck E. Cheese's oh so many years ago.

To a stranger, I might look like a typical sullen, angry teenager, but everyone in town knows I'm the furthest thing from typical.

I'm Lennie Cash.

And my famous name is a big part of why, at this exact moment, instead of dividing my time in English class between clock-watching and trying to figure out exactly how those two crazy kids, Romeo and Juliet, managed to mess things up so badly, I'm sitting in the principal's office while she and a cop give me the "bad blood will tell" glare.

This is the third time I've been called down to the office for one of these sessions since my best friend, Dylan, went missing two weeks ago.

The first meeting was more of a "we're all on the same team" type of chat. That's when the cops thought Dyl was a runaway. I told them I didn't know anything, which was half true, and that I hadn't heard from her, which was totally true. When I left the room, I caught only the slightest hint of "of course the Cash kid is involved with this."

Things were a little more serious the second time. That was after they found Dylan's car at a rather infamous bar on the outskirts of town. They asked me if Dylan went there a lot. If I'd ever been there. Mostly they were fishing, waiting for me to slip up. Or at least that was the only reason I could think of for why they never came right out and said anything about the rumors that Leonard Cash had been spotted at this bar more than a few times. Some people even said he might be the owner.

The one thing they didn't skirt around was the very public fight I'd had with Dylan the day before she disappeared. "I heard you were extremely angry," my principal, Mrs. Kneeley, said, feigning concern.

"Well, yeah, we were fighting," I answered, sounding sarcastic and, yes, angry.

A lawyer probably would have told me to keep my mouth shut. But I didn't have one of those, or anyone else. My mom and her three brothers were my official guardians, but none of them were the school-meeting type.

Which meant that if Dyl didn't show up soon, I could see this getting real ugly for me. Still, I insisted I didn't remember what the fight was about. I was trying to protect Dylan, trying to give her time to do whatever crazy thing she thought she needed to do before they found her and dragged her back home.

In my own way, I was trying to make up for that fight. For saying things I shouldn't have.

This time, though, I think it may be too late, 'cause the cop and Mrs. Kneeley look dead serious. I know from their expressions that we're not fucking around anymore.

All dramatic, the cop slams his hand on the table. After getting a good jump out of me, he moves back again, leaving behind a plastic sandwich bag with a piece of paper inside.

The paper is yellowed with age and red with . . .

Not blood. Please not blood.

"You recognize this?" the cop asks. His name is Detective Otto. He's introduced himself each time we've done this, but I still just think of him as "the cop."

I look past the red smears, to the words.

Yes, I recognize this paper. And I know exactly where they found it.

"It's mine," I tell him. "From when I went to camp a few years ago."

Actually, it was more like seven years. I'd begged my uncles to let me go, thinking I could spend a week with a bunch of kids who didn't know me. Of course, the counselors recognized my name and figured everything else out pretty quickly . . . and the gossip trickled down to every kid there. At the end of two weeks, after being caught at the center of the first brawl in Camp Onawanta history, I came home with my official happy camper certificate shoved into my suitcase. It said: Lennie Cash Earned the Following Camp Onawanta Badges: _____. On that line, the camp director had written: *I'm sorry but I don't think Lennie and Camp Onawanta are a good fit. She will not be allowed back next year.*

I never showed it to my uncles; I just crumpled it up and shoved it under the ripped lining of the suitcase. Now seeing it again, I feel the old shame and embarrassment fill my throat. I want to grab the paper from the cop and rip it to pieces, but he's already tucking the plastic-enclosed piece of my past into his manila folder.

"Do you know where we found this?" he asks.

I nod. "In my old suitcase. Dylan borrowed it."

A few weeks before she disappeared, Dyl had discovered the suitcase at the back of my closet, where it had sat since that disastrous camp experience. She'd declared it "awesomely vintage." I gifted it to her on the spot.

"Do you know where we found that suitcase?" The cop leans in, his voice hard.

"No." I whisper the word, suddenly afraid. The red stains. This new urgent, angry tone.

I hadn't been worried about Dyl before this moment, but maybe that was a mistake. Dylan has always been tough and fearless . . . and reckless. She is exactly the type of person to be stamped with an early expiration date. "Is Dylan in trouble? Did you find her?"

In the moment before he answers, I try to make a deal with God—or whatever it is out there that keeps the world spinning. If Dylan returns in one piece, I'll destroy my uncles' distillery and shut down their moonshine-making operation. If I were God, I'd think that was a pretty good deal. My uncles' moonshine has been the cause of countless troubles and sorrows; seems like nipping it in the bud would save him a whole lot of headaches.

"Yeah, you could say that we found her." The cop glares at me and too late I figure out he's one of those people who hates me on principle.

Still, he's the guy with the answers, so I ask, "She okay?"

"What do you think?" He pulls out another paper from his folder and again slaps it down in front of me.

This is the moment when God laughs at my stupid little deal. When he tells me where I can shove it.

Because this time a photograph lies on the table in front of me. At first I can't make sense of the image. The purple plaid of Dyl's favorite flannel shirt mixed with red red red and then feet and her dyed black hair and a hand . . .

My brain actually refuses to understand exactly what I'm seeing until the cop helpfully adds, "Or most of her anyway."

"Detective!" Mrs. Kneeley, looking as sick as I feel, reaches past him to flip the photo over and hide it from view.

She's too late, though. Much too late.

'Cause that's how I find out that my battered old suitcase, patched up with duct tape and kept closed only with the help of an old leather belt, now holds the butchered remains of my best friend.

BAD

FIVE MONTHS LATER

It had been Dylan's idea to crash Michaela Gordon's party. She'd spent weeks trying to talk me into it last year. I told her no way, no how, over my dead body.

"Next year then, Lennie," she'd said. "You've got a year to prepare yourself, so no excuses."

"Not gonna happen," I'd replied with a roll of my eyes.

And yet here I am, one year later, filling a grocery bag with four mason jars full of my uncles' infamous bathtub moonshine, which Dylan promised would be the magic ticket into Michaela Gordon's almost equally infamous back-to-school Labor Day party.

It's not like I think doing this is gonna bring Dyl back. Or that she's peering down from heaven, cheering me on or something cheesy like that.

It's more like once you see your best friend chopped up

into pieces, it changes you. It makes you reexamine your own life and choices. And after five months of this type of introspection, I've decided that I'm sick of taking the path of least resistance, sick of trying to stay out of trouble when it always finds me in the end anyway, and sick of letting assholes like Michaela Gordon tell me I'm not good enough to play beer pong with their pals.

To put it simply: I'm mad as hell and I'm not gonna take it anymore. So yeah, I'm going to the party to fulfill a dead girl's wish. But that's not all of it. I'm also going to that party to

FUCKING

OWN

IT.

But first I have to get my uncles out of the way.

Unlike most responsible adults, my uncles wouldn't care about me going to a "my parents aren't home so let's drink till we puke" type party or even coming home from that party totally wasted. They would, however, object to me dipping into the moonshine supply for the purpose of handing out free samples.

That's 'cause making moonshine is the way my uncles earn their living. It's a family business, actually. They can't put a sign out front, due to their business being the type of thing that can get you sent to jail, but if they did have one it would say: Hinkton Family Moonshine: Brewing It in Bathtubs and Selling It Out of the Living Room Since 1923.

I realize this sounds sketchy, and you wouldn't know it by the way we live, but business is good. The same people who call us trash behind our backs come knocking at our door with wads of twenties in their fists. You can see the horror on their faces when they're invited in and told to take a seat. And when they finally leave with their brown paper bag clutched in their hands, it's clear they're thinking that Jet and Rod and Dune are more crooked than the falling-down house we live in and as hard to judge as their dogs who, depending on their mood, might lick your hand or bite it. Yet despite all that, most of them come back for more.

So I understand why slipping a few free jars to my friends is a big no-no. It's a rule I never considered break-ing before because when I get in trouble with my uncles, I don't get some sissy punishment like getting sent to my room. My uncles always said that if I'd been born a boy, they woulda beaten the hell out of me, but seeing as how I was a girl and more easily broken, they instead punished me by locking me out of the house until they got over being angry at me for whatever I had done. I just hope that this time I don't make them so mad they change the locks completely.

They'll be real pissed at me, that much is certain. Not only am I taking the shine, but I'm also using one of their favorite things in the world to betray them: Dinty Moore beef stew.

Inspiration struck this morning as I eyed the stacks and stacks of Dinty Moore covering almost every inch of counter space. My uncles had bought twenty cases off a friend of theirs a few days ago. Half the stuff in our house, from the TV to the toilet paper, fell off the back of a truck and was then sold to us at bargain-basement prices. When I was seven years old, I was terrified of driving behind trucks for fear that big leather couches like the ones my uncles had just gotten would come flying out and smash me to bits.

Now I wander into the living room, where the uncs are watching the three flat-screens stuck to the wall. *Die Hard*, SportsZone, and some Food Network show play on the respective screens.

I flop down between Uncle Rod and Uncle Jet and watch with them for a little bit. After we finish cheering as Bruce Willis shoots up a bunch of bad guys, I say in what I hope is a casual tone, "So that's a shit ton of beef stew you got in the kitchen. Which one of you is gonna eat the most of it?"

This seemingly innocent question is all it takes to set

off a series of boasts, put-downs, and finally challenges to decide once and for all which of the Hinkton boys can put away the most Dinty Moore in one sitting.

I reluctantly agree to officiate the contest.

One hour later, Uncle Dune is in the lead by two cans. This isn't a huge surprise. All three of my uncles shop at the Big and Tall store, but Dune's the only one who has to duck when walking through your average doorway.

"Lennie!" he bellows, even though I'm standing right in front of him. "Make me another."

Uncle Jet and Uncle Rod, refusing to fall further behind, shovel their last bites into their mouths and shove their bowls at me as well. "Mine too."

In the kitchen, I open and upend cans thirty-eight, thirty-nine, and forty. The stew plops into the bowls with a wet and rather unappetizing slurping noise. I pull the last three melatonin pills from my pocket and stir them in. I've already given each of my uncles the maximum dose of sleeping pills, but the melatonin is natural so I'm pretty sure a little extra won't cause them to OD.

After a few minutes in the microwave, I put the bowls on the sheet pan I'm using as a makeshift serving tray and carry them back out to my uncles.

I gasp in shock when I turn the corner and see all three of them slumped sideways, fast asleep. I mean, yeah, that's what I was going for, but I didn't expect it to work so quickly or so well, and I feel an unexpected twinge of guilt.

Sure, the uncs may not be the most nurturing people out there, but when my dad disappeared and Mom made it clear she was pretty much useless, they stepped in and took care of me. Of course, you could argue that I've paid them back by mostly staying out of trouble and keeping the complaints to a minimum. I never whined when they skipped out on school events or protested when they thought it was funny to play connect the dots on my arms when I had chicken pox or sulked when I had to remind them it was my birthday. I always sort of understood that my uncles were doing the best they could. Now, I can only hope they extend the same courtesy to me.

I grab a pile of blankets and take a few minutes to tuck them in. I also check their pulses, just to make sure I didn't overdo it on the pills. When I get to Uncle Jet, his eyes flutter open.

"Lennie," he rasps.

Even in his sleepy state, I can hear the threat in that one word and I take a step back.

"Dead," he says, and then repeats it so the message is clear. "Dead." His eyes close again and he begins to snore.

Feeling reassured that my uncles will survive the stew

incident, although considerably less certain that I will, I tip-toe upstairs to get ready for the party.

Fifteen minutes later, I'm in clothes that don't have a noticeable Dinty Moore stink to them, and I've added some pink stuff to my lips and cheeks and sparkly goop to my eyelids. After running my fingers through my half-curled, but mostly just tangled hair, I decide that I am officially as prettied up as possible.

Still, I can't stop myself from taking one last detour— this time crossing the hall into my mother's bedroom.

"Mom," I call, tapping on the door. I don't really expect an answer. The knock is more of an announcement that I'm coming in.

As I crack the door open, I am instantly hit with the stench of stale cigarette smoke.

Mom's in her usual place at the window, her head and shoulders leaning out into the warm night air. Everything about her looks washed out, from the mess of ash blond hair spilling down her back to the gray robe wrapped around her body. It's like she's trying to disappear into the cloud of smoke that always surrounds her.

Walking closer, I notice that she's sucking on the last quarter inch of a cigarette. That's my mom—so dedicated to each cigarette she'll even smoke the filter.

"Mom," I say again.

There is no reaction to indicate she's heard me. All interactions with my mother are like talking with someone over a bad long-distance connection. There are extended lapses between responses, and some things get lost entirely. As has been my habit for years, I start to mentally count: *One Mississippi. Two Mississippi. Three Mississippi.*

"Huh?" My mother mumbles at last. Her head slowly turns in my direction, right as I reach thirty Mississippi.

Her eyes never meet mine, but fixate on a point somewhere beyond my left shoulder. Throughout our conversation they will undoubtedly dart between that point and a similar one hovering in the vicinity of my right ear.

"Got any plans tonight?" I ask.

With one fluid movement, she puts out the burnt stub of her cigarette in the Niagara Falls souvenir mug on the windowsill. I watch the cigarette butt smolder among the dozen or so other stubs, while she taps a fresh one from her pack and lights it.

She smokes.

Meanwhile, I count. *One Mississippi. Two Mississippi.*

She finishes that cigarette and immediately lights yet another. I'd say my mom smokes like a chimney, but I'm pretty sure even a chimney observing this behavior would be like, "Whoa, lady, take it easy."

Out of all my uncles, Dune is the one who makes a

special effort to look after Mom. He talks to her even when she doesn't answer. Brings her special treats that she'll only take one or two bites of. One time I asked him why, and he explained how way back when they were little kids, Mom and Dune were the youngest two in the family and were pretty tight. "Right up until she met your father, I woulda said we were best friends," he told me, sounding super sad and non-Dune-like. It's always weird to hear about my mom from before. I've only known her this way, so I sometimes forget that she was once normal. Well, as normal as my family gets, anyway.

Thinking about all this stuff is depressing, so I go back to counting.

At fifty Mississippi there is still no answer, so I figure I might as well fill in the blanks for her.

"Staying in then, Mom? Well, I'm going out and wanted to know if you'd check on the uncs. They went a little overboard on the beef stew and I'm worried they might not be feeling so good."

Mom sucks hard on her cigarette, then turns away from me to exhale a long plume of smoke out the window. When she turns back, she focuses on my face. It's so strange to have her eyes on mine that I almost look away.

"You're dressed as your father, in his boots made to walk over anyone who got in his way," she says, in her strange, high-pitched voice.

I look down at my feet, practically bare except for the few bits of leather winding between my toes and around the back of my heels. Then I look back up at Mom.

"Yeah, it's a costume party," I tell her. "One where you try to make it real hard for people to guess who you're dressed as."

"Anyone with eyes can see who you are."

"Well, maybe I'll get lucky and some eyes will fall out."

Mom blows a mouthful of smoke up to the ceiling. "If you're lucky." Then she stands and marches toward me and for a moment I'm afraid of that lit cigarette in her hand. Not that she's ever been violent—she usually goes out of her way to avoid me. But she's being weirder than usual, and I have no idea how to predict her next move. So I take one step back and then another and another, until the wall is at my back and Mom is directly in front of me.

Her cigarette-free hand comes up and covers my heart. "I'm a part of you too, Lennie. You were both of ours, but then he took and I gave and you were left between us, but no longer quite of us."

I am not really sure how to respond to this, but Mom doesn't wait for an answer. She takes a step back and holds her cigarette between us, with the glowing red tip pointed toward the ceiling. "Make a wish," she says. As if it's a birthday candle. Or a jar of shine and we're doing my uncles' toast.

I sigh. And then play along. "I wish you'd check on the uncles tonight while I'm gone."

It's like she doesn't even hear me. "You get a chance to make a wish, Lennie, you ask to be bulletproof." Her knuckles rap against the side of my head.

"Yeah, okay," I answer, brushing away the cigarette ashes that were shaken loose onto my shoulder.

But Mom is already wafting past me, out of the room and down the hallway. A moment later, I hear the bathroom door clunk closed and the lock click into place.

"If you're too busy, don't worry about it," I tell the empty room.

Clumping back downstairs, I try to recapture the earlier energy that had every bit of me buzzing in anticipation. Now I feel drained and can sense myself slipping back into the depressed, "I just want to be alone" mood that has been my default setting since Dyl's death.

I need to get my head right. If I walk into that party looking like a kicked puppy, I'll deserve every last bit of the abuse I'll undoubtedly receive.

Trying to once more find the rage that has driven me this far, I pull out my cell phone and dial into my voice mail. "You have no new messages. You have one saved message. To hear your saved message press four."

I hit four. *Boop*, replies my phone. And then this:

"It's Smith. I just wanted to call and say, to call you and tell you, that you should know, in case you don't already . . . It shoulda been you, Cash. Not Dyl, but you. She didn't deserve to go that way. She—" His voice breaks. "Fuck."

That's the end of the message. I replay it three times. Once to hear how Dylan's twin brother carefully enunciates his words in the beginning, the way drunk people do when pretending they're sober. Another time to hear the way he calls me Cash instead of Lennie, like the kids at school, never missing a chance to remind me who I came from. And finally so I can catch the sob at the very end that escapes before he can hang up the phone.

In the month since I received that voice mail, I've listened to it more times than I can count. I know Smith didn't intend for it to be a gift, but in so many ways it was. I cried for days after hearing it the first time. I sobbed and shook and beat my fists against my own body, all with my personal volume level on mute so that my uncles wouldn't hear and tease me about some boy breaking my heart. By the time I finished, I was so drained that I pushed my face into my tear-logged pillow and passed out. I slept for almost a whole day, and when I finally woke up, I realized

I couldn't do this anymore. I didn't *want* to do this anymore.

Dyl was a reckless, fearless idiot and that's almost certainly why she's dead now.

I am a frightened, play-it-safe idiot and will probably live a good long miserable life because of it. Except, at least for tonight, I've decided it's smarter to follow in Dyl's wonderfully reckless fearless idiotic footsteps.

I take a deep breath and feel the banked fire inside of me flare to life once more.

Much better.

After making sure that I save the message, I shove the phone back into my pocket and head into the basement to grab my stash of moonshine.

It's time to party.

BETTER

Clutching the clinking and clanking bag of booze to my chest, I walk as fast as I can in my strappy sandals across the packed dirt scattered with tufts of weeds that my uncles call a lawn. As the dogs begin barking madly and throwing themselves against the chain-link fence, I pick up the pace a little more.

Even with my uncles out cold, I am still relieved to see that Larry followed instructions, parking several houses down and keeping his lights off. Reaching the car, I pop the door open and slide into the passenger seat. As softly as possible, I close the door behind me. "Go, go, go," I tell Larry while grabbing my seat belt.

"Gosh," Larry answers, his usually low voice breathy and high. A moment later the engine revs loudly . . . but the car doesn't move. I reach for the gearshift and move it from park to drive.

"Try again," I say, doing my best to be patient.

"Right. Thanks." He hesitates for another moment, probably trying to remember which is the gas pedal, and then we finally shoot forward.

I twist in my seat to watch my house disappear from view, and as we turn the corner an unfamiliar thrill of energy goes through me. Between my dad and the uncs, getting off on doing something I shouldn't is undoubtedly written deep into my DNA.

"Lennie," Larry says, his gigantic hands squeezing the car wheel nervously. They must be sweating something awful; I've already watched him wipe them on his pants twice. "I don't know if this is a good idea."

I'm too on edge and too angry and too much of an asshole to say something reassuring.

But I also know that I can't scream at him to shut up and grow a pair.

I can't because he's my ride.

And also sorta kinda my friend.

He would say that I'm his best friend. And maybe someday something more. He doesn't think I know about that second one. But I can see the way he looks at me all moony. I know why he gets pouty and sullen if another guy talks to me, even if that guy is only passing along an insult. And once, when we were wrestling after playing paintball, I counted six times that his hands "accidentally" grazed my boobs.

But the "and maybe someday something more" isn't my problem with Larry. My problem with Larry is that I don't want to be his or anyone else's friend. I know it's melodramatic to say that my friends tend to die young, since it's only happened once. But the thing is, I've only ever had one friend. Dylan. Nobody was interested in the position before she came along. And after the way she died, well, I sorta figured she'd be the last.

Larry had been my lab partner in biology for all of junior year. Most of our interactions went like this:

Me: You understand what we're supposed to do?

Larry: No. Do you?

Me: Not really.

Larry: Oh. Huh.

Me: Yeah.

As the year wore on, we sorta bonded over our shared C and D grades. And I was sorta impressed by his ability to laugh no matter what shitty things people said to him. Everything seems to simply roll off his enormous back.

And then Dyl disappeared. The first half of April was lost in a haze of growing anxiety while the rest of it is just . . . blackness. I skipped school as much as possible, and even when I was physically present, I wasn't truly there.

I hardly noticed when Larry started following me around and doing things like meeting me at my locker. And while part of me thought it was pretty fucking presumptuous for him to assume he could slip into Dyl's place, at the same time it was . . . nice. Comforting, even. In the last week before summer break, we hung out a few times after school and got embroiled in an epic *Grand Theft Auto* battle that somehow stretched into late August.

During all this time, he's only asked one gently probing question about Dyl—that I immediately shut down. He's never said shit about my family. I would've torn his head off if he had, so maybe that's just Larry showing some good sense. Or maybe he's a genuinely nice guy. I suspect the latter, and as much as that eeks me out, it kind of intrigues me too. It's like being friends with a creature you've always thought was only make-believe, like a unicorn. It seems too good to be true. So I'm constantly waiting for him to tear the horn off and become an ass like everyone else.

In the meantime, Larry has two other things going for him.

Number one is his size. At six foot five and 250 pounds, Larry is big enough to be intimidating. Not that he uses his size to do anything. He has this idea that it isn't fair for him to hit back because he's so much bigger than everybody else.

Number two is his car. When he turned sixteen, Larry's parents let him pick out any car he wanted. He chose a bright yellow Mazda Miata. I don't know how the salesperson kept a straight face watching Larry climb into that tiny convertible for a test drive. Seeing him in this car reminds me of when I had my Ken doll use a Matchbox car to pick up Barbie at her shoe box house. It's still nice, though, to have a friend with wheels. Especially one willing to drive me wherever I want to go and who never thinks to ask for gas money.

"Lennie." Larry says my name again. Louder. And whinier. "Maybe we should go to my house instead. Watch a movie or play some *Donkey Kong.*" After growing tired of *Grand Theft Auto*, *DK* has become our new obsession. Normally, I'd be all over that suggestion, but tonight—

"No."

"My mom made her amazing chocolate cake."

"Your mom hates me."

"She—" Larry stops. He doesn't like to lie. "*Donkey Kong?*"

"Yes, I have a weakness for *Donkey Kong.*"

"Yeah. *Donkey Kong* rocks."

I laugh, for a moment forgetting I don't *really* like Larry. It happens occasionally. "Yes, he does, but not tonight. Tonight *we* rock. It's gonna happen exactly the way I've been telling you. Once they see what we've brought"—I jingle the jars in the bag at my feet—"they're gonna roll out the red carpet for us. Just trust me, okay?"

Larry wipes his sweaty palms once more, gulps, wiggles his butt in his seat, before finally grinning. "Yeah. Yeah!" He fist-pumps the air. "You're right, it's gonna be great." He sounds like he believes it. As if my saying it makes it true. As if I am someone worthy of trust.

Cleary, Larry is not the sharpest guy around.

. . . Or maybe not, because at first everything does go exactly as I said it would.

We walk in like we own the place, not slinking in the back past the idiots doing keg stands, but strolling right through the front door and straight into the kitchen. One by one I pull the mason jars out of my bag and line them up on the glass table. I can feel a crowd gathering behind me, but nobody says a word. Grabbing the first one, I spin the lid off and let it hit the shiny hardwood floors. Larry snags a plastic cup and holds it out to me, but I push it away. "You always drink moonshine straight from the jar," I say. It's not strictly true—tradition only dictates that the first swig comes straight from the jar— but I like the way it sounds. I push the shine into Larry's hand and then pick up a second one for myself. Off comes the second lid.

"Make a wish," I say to Larry, holding up my jar.

This is another moonshine ritual I've seen performed a million times. Everyone buying shine needs to have a drink with my uncles first. Uncle Rod usually takes the lead, slurping a bit from the jar of shine and then pouring a few fingers into some *Looney Tunes* glasses they got from a gas station years ago. My uncles sit at the kitchen table with the poor schmuck, and as he lifts the glass to his lips they tell him to make a wish. Usually it's some eye-roll-worthy, sad-sack nonsense like, "I wish my wife weren't so mean to me" or "I wish I could get that promotion at work." "Penny-ante shit" is what Uncle Jet calls it, but then he's quick to add it's better that way.

They never miss a chance to remind me to dream small.

I'd coached Larry in the car, not wanting him to ruin our first impression by saying something stupid like, "I wish I was home playing *Donkey Kong*." I told him to say, "I wish I were the king of this party. Bow down, bitches!" He practiced, but every time it came out of his mouth like a question. And he refused to say "Bow down, bitches." He thought it sounded too mean.

Now Larry's eyes meet mine and I can see the panic in them. "Um," he says. Around us people snicker.

Larry gulps. "I hope my mom isn't mad at me tomorrow."

I narrow my eyes, promising retribution, but make my

mouth smile as I give Larry his wish—with a little embellishment. "To your mom and everyone else's parents' staying chill, no matter what!" Then I add the words I've heard my uncles utter so many times: "May all your wishes come true, or at least just this one!"

He clinks his jar against mine. Then in unison, we drink.

The liquid dribbles out the sides of my mouth and burns going down. Smiling, I wipe my mouth with my sleeve. Next to me, Larry is doubled over, coughing hoarsely. I make a big show of taking the moonshine from him and patting him on the back. "Sometimes the first sip's like that," I say.

Another half-truth. The first sip is always like that.

My uncles rubbed the stuff on my gums when I was a teething newborn, poured a finger of it into hot tea anytime I had a cold, and every April Fool's Day they find some way to make me take an unwitting taste of the stuff, whether by soaking my toothbrush in it or mixing it into the milk I pour over my Cocoa Krispies. And yet, despite all that, I have no tolerance for it. The shine leaves a scorched path from the tip of your tongue all the way to your belly. The only reason I'd been able to take a swig without coughing was the bottle of Chloraseptic I'd sprayed onto my throat before leaving the house.

By now the entire party is trying to squeeze its way into the kitchen. Everyone wants to know whether we'll be welcomed or thrown out on our asses.

Here's the thing about Michaela Gordon's party: only the coolest kids are invited. The rest of the school comes to ride it like a bucking bronco—you hold on as long as you can until someone throws you out. For the cool kids, finding horrible new ways to let the unworthy know they're unwelcome is part of the fun. And for everybody else who comes to school the next week with Sharpie-covered faces, or still clutching their stomachs after being force-fed laxatives, there is a strange mixture of shame and bravado in announcing that they were at Michaela's for thirty-eight-and-a-half minutes and three of them were at the exact time the Barney twins performed their topless table dance.

If we're gonna get tossed, this is the moment it's gonna happen.

Just when things can't get any tenser, Michaela Gordon herself comes pushing through the crowd until she is standing right in front of me.

Own it, I remind myself.

I brazenly shove one of the jars at her. "Have some moonshine," I say. Then, holding up my own jar, I officially throw down the gauntlet. "Make a wish."

"I wish this party would never end," she says with a smile that makes her look rather sharklike. "At least for those who last till morning."

Of course, she had to get her dig in, knowing I'll be ushered out long before the sun rises. But I'd rather she talk shit to my face than my back as I'm being tossed out the door, so I only reply, "To a party that rocks all night and forever more! May all your wishes come true, or at least just this one!"

Michaela doesn't bother waiting for me to finish before she tips the jar back and takes a long swallow. A moment later she is bent over and gasping, waiting for the fire in her throat to go out.

I suddenly doubt the wisdom of this whole plan. Michaela Gordon does not like to look like a fool. Gently, I reach down to take the jar of moonshine from her, but she jerks it away and slowly straightens to face me. Her watering eyes have made her mascara run in streaks down her cheeks. I am tempted to apologize, to minimize the damage I've already done. I think about how right my uncles were—the stars in the sky are not to be reached for, but to remind us how small we truly are.

But then Michaela Gordon clinks her jar against the one I'm still holding. "Look out liver, here it comes," she says, her lips tilting into a sly smile.

Grinning, I bring the jar up and take my second deep swallow. And this time—the crowd cheers.

It is perhaps the best moment of my life. I am at the biggest party of the year and I am owning it.

Bow down, bitches.

BEST

After that, things get blurry. Every time a new group of partygoers pushes its way into the kitchen for a taste of the moonshine, I go through the whole routine. Wish. Toast. First sip.

It's a lot of first sips. I lose count after a while.

Even people who make a point of letting me know my place in the universe at least once a week get in line, make a wish, and drink with me. Some of them high-five me when they finish, like we're suddenly best pals.

In between I keep asking for, "Water. I need to drink water so I don't get drunk." Someone presses a glass of it into my hand, and I drain it in a few long swallows.

Then there is dancing. Another thing I hate that suddenly feels good. Larry and I thrash and spin and sing along, not caring that we're getting most of the lyrics wrong.

Next thing I know, I'm lecturing a group of freshmen who were lucky enough to make the official list of invitees about the brilliance of my uncles' moonshine. It's my uncles' sales pitch, which I've heard a million times.

"Making moonshine has been in our family for generations and everyone who knows about it agrees it's the best moonshine around, taking top honors in the three essential moonshine tests." I try to hold up three fingers, but can't quite manage it and settle for all five. "One. Most likely to make a man fight someone he loves for no good reason." I point in the direction of the screaming couple in the next room. "Check."

The freshmen look impressed.

"Two. Most likely to lead to bad life decisions while under its influence." This time I have to scan the room for a moment, mostly because it is spinning around me. Finally, I locate Arnold Tuney kissing Blake Graham. Arnold is out of the closet. He is the cool girl's token gay. Blake is a guy who has been dating the same girl for three years and routinely refers to people, places, and things he does not like as "gay." This time the freshmen don't need me to point, they have followed my gaze and are staring in open-mouthed shock.

"Check. Wow, Arnie could really do better." I shake my head, lose track of what I was talking about, and have to be reminded why I'm holding my hand up in the air.

"Right," I say. "Finally—and most important of all— it's likely to make you so goddamn drunk you don't even care about the other two." I don't have to point to any particular person for this. The whole party is insane. People are puking everywhere and then turning around to get more beer. They are too drunk to know better. Michaela's house may never be the same. It gives me a certain satisfaction. Maybe the freshmen feel it too, because they all look back at me and say, "Check."

By the time I open the final jar of moonshine, I feel certain that my whole life has changed. The crowd cheers me as a hero. We are all best friends, drinking from the communal jar of love. For the last few sips they even pick me up and place me on the dining room table.

Raising the jar of moonshine above my head, a gigantic grin on my face, I know I look like an idiot, but somehow I can't stop smiling. The world isn't the horrible place I thought it was. The world is great. It's awesome and full of possibility that I was simply never drunk enough to see before.

I open my mouth to tell these wonderful people here how much I love them and how happy I am to be here with them tonight.

And then Smith walks into the room.

He has his arm slung around some long-legged girl who goes to another high school, or maybe even college. Smith is so cool he can't date girls who go to his own school. After all, where's the challenge in that?

Of course, half the room turns to stare at him and his latest hottie. *You idiots,* I think, *why do you all fall for his "coolest guy in the world" shtick?* The only problem is that my gaze is also aimed squarely in Smith's direction, drinking in his skinny jeans, worn T-shirt, dark hair that looks casually tousled but has actually been painstakingly styled, and signature smirk. You know the kind of smirk I'm talking about. You want to slap it off his face. Or kiss it off.

Okay, fine. I'm leaning toward the second one and even worse, I'm so drunk that I forget to hold back the drool and naked longing.

And that's when his eyes collide with mine.

Briefly.

It is much too long.

Smith. Dylan's twin. Dylan. Oh, Dyl. Dead, dead Dyl.

It all comes roaring back.

How could he think that I'd had something to do with what happened to her? He should have known better. Maybe he did. Maybe he'd just been looking for an excuse to hate me. For being the one who didn't die. And I hated him for that because once we'd been . . . not quite friends, but close. He hung out with me and Dyl sometimes and we often ended up laughing at the same things, grooving to the same music, reaching for the same potato chip.

All right, so maybe I was inflating small moments.

Smith pivots, dragging his girlfriend with him, back out the door.

"Have a drink, Smith." The moonshine takes over my mouth and I actually yell these words at his retreating form.

Along with the crowd I hold my breath, waiting for his reaction.

Smith pauses the length of three erratic heartbeats and then looks over his shoulder, flipping a lock of hair from his eyes while doing so. The bastard must practice that move in the mirror, it is that good. He raises an eyebrow, which seems a bit over the top at this point, but my wobbly knees don't think so, especially when he pairs it with his trademark crooked smirk.

"Thanks, but I'm not sure if I'm up to date on my tetanus shot."

The crowd laughs loudly, loving it. Stupid drunks, that doesn't even make sense. It's shine, not a rusty nail.

"I get it," I toss back, all casual. "You're scared."

"OOOOOHHHHHH." The crowd obliges.

Now it's my turn to smirk, because I've got him and we both know it.

There is something about the male brain that makes it particularly susceptible to the threat of being called a chicken. They will do the dumbest shit to disprove it.

Smith, though, is worse than the average male. He and Dylan threw dares at each other the way other siblings might've played tennis for sport. Except they volleyed increasingly dangerous challenges, never backing down, always wanting to hit it back harder.

The crowd parts for Smith as he sprints toward the table, charging at me and reminding me of another one of my uncles' favorite sayings: "Mess with the bull, you'll get the horns."

My liquor-soaked reflexes are too slow to do anything except pull the moonshine close to my chest, protecting those last precious drops from harm.

It's a smart move, 'cause Smith leaps and, with the same grace he uses to clear the track hurdles, lands on the table beside me. The whole thing rocks and my free arm windmills, looking for something to keep me on my feet. But there's only Smith.

My fingers brush against his shirt sleeve. I don't grab hold, though. Falling seems safer.

Just when it seems that the floor is my destiny, Smith's

arms circle around me. Our noses brush and his eyes are so close to mine I can see the little flecks of green and gold that swirl through the brown. His hands are warm against my back and the only thing keeping us from being completely sealed together is the jar of moonshine still clutched to my chest.

I swallow loudly, and something flickers behind Smith's eyes. In the romance novels my uncle Dune (not so) secretly loves, the heroines are always reading things in the heroes' eyes. They soften with love, grow hard with anger. Sometimes, if they're really furious, they'll shoot sparks. I can't say what Smith's flicker means, though. Maybe he's thinking about that time we kissed. Maybe he's thinking about that message he left me. Or maybe he's gagging from my booze breath.

In case it's the last one, I close my gaping mouth and lean back so I can bring the jar of shine up between us.

"Make a wish?" The words come out soft and husky, not brash and confident the way I've been saying them all night. The sound of them brings up a bubble of sadness that I quickly swallow back down.

All the while Smith studies me and I can only hope he's no better at reading eyes than I am.

"I wish," he says, his voice pitched low but easily reaching the ears of everyone in that hushed kitchen. "To be there when you get what you deserve."

It's a sucker punch. It shouldn't be, but it is.

So I remind myself of the lessons Smith's little voice mail taught me. Crying doesn't do anything except make me soggy and tired. But getting good and pissed, that's the type of fuel that keeps a person marching through one shitty day after another.

I suck in a gasp of hurt surprise, and breathe it back out as fire.

"And I suppose you're the one who's gonna give me what I deserve?" I laugh like it's a joke and jab a finger into his chest for good measure.

And there's the Smith smirk™. "Nope, not me. I just want to be there watching."

"Kinky."

"It's my wish." Smith shrugs.

"Okay," I say slowly. "Well, I wouldn't want you to miss a thing. So you can have a front row seat when I 'get what I deserve.' Or even better—you can take my hand and deliver me straight to the devil's door yourself. That work for you?"

"It'll do."

I shove the jar at him. "To going to hell hand in hand!" He brings the jar to his lips and tips his head back, letting it flow down his throat. He coughs and gasps, but somehow he makes even that seem cool, 'cause he laughs through it, as if he's thinking, *Ha! Is that the best you can do?*

"May all your wishes come true. Or at least just this one." I spit the words at him and then take a sip, completing the ritual that no longer seems quite as funny.

I hate Smith then. A different type of girl might've given in to the booze blues and started crying. Or asked him what the hell his problem is.

But I only know how to be myself, so I drink more. And this time I toast myself.

"And *I* wish that Dylan was back home, in one piece, alive and safe in her bed." I bring the jar up. Over the lip of the glass, Smith's eyes burn holes through me. Fuck him. It's the wish he should've made and he knows it. I thrust the jar toward him for the second time. His jaw clenches but he takes it nonetheless.

I finish things with a soft, "May all your wishes come true, or at least just this one," while Smith throws the moonshine toward his tonsils. A second later he pushes the jar back into my hand, leaps from the table, and cuts through the crowd where he escapes out the door.

The kitchen is crammed full of people. And every single one of them is staring up at me expectantly, wanting to see how this drama will end.

They'd love to see me bawl my eyes out. I have no

intention of giving them the satisfaction.

I lift the jar above my head. "Bottoms up!" My voice is too loud, clownishly happy, and thiiiiis close to turning into a drunken sob.

"Bottoms up," they yell, and for the last time I tip the jar back and drain it dry.

MUCH
WORSE

The next thing I know, I'm in the bathroom, where Larry is curled up next to the toilet.

"I wondered where you went," I tell him, even though before this moment, I'd sorta forgotten he existed. To make up for that, I gently pat his head.

"I'm dying," he moans.

"No, you're not. It only feels like you are. Give it a day . . . maybe two. You'll be fine."

Leaning forward, Larry dry heaves into the toilet. "I should've listened to my mom."

"Your mom who hates me? The one who told you to stay away from me?" The rage particular to moonshine rises out of me. "Screw you, Larry. Why don't you call your mommy and cry to her, then."

I am screaming, but somehow I still hear Larry say, "Sorry, that's not . . . I just meant that she said not to drink." Except I can't hear it, not really, because it's like every demon I've held at bay my whole life has been released inside of me.

"Sure, Larry, of course that's what you meant." I stomp toward the door, but stop before slamming it behind me, wanting to see his face when I deliver my devastating last line. "You must think I'm as dumb as you are."

I see Larry flinch right before the door slams closed, blocking him from view. I have never called Larry dumb before. It's a thing with us. I think it all the time, but never say it. Except now I have. Before regret can sink in, though, the moonshine churns, propelling me through the crowd until I am outside. The air is wonderful and cool and also I am making out with someone. I realize at some point that it is Blake Graham.

"Hey," I mumble, trying to remember something about him. Before I can say anything more his tongue pushes its way back into my mouth.

That's the last thing I remember.

Then I am in a moving vehicle. Not belted in, but lying on the floor. I open my eyes and see the stars above me. My uncles' truck, I think. But that doesn't make sense. They'd be mad about the party and the moonshine, but coming to drag me away isn't their style. I'm scared, but the truck shakes and shimmies and I pass out again.

The next time I come to is worse. I hear the sound of water. Bodies press against me on either side. I lift my head slightly, just enough to count the ten other people scattered around me in the truck bed. Seven guys, three girls, all splayed out, curled up, or lying prone. I recognize each of them. Like me, they are freaks and outcasts so low on the social ladder they should be ashamed of even *thinking* about Michaela's party, much less attending it.

I slump back down and let my heavy eyes close once more. I've been tossed from the party and while I wish I could say someone made a mistake and that I don't belong here, it's not true. Who was I kidding? Did I really believe a few jars of shine were enough to change my life?

And then, as if the universe wants to make sure that I really and truly got the message, water begins to pour down. We're all soaked in seconds. The deluge ends as abruptly as it began, only to be replaced by soap. I squeeze my eyes and mouth closed too late. From the spitting noises around me, I'm not the only one. Everyone's awake and prepared by the time the scrubbers come down.

Yes, we are at the car wash. After getting watered down, soaped up, and nearly blown away by the drier, we finally emerge back out into the night. Before we can exhale a great big communal sigh of relief, tons of camera phones begin to flash around us as several of Michaela's buddies compete to capture the moment for posterity and Instagram. The cherry on top of all this is someone's car radio cranked up and blasting out that old disco favorite, *"At the car wash, whoa whoa whoa."*

I pull myself into a sitting position in time to watch Michaela saunter toward us. Actually, there are two of her, I think. I squint, trying to bring her into focus, as she leans against the side of the truck and smiles the tight bitchy smile she's known for; Dylan used to do an amazing impression of it.

"I wish I could say that all of you clean up nicely, but . . ." Michaela and her double both laugh.

"Bitshhhh," I slur like an idiot. Michaela laughs again.

"Don't try to talk, sweetie. You've got a lot of liquor inside you still . . . although it does look like some of it's in your hair. Oh, and the cough syrup we poured in your beer is probably messing with you a little bit too."

Furious, frightened, and more than a little betrayed, I try to take a swing at Michaela, but only manage to painfully connect my fist with the side of the truck. Michaela—and now with the clarity of pain, I can see the second girl is not a double, but Blake's girlfriend, of course—gets another giggle out of this. I hate them both, but my eyes are so heavy, and if I let them close for a minute . . . just long enough to gather my thoughts . . .

I wake again, still groggy as hell and now dizzy too. At first I think I'm alone because all I can hear is my own heavy breathing. But there's a hand wrapped around my ankle, and another slowly sliding up my bare leg. The heavy breathing isn't mine. It goes along with the owner of those hands. I squirm, trying to shake him off.

"Don't be like that, Lennie." This voice I recognize instantly.

Walsh Weathers Junior. Otherwise known as W2, which is a nickname his family gave him when he was a baby. They own Weathers Chevrolet, and W2 comes to school in a brand-new pickup truck every month. That explains whose truck bed I'm lying in. The car wash too. Damn.

W2's goal of feeling up every girl in our class is well known. Hell, he even brags about it. "The dykes, the fatties, the nerdies, the Jesus-lovin' super virgins. I want 'em all."

It's gross. And parties full of drunk girls are his main hunting ground.

I know all of this, but for some reason it hadn't even crossed my mind that he might try to cross me off his list tonight.

Because I thought I'd owned that party. I thought that maybe things had finally changed.

I'm an idiot, that's for sure.

Most people would say that right now I'm getting exactly what I deserve. They said the same thing about Dylan when she went missing. That she'd hung out with trash like me and I'd led her to the biker bar where she was last seen. They didn't know that the big fight we'd had was over me telling her to stay away from there. That the uncs had told me that place was bad news, and if they thought so, then it definitely was. Or maybe if people knew that, they'd blame her more. They would say she'd been looking for trouble. But I knew Dylan better than that. We were both looking for the same thing, and it wasn't trouble. Despite her big house, beautiful mother, and heroic dead father, what Dyl and I both longed for was escape.

When she was still missing, I overheard a group of teachers whispering about how she might be "dead or worse." I don't know what's worse than dead. Even now with W2's hand slithering north of my kneecap, I wouldn't prefer death. And I'm not going to lie here like I'm dead while he gropes me as if I'm his own personal blow-up doll.

Filling my lungs, I scream. One of his hands quickly covers my mouth. I wiggle and thrash until he removes it. For an instant I think I'm winning, until W2 squeals. "What the hell, Smith?"

I look up to see that Smith has W2 in a headlock.

Smith has come to my rescue. My eternal flame of hope flares to life once more.

And then Smith . . . laughs.

Laughs at me, lying there soaking wet and helpless.

"Not the plan," he says, releasing W2.

All hope is fully extinguished as W2 whines, "But I didn't get to the boobies yet. Come on, bro, ya know I need the boobies for the list."

Smith and I were never friends, but he always treated me kindly. He probably knew I had a crush on him. One too many times he caught me staring at him, especially when we all sat basking beneath the summer sun beside their Olympic-size swimming pool. His bare chest, tan and muscled, water dripping down as he did pull-ups on the edge of the diving board . . . Of course, I stared then.

But that wasn't the only time.

Or the worst of it.

No, that was a few months before Dylan went missing. She'd sent me downstairs to steal some wine coolers from her mom's booze fridge out by the pool. Her mother knew we took them, but didn't want to see us doing it, so stealth was important.

On padded feet, I snuck through the gigantic house until I reached the kitchen and sliding glass door that opened to the backyard. At the other end of the house, an addition had been specially built for her mother's office. It was mostly just a space to display the pictures from her days as a model, but that night Teena and Smith were inside and they were dancing. They looked so elegant together and . . . sweet.

I knew Dyl hated her mother, said she was twisted and strange. And Teena never seemed terribly fond of her daughter either. She was always happy to see me, though, when other mothers hadn't even allowed me in the front door. Told me to call her Teena and sometimes even touched my hair and said things like, "Why do you and Dylan insist on looking ugly when you could be so pretty?" Okay, so maybe that wasn't so nice, but it was more motherly than anything I'd ever heard from my own mom. And she was beautiful, so beautiful, even though she was years past her time as a model. I couldn't help but romanticize her, and this scene with Smith fed right into that.

I imagined her teaching him the steps when he was just a little boy, wincing when he stepped on her feet. And as he got older, slowly showing him how to lead. I watched them finish their dance with a whirling turn, and I would've clapped if not for the wine coolers in my hands.

I kept watching, indulging myself with a wistful sigh, and so I saw the exact moment when things transformed into something terrible.

Teena took Smith's face in both hands and kissed him on the mouth. It was not a motherly kiss. Not with her other hand trailing down his chest and seeking more southern territory even as Smith shoved her away.

A wine cooler slipped from my suddenly sweaty hands and smashed against the cement. I left it, and went running back inside the house.

I hid in the bathroom, trying to make sense of what I'd seen. I decided not to tell Dylan anything, even though I had a feeling, from things she'd said in the past, that she wouldn't be all that surprised.

Decision made, I opened the bathroom door and came face-to-face with Smith. He leaned against the wall opposite the door, arms folded over his chest.

"Hey, Smith," I said. It was times like that when I was actually thankful for my upbringing in a family of law-breakers. My face didn't go red, my voice didn't squeak, and my hand, raised in a casual wave, didn't shake. "Were you waiting for the bathroom?"

"No," he said. "I was waiting for you."

"Oh?" I asked. "Why's that?"

He didn't answer. Instead, he walked toward me, two

deliberate steps and then his hands were on my shoulders, propelling me backward into the bathroom until the bathtub pressed against the backs of my legs and I couldn't go any farther. Still he leaned against me, so that I had to grab hold of him or fall onto my ass. I clutched at him and was about to say his name, demand he stop, when his mouth found mine.

He didn't kiss me the way that a high school boy kisses a girl, hesitant and too moist or too dry and generally making it clear that he isn't really interested in your lips, except that they give him an excuse to be closer to your boobs. Smith kissed me like he was trying to prove something. He made my mouth a roller coaster ride that did loop-da-loops and caused my stomach to jump and generally scared the hell out of me.

Like all roller coaster rides, it ended way too soon.

Just as I kissed him back, he pulled away. I was left grasping air, and then the shower curtain, trying to stay on my feet, but ending up in an ungraceful heap at the bottom of the bathtub. I stared at Smith, who stood in front of the sink with his back to me, taking a giant swig from a bottle of Listerine. He gargled and spat. Our eyes met in the mirror above the sink. I had a thousand words, but couldn't get a single one out. Smith didn't say anything either. His stare was almost hollow and as my senses returned I realized it was whiskey that I'd tasted in his kiss.

"Are you drunk?" I asked.

He turned and walked out of the bathroom. His feet pounded down the steps before he bothered to call out a reply. "Believe what you want."

I'd figured he was referring to more than just my question, but I never had the guts to find out for sure.

"Let's get this over with," Smith says now, and I am lifted and flipped over so that I am upside down over his shoulder with my ass in the air. I close my eyes, fighting nausea and something else that feels like my heart breaking.

We walk long enough for me to hear the sound of gravel underfoot and to count only one set of footsteps. Wherever he is taking me, he is doing it alone. This, then, is my only chance for mercy.

"Smith, please," I whisper. "Don't do this."

He stops, and I stupidly hope I've gotten through to him, but then he lowers me to the ground and I am lined up with the rest of the party rejects on a curb at the edge of a nearly full parking lot. I squint toward the squat brown building at the other end of the parking lot that seems to pulse with some sort of dark energy.

My stomach sinks as I realize this is the biker bar where Dylan's car was found. The one where my father and various other lowlifes have supposedly been spotted. And they are leaving us here, which means that one of us will have to go inside and ask to use the phone or else we'll have to hike at least a mile down the road to the nearest gas station. It's the perfect combination of clever and cruel. I look down the line of my fellow party evictees huddled on the curb. The ones who meet my gaze glare back. They know as well as I do that they've been dragged into a punishment meant for me.

Pulling myself to my feet, I lurch forward and grab hold of Smith's shirt. "I had nothing to do with what happened to Dyl. Smith, come on, you know that. She was my friend. I—"

At last Smith's eyes meet mine. "You what?"

I was going to say I loved her, but with Smith glaring at me I can't get the words out. "She was my friend," I repeat lamely.

"And she was my sister."

"I know. I'm sorry."

"Are you?" Smith says, and I finally detect a slight softening in his tone.

"Yes! Of course."

"Then why did she have your crappy old suitcase, Lennie? And a fake ID with your name, but her picture on it? What do you know about that?"

I'd had no idea about the fake ID, but I can't say I'm surprised. *Oh, Dyl, what did you do?*

"Well?" Smith presses, and I'm about to spill everything I know, when a gigantic arm circles Smith's chest, picks him up, and carries him away as if he weighs nothing more than a rag doll. The white letters on the back of his T-shirt read Security. I start to chase after them when a second bouncer grabs me. I struggle as he drags me in the opposite direction as Smith.

"Smith!" I yell, uselessly kicking my legs against the mountain that has me in his grasp.

I can't help but wonder if I'm going to end up like Dyl.

The thing is, I'm not Dylan. Dyl wanted lots of things. So many things. She was a black hole of wanting. But— with the exception of tonight—all I've ever asked for is survival. During that last fight when I accused her of having a death wish, she called me the living dead. Said that I didn't know how to truly live. Maybe this whole night was to prove something to her.

In the end, though, I am proving something to myself. Survival is sometimes more than enough.

Since I cannot overpower this guy, I decide to use my words instead. "My uncles," I gasp. "My uncles are the Hinkton brothers."

He hesitates and I feel laughter through his chest.

"Maybe you'll taste like moonshine."

I go cold. We are directly in front of the bar and he is reaching for the door, no doubt ready to carry me in and offer me as a virgin sacrifice. Squeezing my eyes closed, I blurt out the only words that might save me. "I'm Leonard Cash's daughter. He'll kill anyone who touches me."

And just like that, I'm released. For the first time in my life that name is not a curse. For the first time I am happy to have it.

My legs wobble beneath me and I sink to the ground. I need to get up. I need to get away from here. I take three, four, five steadying breaths and then, using the wall behind me, I get my feet beneath me once more.

A tiny man stands before me. The overall impression he makes is that of a small, harmless woodland creature—like a chipmunk or a squirrel. A large part of that is due to his hair, which flows from the top of his head and down around his shoulders. As if this wasn't enough, his beard seems to cover most of his face too, giving the impression of a veil that allows only his eyes and his nose to peek out. His clothes seem like they were picked to match his hair—both in color and texture. Several layers of pilly brown sweaters make him appear almost cuddly, while the frayed cords covering his legs have wear marks at the knees.

"I'm a friend of your father's," he says, as if this explains everything. "Well, perhaps more of a business partner. An associate of sorts. Or an employee." He flashes a gummy smile at me. "It's a shifting role, to be honest."

"Um, okay," I say.

"Sorry about the boys. They get a little overzealous sometimes."

"It's okay," I say, then step sideways to go around him. He moves with me, blocking my path. I slide in the other direction, but he follows me again. I try a last-ditch quick dodge to the right and still cannot shake him. Frustrated with the ugly twists and turns this evening has taken, I finally lose it. "What the hell? Get outta my way, dude!"

My outburst is enough to shake him. He stumbles backward as if my words are a physical blast, and I take the opportunity to slip around him. Except he snatches at my elbow, with a surprisingly strong grip. "Lennie, please. If your father were here, he'd roll out the red carpet and gilded cage. And if he knew that in his absence you'd been treated with anything but the best, well, he'd kill me." The man titters nervously. "I'm joking. Probably. I hope. Right?"

His voice trembles. I don't want to feel sorry for him, but I do. "Look, it's okay. He's never gonna know about any of this. I just, I gotta go," I give a little tug, removing myself from his grasp. "I have to find my friend."

"Oh, don't worry about him. He's been taken care of."

I freeze. "Like cement boots sending him to the bottom of Lake Erie taken care of?"

"Heavens, no." He chuckles nervously. "He's been sent home. Unless . . . did you want him taken care of in that way?"

"No!"

"Oh, well, good, good. That keeps things simple." He clears his throat and then does this little weird half-bow thing. "As for you, young lady, I have a driver who can take you and the rest of your friends home. I'm pretty sure it's past your bedtime. No need to pay or tip. The driver will be taken care of. . . . Oh, dear, maybe I shouldn't use that phrase anymore."

"Yeah, it's a little confusing." The man remains by my side as I slide around the cars with the goal of returning to my far corner of the parking lot. He refuses to be shaken loose, so with the hope of getting rid of him, I stick out my hand. "So, um, thanks, I guess."

"Rabbit. The name's Rabbit," he says. "If you do run into your father one day, I'd prefer if you didn't mention that we met. Also, you should probably avoid running into your father."

"Sure," I easily agree, knowing the chance of seeing my

father is pretty much zero. "I'll do my best to avoid him."

"Wonderful. Wonderful." Rabbit grabs my hand and shakes it enthusiastically. "It was a pleasure to meet you, Miss Cash. A real pleasure. If you ever need anything taken care of, er, that is, if I can ever be of assistance, you can ask for me at the bar anytime."

Right on cue, a minivan with a taxi logo on its side door pulls up in front of me.

The driver collects the other ex-partiers still lined up on the curb. A few of them mumble thank you to me when they climb inside. As we pull out of the parking lot, I look for W2's truck, but don't see any sign of it. A last ember of anger flares and for a moment I regret not asking Rabbit to have that sleazeball taken care of.

It is four a.m. by the time I get home, and I nearly cry with relief when the door opens easily under my hand. With heavy feet I climb the stairs to my room and collapse onto my bed. I expect sleep to come quickly, but even as the approaching dawn begins to eat away at the night's darkness, my brain won't stop replaying the evening's events.

I keep coming back to the moment when it was all going right, when I got to have just that little taste of what it felt like to be winning. I'd had this crazy hope that maybe the tide was finally turning. That maybe for the first time in my life, things were gonna go my way.

It was a short-lived fantasy, but I can't stop myself from trying to hold on to it as I fall into sleep. Hoping that maybe, in my dreams, I can believe in it once more.

WORST

I wake to the sound of someone doing their best Big Bad Wolf impersonation on our front door.

BAM. BAM. BAM.

Some people say bad things happen in threes.

Those people must be luckier than me. In my life, bad things don't feel the need to limit themselves this way. Which is how I know trouble has a distinctive knock. And this is trouble times three.

My suspicions are confirmed a moment later, when the banging becomes interspersed with someone yelling my name.

"Cash! Cash! CAAASSSHHHH. My dad's gonna sue you for every sorry thing you own!" It's impossible not to recognize W2's distinctive holler. He's one of those people who doesn't have an inside voice.

Bleary-eyed, I find my alarm clock. It is seven a.m. We

are a night-owl family and nobody is ever up before ten at the earliest.

The uncs will not be pleased.

Hoping the pills still have them sleeping peacefully, I hop out of bed, throw on some clothes, and shove my cell into my back pocket. I have to take several deep breaths while my head swims and I resist the urge to hurl.

"LENNIE!"

That is Uncle Jet's bellow. The "you're in deep shit" one.

Oh, good, the sleeping pills have worn off. Perfect timing. Once again my luck is the worst ever.

Stomach churning, I gingerly slink downstairs while trying to think of a cover story for damage control, but when I spot the tableau in the middle of the living room my entire mind goes blank.

W2 stands with his arms crossed over his chest, flanked by my oversized uncles. He looks pitiful and small. I would laugh except for the looks on my uncles' faces. They are not red-faced and furious as I expected them to be. No, what I see is much worse.

They look scared.

No one says anything for a long moment.

"What did you do to me?" W2 whines, breaking the silence.

Uncle Dune slaps a hand against the back of W2's

skull, accompanied by a soft, "Shaddup."

W2 is an idiot, so instead of shadduping, he clutches the back of his head as if mortally wounded and wheels on Uncle Dune. "Do you know who I am?" he demands.

There's a hole in the garage wall the size of Uncle Rod from one of Uncle Dune's punches. For all their power, though, Uncle Dune's fists fly incredibly slowly, which at this moment is very lucky for W2 as Uncle Jet quickly steps in and grabs hold of the fist headed toward W2's stupid face.

"Not now," Uncle Jet tells Dune. Then he looks at me. "This boy says you were at a party last night."

I know better than to try and lie, but that doesn't mean I'm gonna volunteer information. I simply nod in response.

"And you brought moonshine with you?" Uncle Jet continues.

Damn, how did W2 manage to blab so much so quickly? I nod again.

"And you gave this boy some of that shine? Personally drinking and toasting with him?"

"Yeah, we did the toast." I sigh and roll my eyes like a petulant asshole, trying to convince everyone *I'm* the wounded party here.

"What did I tell you?" W2 exclaims, pushing past

Uncle Jet. I wince, waiting for blood to flow, but for some reason Uncle Jet not only allows W2 to interrupt his interrogation but lets him get in his space too. "She said, 'Make a wish.'"

Now it's my uncles' turn to wince.

"And I said, 'I want brass balls so when some pissy girl tries to knee me in the nuts you'll just hear a loud old *gooonnggggg*.'" W2 makes the gong noise all dramatic, his mouth open in a wide O and his whole body vibrating like it's been rung. "And then she said, 'Wish granted.'"

"That is not what I said!" I explode.

W2 shrugs. "Right, right. You told me stainless steel would be better, it's dishwasher safe and lasts forever. And I was like, 'Yeah balls of steel. I like that.' Then you said some alla-kazoo wish bullshit and we both drank that nasty booze you brought to the party."

Uncle Dune growls low in his throat, but W2 doesn't seem to notice.

"And I thought, 'Well this swill is sure as shit gonna make my head pound tomorrow.' But instead when I woke up this morning to take a piss, you know what was aching?" W2 grabs his junk. "My balls! My freaking balls were killing me, and when I scratched them they made this weird clinking noise." Of course, he demonstrates. "So I jerked down my shorts, took a peek, and guess what I saw?"

I say nothing. This is a joke. I mean, of course, it's a joke. It has to be a joke.

W2 hooks his thumbs inside his track pants and jerks them down. "This is what I saw!" Both hands gesture to his crotch, in case anyone was confused about where exactly to look.

I throw my hands up to cover my eyes.

"You scared to see what you did?" W2 yells. I can hear him coming closer. "Look, bitch. Look, you little cu—"

W2 is cut off by the thud of flesh and bone colliding, immediately followed by the louder crash of a body plowing through drywall.

I peek between my fingers to find the solid wall of Uncle Dune's back between me and everything else. Leaning slightly to the left to see around him, I immediately spot the new dent in the wall and W2's slumped form beneath it. Uncle Jet and Uncle Rod are leaning over him on either side. At first I think they're checking his vitals to make sure Dune didn't kill him, but then I realize their attention is focused between W2's legs.

Uncle Rod gives a long whistle. "She's done it now," he says in a low voice as he bends to pick up W2.

I suppose after last night, the sight of W2's bare white buttocks slung over Uncle Rod's shoulder on their way out the door should give me some satisfaction, but all I feel is dread. And it grows when Uncle Jet says, "Put him in the basement."

I open my mouth to protest, but realize the alternative is to put him outside, where he'll run to his daddy as soon as he regains consciousness. And then we'll really be in trouble.

"Need me to open the door?" I call after Uncle Rod.

"You're staying right here," Uncle Jet says in a tone that leaves no room for argument.

Not wanting another interrogation, I decide to argue anyway. "That guy is a slimeball. I mean, obviously. You saw for yourselves. Look, yes, I went to a party last night. I took some moonshine. I only wanted to have some fun. It's my senior year and . . ." I choke back the words I was going to say. That after this year my life feels like a dead end. That I have nothing to look forward to except having a life exactly like theirs.

"It's my senior year," I repeat lamely. "And W2's just pissed that nothing happened between us last night, so he came here to get me in trouble. Whatever he did to himself down there is some stupid prank he thinks we're all dumb enough to fall for."

Uncle Jet stares at me long and hard, looking a little perplexed. "That was no prank." His brows furrow even further than before. "Lennie, you do know what your uncles and I do for a living, right?"

I laugh more out of nervousness than anything else. "You sell moonshine and it's illegal. And I know it was bad to take it to the party."

Uncle Jet looks angry now, but thankfully his stare isn't directed at me. He's pointing a finger at Uncle Dune. "I thought you talked to her. What was it . . . three or four years ago? You drew the short straw and then a few days later said you and Lennie had a good talk."

"I was gonna!" Uncle Dune roars. "But then you had to stick your nose in and tell her first!"

"I sure as shit didn't!" Uncle Jet shoots back. "Who told ya I did?"

"Well, Lennie . . ." Uncle Dune's voice trails off and once again the focus is on me. Worse, Uncle Dune is looking at me with a look reminiscent of Bambi after his mother got shot. "Lennie . . . you lied to me?"

I gulp. "A little lie. I thought you were trying to give me the sex talk."

I can still clearly remember five years ago, looking up to see Uncle Dune standing in my bedroom doorway. He'd cleared his throat before announcing, "Lennie, you're old enough now. It's time you were told how things really work."

I assumed that *things* was a euphemism for penises.

And I really did not want to discuss the ins and outs (excuse the pun) of such things with my uncle Dune of all people. In a panic, the lie popped out. "Oh, Uncle Jet already told me all about it."

"He did?" Uncle Dune's face got all crinkly and confused then.

"Yeah, we were watching *Road House* together and you know how that movie always makes him real emotional and he just sorta told me. Everything. All the details. More than I needed to know really. So there's nothing more for you to tell me. It's been covered like a plate of extra-cheesy nachos."

"Oh," Uncle Dune said. Then came the dreaded follow-up question. "And do you think that's something you'll want to do sometime soon?"

"No! God, no! I'm way too young for that. In fact, I think I'm one of those late bloomers who end up waiting till I'm thirty or forty to do it for the first time."

Uncle Dune finally cracked a smile at that. "Okay, I get it. You're freaked out. I was the same way at your age. It seemed impossible that it all worked that way. I promise, it all comes together how it's meant to. But look, when you're ready, I'd like you to grant a wish for me."

Assuming Dune meant that he wanted me to practice safe sex or something like that, I'd quickly agreed just to get him out of my room. "Sure, sure. You'll be the first to know when I'm ready." *As if.*

"Damn it, Lennie!" Uncle Jet explodes now. "That wasn't sex ed! He was explaining how the shine works. He was preparing you for the day when you'd start granting wishes and take over for us so we could retire. Are you telling me that every time since then, when I've told you about carrying on an important legacy, you thought I was talking about plain old bootlegging?"

Oh boy, I hope that's a hypothetical question, 'cause to be honest, Uncle Jet likes to monologue sometimes. Especially when he's had a few. And I usually tune him out.

"Did you?" Uncle Jet demands. Shit. Not hypothetical then.

"Ummm . . ." I stall.

"Let me make this clear. Are you listening real good right now?"

I nod.

"We. Grant. Wishes. 'Make a wish' isn't a way of saying, 'Down the hatch.' It's our way of saying, 'What do you wish for?' That's it. Right there. We grant wishes. Do you think you maybe got that now?"

I blink at him several times. But nothing he said makes any sense no matter how many times I flap my eyelids. At last an idea slowly takes shape in my head. "Did you put

W2 up to this? Is this your way of teaching me a lesson about sneaking out with shine?"

"Teaching you a *lesson?*" Uncle Jet's face grows redder with every word. I don't think I've ever seen him this angry before. He takes two steps toward me, and I can't help it—I flinch. He freezes. "I'm not gonna hit ya, Lennie. But I am gonna throw you out." He points toward the door. "Get out. Get out and don't come back."

I should run, but I can't because Uncle Jet's suddenly on his knees, clutching his chest. "My heart." He grinds the words out between his teeth.

I put a hand on his back. "It's okay, it's only a panic attack. Remember what the doctor said? Your heart is fine."

"Strong as a horse," Uncle Dune booms behind me.

"Put your head between your knees," I remind him. "You don't want to faint like the last time."

Uncle Jet staggers toward the stairs and lowers himself so that he's sitting with his head hanging between his knees. "I didn't faint. I've never fainted in my life." He mutters.

I go into the kitchen, pour a few fingers of shine into a glass, and bring it back to Uncle Jet, setting it between his feet. I know he sees it, but it takes a long moment for his hand to find the glass. "Thanks." He practically whispers the word, but I hear it just the same.

"You're welcome," I say at precisely the same volume.

This is usually the point where I would escape back up to my bedroom, but since I was only moments ago sort of kicked out I'm not sure if I even have a bedroom anymore.

Luckily, Uncle Rod returns, throwing the door open so that it bangs against the wall. "Holy shee-it." He gives a long exaggerated whistle. "That kid's got stainless steel nicer than what we got in the silverware drawer wrapped around his boys. Lennie, that is some—" He stops suddenly as the scene by the staircase penetrates his brain. "What did I miss?"

"Nothing," Uncle Jet and Uncle Dune say at the same time.

I force a weak smile and shrug when Uncle Rod's raised eyebrows swing in my direction.

"Okay, then," he says. "Well, I locked the man of steel in the crawl space. He's about as sharp as a bowling ball—"

"Or his own balls," Uncle Jet, still in the prone position, cannot resisting inserting. All three of my uncles giggle over that one. Uncle Jet even recovers enough to pull his head out from between his knees.

"Ain't that the truth," Uncle Rod finally says. "He won't be happy when he wakes up. And when I came up the stairs I found this one, hovering at the back door." He jerks his thumb behind him and I look past Uncle Rod to see Smith standing in the doorway. His face looks like someone mistook it for a piñata and refused to stop hitting it until some candy fell out.

There is nothing good about the feeling in my chest. Part of me wants to walk over and press a finger into the angriest blackest bruise just to watch him wince. The other part wants to hand him a bag of frozen peas and stroke his forehead.

Ignoring both impulses, I cross my arms over my traitorous heart.

"Aw, shit," Uncle Jet says, slowly rising to his feet. "You got brass balls too?"

"*Stainless steel,*" Uncle Rod interjects.

Uncle Jet waves a hand Uncle Rod's way, silencing him. Then we all stare at Smith and he stares back at us with his one eye that isn't swollen shut.

"I woke up this morning," he says, but then stops and starts again. "Something woke me up this morning. My hand." He holds up his right hand. Unlike his face, it seems to be in good shape. Looks like whoever beat him up didn't give him much chance to return the favor. "I tried to ignore it, but the feeling wouldn't go away."

"I think we know where this is going," Uncle Jet groans. "Damn it, Lennie. Maybe we shoulda given you some sex education so you'd know it ain't right to mess with a man's manhood."

"No!" Smith lets his hand fall. "That's not what . . . My hand didn't want . . ." He clears his throat. "Last night, I made a wish. And now . . ." Smith's gaze drops to his shoes as he mutters something unintelligible.

"What was that?" Uncle Rod asks.

"He said he needs to hold Lennie's hand."

You wouldn't think it from his own lack of volume control, but Uncle Dune has superhuman hearing. When I was a little kid we used to play a game called Can You Hear This? I'd stand at the opposite end of the room from Uncle Dune and whisper something as softly as possible, then he'd bellow out what I'd just said. He almost always got it right. So instead of questioning Dune, my uncles simply look from Smith to me and then back to Smith again.

"Well, Lennie," Uncle Jet says at last. "Give the boy your hand."

I shove both hands up into my armpits. "No."

"Did that boy make a wish to hold your hand?"

"No. Yes. Sort of. I guess."

"Which one?"

I glance at Smith, waiting to see if he wants to jump in, but he's still examining his shoelaces. "I didn't grant any wish. This is crazy. It's insane. Smith's screwing with me. He probably cooked it up with W2. I keep telling you it's some weird practical joke."

Uncle Jet shakes his head. "I'd get the moonshine and have you grant my wish that the truth would penetrate your thick skull, but it wouldn't work till sunrise tomorrow and I hate to think of what kind of hell you'll unleash between now and then. So let me explain this to you, one more time." He shoots an accusing glance toward Uncle Dune with this last bit, who merely shrugs in response.

"We grant wishes. Nobody knows how it started but it's been going on for generations, at least as far as Pop Pop knew. He always said someone up the family tree must've screwed a leprechaun. Whatever it was, we got this thing where we can grant wishes through the moonshine. None of that genie giving you three wishes crap. Everyone gets one wish per wish granter. Even the wish granters themselves only get one. That means I could grant a wish for Rod and Dune and myself. And they could each grant one for themselves, for me, and each other. We're more like fairy friggin' godmothers in that way. You got that?"

"You and Uncle Rod and Uncle Dune grant wishes," I repeat. It sounds just as insane coming out of my mouth.

"Wrong!" Uncle Jet crows. "We used to grant wishes. The power gets passed to the next generation once someone has granted three wishes. That means you're it now, Lennie. Us three can't grant any more wishes."

"That can't be real," I whisper, even though I have a terrible feeling it is.

Uncle Jet's told me lies before. Whoppers, too, like that a monster would eat me if I got out of bed in the middle of the night. After I spent most of grade school with recurrent bladder infections from being too afraid to use the bathroom in the middle of the night, Uncle Rod took pity on me. In exchange for no longer stealing the poker from the fireplace to keep it at my bedside, he broke down every single one of Jet's tells that he'd observed after years of playing poker together. The nose scratch with his middle finger. The chin stroke. The fake cough. The throat clearing. The rapid blinks. The loud honking nose blow. Actually I'm pretty sure some of these were Uncle Jet's allergies acting up, but I watched for them all the same. As a result I don't trust most things that come out of Uncle Jet's mouth. Right now, though, he's as still as a statue.

A hand slips into mine and holds tight. It is amazing how much comfort can be gained from such a simple touch. That is until I look to my left and realize it's Smith.

"Oh, wow, that feels so good," he says.

I don't like it. I don't like any of this, especially the idea that Smith is only holding my hand because of some wish.

"Let go," I demand, jerking my hand away. Smith doesn't come loose.

"I can't."

I pull away with my whole body. Smith's hand doesn't get any tighter, but it doesn't relax either. "LET GO!" I screech in a high-pitched voice that immediately sends my uncles into action. They each reach in and begin to pull back Smith's fingers. One. Two. Three. Four. I finally escape while Smith whimpers like a kicked puppy and sinks to the floor.

Quickly, I stuff my hands into my pockets. Not so that Smith won't take them, but more so that I won't be tempted to give them back.

"What wish did you grant that boy?" Uncle Jet demands.

"A curse," Smith spits out, still curled at our feet.

"Same difference," my uncles respond as one. They turn to me, waiting.

"He wanted to hold my hand till the end of time," I lie. I'm not sure why, but I don't want the uncs to know Smith's wish. To know how much he hates me. That he wanted to see me suffer.

Smith is a jerk, but not an idiot. He's seen the size of my uncles and probably overheard how they dealt with W2. He shoots a questioning glance my way, but doesn't open his mouth to set the record straight.

Meanwhile, the uncs groan and roll their eyes like a bunch of eight-year-olds worried about catching cooties.

Deciding to change the topic, and get some more answers, I step in front of Smith so that all attention is back on me. "If this is real, then show me what you three wished for yourselves."

"Maybe we never did," Uncle Jet says.

"Nah," Uncle Dune says. "We did. Almost soon as we got our powers. Couldn't resist. I got super ears, super eyes, and super nose. To see and hear trouble coming."

"I wished for enough stuff and money to keep us comfortable." Uncle Rod adds.

I look back at Uncle Jet. "And you?"

He stares back at me for several long moments, before giving in. "I made a wish to keep us safe and hidden from anyone wanting to use what we could do the wrong way. And if you're smart, you'll make a similar wish. We were lucky, though, there were three of us and we were able to multiply our wishes. You don't have that luxury."

"Okay," I say in a small voice as inside me the truth hardens like cement. I always wondered how my uncles had enough money and got all the stuff that fell off the back of trucks and how everyone knew about the moonshine but never bothered them about it and how Uncle Dune could smell rain in the air when the skies were blue.

"Um, Lennie . . ." Smith says, slowly pulling himself to his feet.

"What?" Uncle Jet demands.

"I think, I'm not sure, but I think Lennie did make a wish. She sorta tacked one on after mine."

"That is such crap—" I start to deny it, until I realize . . . Oh, hell, he's right.

I wished for Dylan to be alive again.

Holy shit. Holy holy holiest of shits.

I wished for Dyl to be alive and if everything is fucked up the way my uncles say it is, then that means . . .

As one, Smith and I sprint toward the door.

"Hey," Uncle Jet hollers behind us. "Where do you think you're going?"

I turn to see all three of them running down the porch steps, ready to jump in their truck and come racing after us wherever we go.

It's easier to simply tell them the truth. Or at least part of it.

"He's right. I made a wish," I say. "And it was a big one."

Uncle Jet stops and stumbles and then finally sinks to his knees.

"Breathe," I yell as I climb into Smith's Jeep. "Put your head between your knees and breathe!"

Then the engine is revving and dirt is kicked up

everywhere as we fly down the drive and with a screeching turn hit the road.

Taking my own advice, I let my head fall forward and focus on taking steady strong breaths, one after another. As I do this, I try to recall the wording of my wish. Something about Dylan being alive. Or safe. Or maybe both?

I can't remember exactly what I said, but that doesn't stop me from hoping that no matter what else I screwed up last night, I might've actually gotten this one thing right.

At least that's what I hope.

But another part of me can't help but remember the uncs' grim response to Smith's accusation that his wish was a curse.

I've already used up my wish, but I still try to make another one.

Let them be wrong. Please, please, please let them be wrong.

Let that wish be an answer to a prayer and not just another nightmare.

GOOD
GOD

The silence in the car is so full of unsaid words that talking seems redundant. I stare out the window, pretending I don't notice, like I'm so lost in my own thoughts I'd need a map to find my way out.

The truth is, my thoughts are pretty clear right now. *This is fucked this is fucked this is so fucked* is the nonstop refrain swirling around in the space between my ears.

After ten minutes of this I realize I can't sit here stewing while we spend the next twenty minutes driving from my neighborhood full of weedy lawns and boarded-up windows to the complete opposite end of town, where Smith's house is the shining jewel of Dalton Lake Estates.

There are so many things I could use to get the conversational ball rolling. I could ask about Dyl. Or what happened to his face. Or if he thinks this whole wish thing might possibly be for real.

Instead I say, "I think I'm still drunk."

Smith glances over at me. "Nah. You puked a lot up last night."

"How do you know?" And then I realize. Of course, while he and his horrible friends were driving me to the bar. "Never mind," I say when Smith doesn't answer. "I figured it out."

Smith sighs. "Lennie, I'm . . ." for a second I think he's gonna say he's sorry. But Dyl always said that word wasn't in their vocabulary, and I guess she was right, 'cause instead he says, "I'm glad you got home okay."

"No thanks to you," I snap back.

"I wasn't gonna leave you there."

"You should never have brought me in the first place!"

"I know! Okay? I know. I just . . ." Smith takes his right hand off the steering wheel and flexes the fingers open and closed. "I wanted to shake you up. Scare you. I thought you knew something about Dyl, and I wanted you to spill it."

I don't answer right away, because he's right. I didn't tell the cops everything I knew. I would've if it could have saved Dyl, but by the time I realized, she was already dead. Then it seemed pointless. Everyone already blamed me, why make it worse?

There was only one person I would've willingly given

all the details to. "You could've asked me, Smith. But you didn't want to. You wouldn't even let me in the church for her funeral." I close my eyes as my hangover suddenly catches up with me. Or maybe it's the memory of standing in the parking lot, watching the church slowly fill up with people who'd barely given Dyl the time of day when she was alive.

Silence stretches between us once more and I'm pretty sure it's the end of that conversation when Smith says, "You're right." It's as close as he's gonna get to an apology, I guess.

I could throw it back at him, say something like, "Of course I'm right." But that's what you say when you're angry, not when you feel as if you've been chopped into pieces just like your best friend. And I can't say, "It's okay," either, because it definitely is not.

I settle on a shrug. "Whatever, Smith."

He doesn't reply, but after another pregnant pause, I feel his fingers brush against mine. I'm not falling for that again. I quickly jerk my hand away.

"Come on, Lennie, please," Smith says, and I can hear the strain in his voice. "Let me have it for a few seconds. It feels like someone is sticking needles into my fingertips and fire ants are crawling over my knuckles. I need your hand for a tiny bit, just to make the feeling go away."

I tuck both hands under my butt. "It's a part of my body, Smith. Not hemorrhoid cream."

"Yeah, well, I already tried hemorrhoid cream. And a bag of frozen corn. Then I thought maybe I could burn the feeling away."

"But you didn't," I quickly interject.

"No, I didn't." Smith glances over at me. "I flipped a coin and it landed heads up, so I turned the gas on the stove off and drove over to your house instead."

I can't help it. My mind conjures up a vision of Smith's hand in the blue flame of the stove, his skin bubbling up beneath it. I wince. "You wouldn't have done it."

Smith laughs in response, this hoarse jerky sound. "I've been eyeing the cigarette lighter for the last five minutes, and not because I need a smoke."

"Smith!"

"Yeah, well, I'll warn you when I'm gonna do it so you can look away. And feel free to roll down the window so you don't have to smell my burning flesh."

I'm being manipulated. I know that. But at the same time, I understand that Smith's desperation is real.

"Okay, fine. This is what we're gonna do. Put your hand on top of the drink holders." Smith instantly obeys, placing his hand palm up on the center console. "Good. Now keep your fingers spread out and fully open. A single twitch and we're done. Got it?"

Smith nods. "Yeah, okay. Deal. Just do it alreadeeeee-oooooooohhhh."

The exact instant the tip of my finger connects with the soft center of Smith's palm he loses it. Fingers curl in as his hand clenches and I immediately pull away.

"No, Lennie, c'mon, don't stop."

"You moved your fingers."

"Gimme one more chance. Come on. Please."

I try to stay strong, but the "please" unravels me.

"Fine," I say. But I hesitate, looking down at Smith's large hand and long, square-tipped fingers. How many times have I dreamed of touching him? And of him reaching back for me?

My hand hovers over Smith's palm and then I let my thumb fall and slowly brush along his lifeline. Smith exhales sharply, a hard hiss between his teeth, but he keeps all five digits frozen in place.

Feeling a little bolder, I run four fingers from the base of his palm all the way up to his fingertips. Smith's arm trembles and I can see his biceps bulging beneath his short-sleeved tee, but he still doesn't move his hand. My mouth goes dry and I realize that I am trembling a little too.

Suddenly, this feels much more intimate than two

hands simply touching.

I should stop, but instead I do the same move again, this time sneaking a look at Smith's face as my fingertips connect with his. His eyes are clenched shut and his jaw is tight. I have a sudden urge to kiss him, but it is quickly overwhelmed by panic as it sinks in that he is driving with his eyes shut.

I scream his name while at the same time grabbing the steering wheel and moving us back into our own lane. We fly toward the red light at a busy intersection with several cars lined up ahead of us. Smith opens his eyes just in time to slam on the brakes and stop the car inches away from the back bumper of a semi.

"Shit." Clenching his right hand into a fist, Smith punches the window beside him hard enough to make the glass crack. He must want to put his hand all the way through it, though, 'cause he hits it again and again and—

I grab hold of his arm, wrapping both my hands around his bicep and pulling back with all my weight. "Smith, stop."

He jerks away from my hold, and lets his hand fall into his lap.

"Next time roll the window down if you need more air." It's a lame attempt at humor, but I don't know what else to say. Smith doesn't react. It's like he doesn't even hear me.

"Hey, you okay?" I reach toward his bloodied hand, which is now resting on his lap.

"Don't touch me," he snaps. "It only makes it worse."

I snatch my hand back, hurt despite myself, but all I say is, "Light's green."

As the car rolls forward once more, I cross my arms over my chest and go back to looking out my window.

This is fucked this is fucked this is so fucked screams the chorus in my head once more.

This time I don't even try to tune it out.

WELL

When we reach Smith's house, neither one of us makes a move to get out of the car. "Beep the horn," I say impulsively.

"What?" Smith gives me a disdainful glance.

"Maybe she'll hear it and come running out." It sounds lame when I say it aloud. I was hoping the opposite would be true, since it had also sounded pretty bad when I'd tried it out in my head.

"What, you think she's inside, like, watching TV or something right now?" This time he twists in his seat and faces me full on so that I cannot possibly miss how monumentally stupid he thinks I am. You'd think a guy with a black eye and busted lip wouldn't be able to pull that look off, but if anything the bruises enhance it.

"You're an asshole," I say, and finally I find the momentum to climb out of the car and slam the door behind me. Still pissed, I march up to the front door and . . . it's locked. Luckily, I've seen Dylan retrieve the spare key from behind the loose brick enough times to get it in my hands and start fitting it in the lock by the time Smith saunters up behind me.

"You'll set off the alarm," he says.

"You don't have an alarm," I shoot back as I push the door open. Immediately an alarm begins to shriek. Pushing past me, Smith punches numbers into a keypad beside the door.

"So that's new," I say as the alarm goes quiet and Smith turns to face me.

"Actually, we've always had it, but Dyl was constantly setting it off accidentally so Teena had the service disconnected. Then after Dyl . . ." Smith shrugs, letting me fill in the blank there. "Teena was freaked out and had it reactivated."

"Is . . ." I glance around. "Is Teena home?" It's weird even mentioning her around Smith, but if he is bothered, he doesn't show it.

Smith shakes his head. "She's out of town for the weekend."

"Oh." I nod, and then realize that neither of us has taken a single step away from the front door. "I guess we should check Dyl's room, right?" I ask, knowing I'm risking Smith biting my head off again.

But he just looks up at the ceiling, as if searching for some sort of sign. I'm guessing he doesn't find one, 'cause his gaze returns to me. "Yeah, I guess. I mean, you wished for her sleeping safe in her own bed, right? So that's where she'd probably be."

"I don't think I said sleeping. Did I say sleeping? 'Cause then would that mean that she never wakes up?"

"How the hell should I know? It was your wish."

"I didn't know it was a real wish! And I was drunk so I don't remember what I said!" I close my eyes, knowing if I see Smith smirk at me one more time I'll punch him in the face. And then I remember the wish with such perfect clarity that I can recall the exact way that the words felt on my lips. "'Alive and safe in her own bed.' That's what I said. Not sleeping. Just alive. And safe."

"Okay then," Smith says. "That's good." He hesitates a moment longer, then suddenly turns and plants his fist into the wall behind him. Pulling it out of the crumbly drywall, he nods. "I'm ready." And with his usual long strides, Smith heads farther into the house.

I chase behind him. "Hey, maybe you can give me a warning the next time you're gonna do that? It's kinda freaking me out."

"Can't," Smith throws over his shoulder. "It's an impulse. Just do it. You know?"

I roll my eyes, but don't respond because we are climbing the stairs and as soon as my foot hits the first step my whole body gets Jell-O shaky. At the top of the stairs, we both walk as softly as possible across the creaky hardwood floors until we come to a stop outside Dyl's closed bedroom door.

Smith exhales a long, shaky breath before lifting his non-bloodied left hand up and softly tapping his knuckles against the door.

"You're knocking?" I whisper.

"Yes," he hisses back. "We always knock. You don't barge into someone's room without—"

Ignoring Smith, I turn the knob and walk right in. Dyl's room is unchanged from the last time I was here. The same mixture of posters and rough charcoal drawings cover the walls. Clothes are strewn everywhere except for the corner where her record player and several messy piles of vinyl take over.

I finally turn my attention to Dyl's bed. She always tried to be so tough, so hard. Hair dyed in various color streaks, most recently a mixture of white blond and purpley black. Spiked piercings in her lips and brow and ears. Dark red lipstick, heavy black eyeliner, and chipped black and blue nail polish. She sometimes wore the preppy clothes her mom bought, but only after attacking them with bleach and sandpaper and who knows what else, until they were completely her own right down to the homemade labels she'd sew on that read, Screw You Clothing.

So you'd think Dyl's bed would be something with leather and nailhead accents or, on the opposite end, a little more boho, like a simple mattress on the floor covered with a heap of mismatched quilts. Instead, it's this magical white iron canopy bed, covered with a ruffly comforter and about twenty pillows of all shapes and sizes. Once when we were really drunk, Dyl told me the bed made her feel like a princess in a fairy tale, waiting for her prince to wake her with a kiss. I'd started laughing, certain it was a joke, and only realized it wasn't when she went stomping from the room.

Heart pounding, mouth dry, I take one step closer and then another and another until I am beside the bed and looking down at my best friend, sleeping peacefully beneath the covers.

My eyes fill with tears and Dyl blurs but does not disappear. This horrible choked sound gurgles from somewhere inside me as my legs give out and I flop to the floor.

Smith rushes over from where he's been hovering in the hallway. "What? What?"

He stumbles to a halt beside me, and I peer up at him. It's impossible to get a good look at his face from this angle, but when I hear him choke out her name, his voice cracked and broken and raw, I look away, lowering my gaze to the nail polish stains on the rug. This is way too personal a moment for me to witness. Uncertain if my legs will hold me, I'm ready to crawl out on my hands and knees to give him some privacy, when Smith turns and bolts from the room. I listen to the sound of his feet pounding down the stairs, and then there is only silence.

I pull myself up, just enough to see Dyl again, to confirm I didn't imagine her. And there she is. Curled up small, face buried deep in her pillow and covers pulled up to her nose.

Dyl in her bed. Alive. Exactly the way I'd wished she would be.

Except why isn't she waking up? Smith and I haven't exactly been quiet.

I lean in closer, suddenly afraid that only half the wish was granted. I mean, bringing someone back to life is way bigger than steel balls or an itching need to hold someone's hand. I stop breathing, listening for one of Dyl's. No matter how I strain, I can't detect the slightest sigh or inhalation.

Trembling, I slide my hand beneath the blankets and rest two fingers against the side of Dyl's neck. Her skin is warm to the touch, which is reassuring, and after shifting my search slightly up and to the left I find the faint but unmistakable beat of Dyl's pulse.

I hold my hand there, counting the beats and daring Dyl to wake up. I can imagine the way her eyes would fly open. "What the hell are you doing?" she'd say. "That's some creepy shit, Len."

She just lies there, though, so still and silent that even with my fingers tracking the beats of her heart, I still am not sure whether she's dead or alive.

Something in me snaps. "DYL!" I scream in her face. "Wake up, Dyl! Dylan. Wake up!" I grab her shoulders and give her a good shake. Her head wobbles on her neck, and worried that I might snap it, I snatch my hands away. Limp, Dyl flops back onto the pillow, her striped hair floating outward in a halo around her. And yet, not so much as an eyelid flutters.

"What the hell are you doing?" Smith, using the same words I'd imagined coming from Dylan, grabs my arm and pulls me away. I jerk back, but he grabs me again and this time puts his face only an inch from mine. "Leave her alone, Lennie."

His breath stinks of alcohol. Whiskey or bourbon or something strong, that's for sure.

A rush of rage fills me. He ran out of here to get a drink. While I've been trying to decide if Dyl is alive or dead or something weirder and in between, he's been doing his best to get drunk. From the glassy look in his eyes, he's been pretty successful.

I bring my hand up and jab two fingers into the blackest part of the bruise below his right eye. Then I push past him to Dyl's record collection and begin digging into the pile of vinyl, already knowing the exact one I want. It's the pride of Dyl's collection, a first pressing of Led Zeppelin's self-titled debut album. Spotting the distinctive turquoise lettering on the sleeve, I slide the record out.

Despite her haphazard storage methods, Dyl is particular about her collection and never lets me handle them. I've seen her do it a million times, though, so I know the ritual. First, she blows across the surface of the record to remove any lint or dust. Then, keeping her fingers carefully on the rounded edge, she gently settles it onto the player. Finally, the needle is lifted and with the softest of touches placed at the edge of the record.

As "Good Times Bad Times" starts to play, I reach down to crank up the volume.

I stand there for a moment watching the record turn, listening to the music, and wishing . . .

No, I don't make wishes. Not anymore. It's too dangerous.

So when I slowly turn back toward Dylan, I don't wish,

but merely hope to see . . . what?

Dyl dancing on her bed while Smith gazes at me with a mixture of gratitude and love in his eyes?

Yeah, that doesn't happen.

Dyl remains frozen in bed, and Smith is once again nowhere to be seen.

I rub my eyes, suddenly exhausted. I'm tempted to crawl under the covers next to Dyl. When she was alive I wouldn't have thought twice about it, but now it feels too much like sharing a grave.

"Gah, Lennie, mope why don't ya." I can hear Dyl saying that so clearly that I almost go over to the bed to shake her again. Dyl believed in action. She dared life to knock her down, just to see how quick she could get up again.

"Get up, Dyl," I urge in a soft voice. "Get up."

Still nothing.

"Okay." I nod. "It is way too early to be up. Excellent point. I'll go downstairs and have a little breakfast while you sleep in. All righty then?"

I turn away before she can not answer.

Actually, breakfast isn't such a terrible idea. I've been too nauseous to even think about food up to this point, and even though the sick feeling hasn't gone away, I'm determined to make myself eat something, because whatever else happens next, I have a feeling I'll need all my strength to face it.

I clomp down the stairs and head into the kitchen where as usual the cupboards are mostly empty and the fridge is full of old takeout boxes. After digging through various drawers, I end up with a small pile of fortune cookies and three bags of potato chips with nothing left in them but broken shards.

As I crack open two of the fortune cookies, Smith saunters in. I brace myself to be bitched at again, but he simply stands there sheepishly with his hands shoved deep into his pockets. Dyl always said Smith's anger came on fast and melted away almost as quickly, whereas she was the type to hold a grudge. I must be more like Smith than Dyl, 'cause as soon as I notice how wrecked and thoroughly exhausted he looks, I can feel my anger start to fade away. I don't want him to know that I'm a total pushover, though, so I just stand there and chew on my stupid stale cookies.

Smith falls into a chair and then looks up at me with his gorgeous eyes framed by thick long lashes. "What's it say?"

"Huh?" I reply as my heart misses a beat.

"Your fortune. Things gonna start looking up?"

"Oh." I twist around to pluck the two fortunes off the counter, and hold both out to Smith. "Take them. I honestly don't want to know."

His hand closes around mine and when I hurriedly snatch it away, Smith gives me a wicked smile. "Lennie, I thought you liked me."

"Sure I do, Smith. I mean, I'm a girl and not a single one of us can resist you, right?"

The minute the words clear my lips, I know he thinks I'm referring to the whole thing with Teena and the smile goes out like I pulled a plug. For the second time since he walked into the kitchen every muscle in my body tenses, waiting for Smith to strike back. Instead, all he says is, "Well, you got my number."

"Smith," I say, an apology on the tip of my tongue, even though I'm not sure he deserves it.

"Let's see what our fortunes have to say." Smith talks right over me, and I remember that he doesn't just refuse to hand out apologies, he also has a policy against receiving them. He holds out two hands curled into fists. "Pick a hand."

I work hard to resist the urge to touch him. "Left."

Smith opens his left hand and I watch as he reads the fortune. His lips quirk in a little smile and he looks up to share it with me. *"You have unusual equipment for success. Use it well."*

"Shut up. It does not say that." I grab the fortune from his hand. And holy shit, it really does say that. It says that exactly. I look at Smith, expecting to see him laughing at me, but instead he's reading his own fortune. "What's yours say?"

Smith gives me a lopsided grin. "You gonna tell me to shut up again?"

"Probably."

"Never underestimate the power of the human touch."

"Shit," I say.

"Yeah." Smith drags a hand through his hair. "You think the universe is laughing at us, Lennie?"

I scrub my eyes, which feel tired and sticky, even though it's not even nine a.m. "I'd guess it's laughing so hard it's crying by now."

OKAY

Smith and I silently chew our way through the burritos he found at the back of the freezer, stretching out every bean-filled bite as long as possible. Neither of us needs to say that we don't know what to do next. Or at all.

Okay, I do have one idea. Go home. Tell my uncles everything. Beg them to help. Hope they have answers and a way to fix everything. Only problem there is I'm pretty certain right now they're crossing my name out of the family bible, changing the locks, and putting all my stuff in boxes on the front lawn.

It's actually sort of a relief when my phone, still tucked into my back pocket, starts vibrating. As I pull it out, I make sure to curl my hand around the beaten-up old iPhone, not wanting Smith to recognize the grinning pink skeleton on the plastic cover.

It's possible he'd freak out.

Dyl gave me this phone the week before she disappeared. She'd gotten an upgrade and knew I'd been dying for something other than my crappy old flip phone. So she gifted me her old one instead of trading it in. Never mind the giant crack running the length of the screen or that the battery couldn't make it through a whole day. I loved it. I was supposed to wipe the phone of Dyl's photos and playlists and all that other stuff, but I never got around to it and then Dyl was dead and the phone became a sort of digital memorial to her.

The phone buzzes in my hand and I glance down at the screen. Larry's picture grins back up at me.

Guilt hits me hard. I haven't given Larry a single thought since last night when we had our little fight. Knowing him, he's probably calling to make sure I'm not mad at him. Or . . . a worse possibility occurs to me. Has his life been royally screwed by a wish too?

It takes me a minute to remember what his wish was for, and as soon as I recall it my shoulders sag with relief. He didn't want his mom to be mad at him. Lame Larry and his lame wishes. If the idiot was standing in front of me right now, I'd hug him.

I quickly pick up the phone call, a little surprised by how happy I am at the prospect of hearing Larry's dopey normal voice.

"Hey," I say.

In response, Larry whispers something so quietly that all I can make out is my name and the word *help*.

A shiver of something—I guess you'd call it foreboding—goes through me. I shake it off. "Larry, use your big boy voice and talk louder."

"I can't," he whispers back in a slightly louder whisper. "I'm hiding." With his volume raised, I can hear the tremble in his voice.

"You grounded or something?" *Please, let that be it.*

"I wish," he squeaks back. "I'm at Michaela's house. We all are."

I shove myself away from the table. My chair tips and hits the floor with a bang. "What are you still doing there?" I ask, trying to contain my panic.

"No one can go past the end of the driveway. It's like there's a force field or something. And people are acting weird. Everyone's gone crazy. I'm afraid, Lennie. I'm really afraid."

I wait for him to connect the craziness to the wishes and say it's all my fault. But this is loyal-till-the-bitter-end Larry, so of course he doesn't.

"It's okay, Larry," I say, although I feel 99.9 percent certain that it's not. "I'll be there in a little bit. Other people can still come in, right?"

"Yeah, I guess. I don't know."

I press a fist to my churning stomach. "All right. I'm on my way. Do you need me to bring anything?"

"Lennie, no. It's too dangerous. You should stay away. I only called 'cause I wanted someone to talk to. I tried calling my mom, I thought she'd be worried, but she said I wasn't a baby anymore and I should learn to take care of myself." There is a snuffling sound on the other end of the phone and I suddenly realize that Larry is crying. "Lennie, my mom always said I'd be her little baby boy forever."

Oh, shit. Larry's wish. Damn it all.

I want to cry with him and beg his forgiveness. Instead, I take a deep breath and try to sound strong and certain when I tell him, "I'm gonna come get you, Larry. It'll be okay. I promise, everything's gonna be fine."

Another loud sniffle before Larry speaks again. "Thanks, Lennie, you're a great friend. Just be careful, okay?"

"Don't worry about me," I respond. "Sit tight and I'll be there soon."

I press the end button before he can thank me again and make me feel a million times worse.

Then I turn and come face-to-face with Smith.

"What's going on?" he demands in this hard "what the hell have you done now" sort of tone.

Pissed off, I spit the words at him. "My friend is still at Michaela's party and a bunch of other people are too. He says no one can leave and the place is a mess. I told him I'd come get him, 'cause it's all screwed up and—" I stop before I can add "and it's all my fault."

Although, it's not like that's some big secret. No one else was granting crazy wishes last night.

"Holy shit." Smith releases me and takes a step back. "Your friend Larry?"

"Yeah," I answer, surprised that Smith guessed he's the one friend who would call me—the two of them don't exactly run in the same circles.

"And you told him you'd go straight into the shit storm. For him."

I shrug, a little uncomfortable with this line of questioning. "Yeah."

"Okay." Smith nods. "So what should we expect at Michaela's?"

"You're not coming with me."

"Technically since I'm driving, you're coming with me."

I shake my head. "I'm calling my uncles. I gotta ask them what to do about Dyl anyway."

"What do you mean, 'Do about Dyl'? No offense, Lennie, but I'm not gonna have your uncles locking Dylan in the basement with W2."

"They wouldn't," I protest, but when Smith gives me a skeptical look, I can't help but modify my defense of the uncs to, "probably."

"Right," Smith says. "So here's the plan. You'll stay in the car with Dyl, while I run into Michaela's and grab big dumb Larry." I might agree that Larry is big and dumb, but Smith sure as hell hasn't earned the right to say so.

"Fuck. You. *That's* why you're not going."

Smith scoffs. I've never actually heard someone scoff before, but he makes this throat-clearing noise that can't be described in any other way. "Because I don't like your boyfriend?"

"No, because—" I stop as I realize what Smith just said. He thinks Larry and I are together? Ugh. The high school attitude of believing that a boy and a girl can't be friends without sucking face is so stupid, and I should've guessed that people would've interpreted my relationship with Larry that way. For some reason, though, I thought that Smith of all people would've known better. "Whatever. He's a good guy and you're—"

"Not?" Smith cuts in finishing my sentence for me. Except that isn't even what I was going to say. I'd meant to repeat that he was not going with me to rescue Larry.

I glare at Smith, wondering what is going on in his head. As usual it's impossible to tell. He looks angry and dark and complicated and not at all like someone I'd describe as a "good guy." Which is, of course, a big part of the reason I've always been so drawn to him. Hot mess—emphasis on the hot—seems to be my type.

And just like that, I give in. Because who am I kidding? If I'm gonna walk through hell, I want Smith at my side, trying to convince me to let him hold my hand.

"Fine." I throw my hands up in the air, so my complete surrender is clear. "We'll both go. But forget the whole me sitting in the car with Dyl while you run inside. Actually, I don't think it's a great idea to bring her along at all."

You'd think Smith might meet me halfway on this. But like me, you'd be wrong. "Yeah, well, it's a worse idea to leave her here. Let me paint you a real quick picture. Teena and her guy of the week have a fight. She storms off. Most likely comes home to get drunk. And when she's had too many, there's nothing she likes more than tottering into Dyl's room and playing up the grieving mother bit. Screaming. Crying. Shaking her fist at the ceiling. All while asking, 'Why why why . . .'" Smith stops and takes a deep breath. "Half the time she passes out on Dyl's bed."

"Okay," I say. "I get it. But . . . we can't hide Dyl from her forever."

"Maybe. Maybe not." He sighs. "But for now, at least until we figure out what's going on with her, I think we should keep Dylan close to us." Springing to his feet, Smith holds a hand out to me. "Come on."

I almost put my hand in his. It feels so natural, like an agreement that we are in this together. I even go so far as to stretch my arm out, before I remember and recoil. "Why don't you lead the way?"

"Damn. I almost had you," Smith says, flexing his hand so that I can see his torn and bruised knuckles. Then with a shrug, he grabs our plates and tosses them into the sink before heading back upstairs.

We find Dyl in the exact same position as we left her.

"Now what?" I ask, making sure to keep my voice low.

Leaning forward, Smith grabs hold of the comforter and whips it off the bed. "Now we—"

He chokes on whatever he was going to say next and we both stare in horror.

Dylan is wearing the same thing she'd had on when she disappeared: a threadbare Mickey Mouse tank top, paired with short black denim shorts. Curled on her side with her arms crossed over her chest, she looks so vulnerable.

But this isn't what has Smith and me so shaken. No,

that would be the red streaks slashed through with black, like lines of stitches, encircling her ankles, her knees, her wrists, her elbows, her shoulders, and—worst of all—her neck. There are probably even more we can't see beneath her clothing. We both know instantly that each of them marks a place where she'd been chopped apart, and the black lines make it look like she's been crudely sewn back together.

As Smith and I stare, unable to tear our eyes away, I hear this horrible high-pitched whistle, like a distant tea-kettle coming to a boil.

Smith steps in front of me, blocking my view. His hands curl around my head, gently applying pressure as if he knows that my skull is in danger of exploding. "Breathe in, Lennie. Come on now. Don't freak out."

It is only then that I realize the terrible sound is com-ing from me. I was trying to scream but a shrill whisper is all that can make its way past my closed throat. Shudder-ing, I make the horrible sound stop and try to take deep, calming breaths, but I choke on the air, unable to remem-ber how to get it into my lungs.

"Breathe." Removing his hands from my head now that it seems like it'll stay in one piece, his magic touch moves lower, one hand pressing on my back and the other flat against my lower ribcage. "Come on, Lennie. Don't do this. Breathe."

My throat loosens enough for me to sneak a bit of air in and then a little bit more. The world comes back into focus, and that's when I realize that the fingertips of Smith's right hand are parked directly beneath my boobs.

"I'm okay," I say, pushing his hand away and taking a step back. "It was only that . . ." I swipe the back of my arm across my eyes, not wanting Smith to see the tears there. "I saw the picture. The one of Dyl . . . after."

"No way." Smith's response is immediate. "Who would show that to you?"

"A cop. He was asking all these questions. Then he just put the picture in front of me."

"That's fucked."

I make a little squeaking noise that I hope Smith thinks is a sad laugh and not a choked back sob. "Yeah, I guess. I mean, they thought I did it."

"They didn't, Lennie." Again, there is no hesitation. "They thought you knew something. That's it. You were never on the official suspect list."

For some reason this makes me feel better. Not weight-lifted-off-my-chest better, but slightly better, which it turns out is enough to keep from falling to the ground and sobbing.

"Okay, thanks," I say, finally able to meet Smith's eyes

again. "Okay," I repeat, trying to regroup. "We need to get her out of here, right?"

"I'll carry her," Smith answers. "I need you to scout ahead and make sure the coast is clear."

I nod. "I can do that. One thing first, though." I cross the room to Dyl's closet and then dig through until I find her favorite pair of Pumas, a red-and-black-plaid baseball hat, and a hoodie. After shoving all of the items into a canvas bag and slinging it over my shoulder, I turn back to Smith and give him the thumbs-up sign. "Let's do this."

Smith scoops Dyl into his arms so that she is cradled close to his chest. I ease the door open and peer out, feeling paranoid. The hallway and the rest of the house are as silent and empty as before.

"It's clear," I whisper, twisting around to where Smith is now directly behind me. "You go first and I'll cover your back."

The corner of Smith's mouth kicks up in a half smile. "No one's coming after us with an MK16, Lennie."

If he wasn't holding Dyl, I'd be tempted to poke his bruise again. I settle for giving his shoulder a shove. "Go already, Smith."

For a bigger guy, who's also carrying another person, Smith really nails the quick and quiet combo. We make it to his Jeep Cherokee in record time. Smith gently lays

Dyl across the backseat and tucks a blanket around her. A lump fills my throat so full that I have to turn away and busy myself with getting into the car and buckling my seat belt.

Smith lingers behind me while I stare straight ahead and pretend to not hear the suspicious sniffling sounds coming from behind me.

Or maybe I was imagining them, because when Smith swings into the driver's seat and begins driving us to Michaela's, he appears to be as in control as ever.

"Look," he says. "The day after one of these parties everyone's tired and hungover. Any craziness is probably fights over the ibuprofen and pizza delivery menus."

"Sure," I say, and then I laugh. It sounds fake. And horrible. A stupid lie just like the one Smith's trying to feed me. It's still relatively early in the day, but at this point we both know that things are messed up in the kind of way that isn't gonna go away or get better. . . .

Not today.

And maybe not ever again.

BAD
IDEAS

The creepy "this is bad" feeling increases as we approach Michaela's gigantic mansion. Trying to distract myself, I twist around in my seat to check on Dylan. Seeing that one of her arms is dangling down at an awkward angle, I reach back and gently take her hand.

And then I scream.

I am jerked sideways as the car swerves, and thrown again when it screeches to a stop.

"What?" Smith demands. "What?"

I can't answer him, because I am too busy flinging my door open, unbuckling my seat belt, and finally diving out of the car to puke all over someone's perfectly maintained lawn.

"Here," Smith says from behind me. Glancing over my shoulder, I see he's offering me a bottle of water. Gratefully, I grab it and then spit and rinse. After a few minutes, I'm steady enough to stand.

I lean against the side of the car taking deep breaths while Smith waits beside me. I give him credit for waiting at least two full minutes before asking, "You gonna tell me what that was all about?"

I wonder if I should tell him, but he'll probably notice eventually, so I decide to spill. "Her hand. Her fingers. She's missing her pinkie and her middle finger. They're just . . ."

"They're gone." He says it almost nonchalantly, like we're discussing a change in her hair instead of how Dyl can no longer use her fingers to count to ten. "I noticed right away when her covers came off, but you wouldn't have known to look."

"To look for missing fingers?"

"Yeah. It was sort of a secret," Smith explains. "When the cops found Dyl, they reassembled her and did a body parts count. That's when they realized she was all there except for two fingers. We were told to keep it quiet, so if the cops found a suspect who knew about those missing fingers, they'd be able to prove that was the guy who did it. But they never got close enough to any suspects, so it didn't make a difference." He sounds calm, almost clinical, but when I glance over I notice how the sunshine highlights the tautness in his face. He's only barely holding it together.

I know the last thing he wants is for me to see the million vulnerabilities he has bubbling beneath the surface, so I look away and press my forehead to the cool glass on the side of the SUV. Regrets fill me to overflowing and the words explode out of me before I can even think to stop them. "It was my fault, Smith. You were right. The whole time. It was my fault."

He says nothing. Unable to take it anymore, I turn to face him.

I immediately wish I hadn't. I'd been expecting anger. I could've dealt with that. But he looks . . . pained. Like breathing hurts. Like *being* hurts.

"Talk. Now." He bites the words out.

The truth gushes out of me. "She met a guy online. He was a fan of my father's. He wanted to meet me. Dyl promised to set it up, but I told her I wouldn't do it. She kept bugging me for months, telling me what a great guy he was and all this stuff and I could tell she really liked him. But I didn't want to do it and I got mad and said he probably didn't want to meet me, he just wanted an excuse to meet her in person—'cause it was pretty obvious they were both crazy about each other. And then she told me that she'd been pretending to be me the whole time and that was the only reason he liked her and we got into a huge fight. I told her to go ahead and be me and see how much she liked it and she said that it was only terrible being me because I sucked at it and made things harder for myself and . . ." The stream of words suddenly halt, caught in my throat. Somehow, though, I push them out. "That was the last time I saw her."

"Jesus, Lennie," Smith whispers.

I sink to the ground, burying my face in my hands. "I know. I should've told someone. But I didn't really know anything worth telling, and anyway I'd thought she'd run away with this guy. That she was having the time of her life. And even when it got more serious, I figured the cops would've searched her computer and figured it out for themselves. They were already so sure I was involved, I worried that if I told them anything it would be evidence that I'd caused it and then by the time I realized how serious it was . . . well, Dyl was dead, so it wasn't like they could save her."

Smith's hand lands on my knee, in a surprisingly soft and comforting way. "Lennie, some dude wanted to kill you. Maybe that would've been a good thing to tell the cops about."

I peer up at Smith from between my fingers. "Maybe he killed Dyl 'cause he found out she wasn't me."

"Or maybe the shady internet guy wanted to kill you the whole time. What if he came after you? Did you even think of that?"

"Of course," I admit in a soft voice. "But . . . I sort of had it coming, right?"

Smith grabs a chunk of my hair and yanks it—hard.

"Ouch!" I scoot away from him.

A clump of dirt hits me in the chest. Another gets me in the shoulder, as Smith tears apart the pretty flower bed around someone's mailbox.

"Stop, Smith! Fuck!"

"Oh, sorry, Lennie," he says, while chucking another bit of dirt at me. "I didn't think you'd mind. It's not as if I'm trying to kill you, you know, like you really deserve."

He hits me again, this time on the side of my head.

"Okay!" I stand up, and then quickly duck away from another dirt ball. "It was a stupid thing to say. I'm sorry!"

"Nope." Another dirt clod, this one the size of a softball, explodes against my back as I try to run. "I want to hear you say that was some major bullshit." Giving chase, Smith hits me again. "I'm not stopping until you say it, Lennie."

"Fine!" I spin around, putting my hands in the air to signal my surrender. "I was feeling sorry for myself and it was bullshit. Are you happy now?"

Smith pauses with another giant clump of earth waiting in his fist. Letting the dirt trickle to the ground, he nods. "Totally happy."

"Great," I grumble as I run my fingers through my hair, trying to shake all the dirt free.

"Of course, you had to find the dirtiest way possible to make your point."

He grins, totally unrepentant. "I work with what I got."

"Jerk," I respond, the word coming out gentle, maybe even affectionate. Some subtle shift just happened between me and Smith, one I'm gonna need a little more time to fully understand. But already I know enough to tell that I like it. "We should go," I say, reminding myself of Larry waiting only a few houses away.

I spin to head for the Jeep, but before I even make it two steps Smith snags the hem of my shirt and reels me in until the back of my shoes hit the tips of his. His knuckles graze the sensitive bare skin at the base of my spine. It's only the slightest of connections and yet my neurons race up my spine to my brain screaming TOUCH TOUCH TOUCH. I feel his breath, warm against the back of my neck. "I should've said it earlier, but thank you. For the wish. For Dyl. For—"

I whirl around, needing to see his mouth moving and these hushed and humble words flowing out of it, just so that I know for sure that I'm not imagining this. But as soon as I face him he goes silent and almost glares at me in this smoldering way, which is annoying but also sort of hot, which also makes it even more annoying . . . and hot. It's a vicious cycle.

Dumb, I know. Stupid that I have to keep reminding myself that having my hand permanently connected to Smith's would be a bad thing. And when he acts protective and nice and actually worried about me . . . well, that makes it so much worse. If I don't get away from him pronto, the next thing you know I'll be cutting off my hand and giving it to him, insisting that he needs it more than me.

And yet I can't seem to stop myself from crossing the few inches of distance between us and giving Smith a "you're welcome" kiss.

Actually, I'm not even sure if it qualifies as a kiss. It's a brush of lips against his rough cheek, so short that I barely connect with the warmth of his skin beneath the dark stubble. And then I am stumbling backward, as if he'd pushed me away, but it's only my own mortification chasing me, while Smith follows, reaching out, and I reflexively give him my own hand in return, our fingertips brush—

Remembering, I snatch my hand away again.

Smith's outheld hand falls as if it's suddenly made of lead. "I wasn't—" He gives a sharp shake of his head. "Never mind."

And just like that, I can feel all the progress we made crumbling away.

"Right. Yeah." My head pumps up and down a few times in enthusiastic agreement. "Larry's probably wondering what happened to me," I say, unable to deal with this moment.

Smith nods, then turns, strides across the grass, and gets back into the Cherokee without another word. And I am left feeling like I somehow lost the one thing about this whole situation that didn't totally suck.

And that sucks even worse.

HELL

Michaela's driveway is still packed with cars, but other than that, nothing looks weird or out of place. "Who's that?" Smith asks as we pull to a stop.

A tall skinny guy plays basketball on the half-size court on the side of the house. And he's good—no, he's amazing. Sinking every basket, dribbling and running the ball like he was made to do it. The sun high above us makes his wild red hair look like it's alive.

That's when I realize who he is. And I remember another wish.

Seanie O'Hara standing in front of me, so short that the top of his head just barely reached my chin. I remember he had to sorta lean back to look up into my eyes, before he said, "I wish I was a little bit taller, I wish I was a baller."

"Holy shit," Smith says, finally putting it together. "That can't be . . ."

"Seanie O'Hara? Actually, it is."

"I've had gym class with that kid. He couldn't get half-way across the court without tripping over his own feet." Smith shakes his head. "He's a genius. Why didn't I make a wish like that?"

"Because you're an idiot," I immediately reply and then jump out of the car to get a little closer to Seanie and see up close the graceful miracle he's become. For a minute I worry I'll see a grimace of pain on his face, like maybe he can't stop playing or maybe the sudden growth was painful. But he looks happy. Unmistakably, irrefutably happy. If there was some terrible side effect, it doesn't seem to be bothering him.

I did that. It was a good thing and I made it happen.

For the first time it occurs to me that this whole wishing thing could be okay. I mean, obviously, I have a few things to figure out before I try it again, but maybe this is the answer to the black hole that is my life after high school. While everyone else is going to college and looking for jobs, I can travel the world or find a nice little house on the beach—hell, maybe both! And to keep the cash rolling in, I'll grant wishes. Only nice ones like Seanie's. Nice little wishes that make one person's world a little bit—

Seanie screams in this shrill voice and then takes off running. The glare from the sun momentarily blinds me, so I'm not sure what Seanie's yelling about until a dark form with gigantic wings leaps from the roof and swoops down toward the basketball court.

In the end, Seanie's not quite fast enough. The bat person picks him up and carries him away, beyond my line of sight. The scream, though, lingers long after he disappears.

My heart beats like mad and I can actually feel it sinking down down down from its earlier hopeful elevation to its new location closer to my knees.

"Did you see that?" Smith asks in a shaky voice.

"Devon Stringer wanted big scary bat wings."

"Emo Devon Stringer with the skinny jeans and guyliner?"

"Uh-huh."

"Shit."

"Uh-huh."

I begin trudging toward the front door and Smith falls into step beside me. "It's gonna be even worse when we get inside, isn't it?"

"Uh-huh."

"Okay."

We reach the stairs leading up to the front porch and for the second time in as many days, I walk uninvited into

Michaela Gordon's house.

And it is chaos. Not the drunken bacchanal chaos of last night that even at its rowdiest felt like a party. This . . . this is something else entirely. Like a scene out of a disaster movie.

To the right of the entrance, a group of girls I recognize from the three-time state champions girls' lacrosse team wield broomsticks and golf clubs. Mercilessly, they bash skulls and whack the shins of anyone foolish enough to enter their territory. Most of the invaders quickly retreat back the way they came. The few who get past are chased by one of the girls who insists on checking the bottom of their shoes before finally letting them go.

Worse, judging from the screams, thuds, and crashes coming from the rear of the house, the lacrosse girls' skirmish is only the tip of the shitberg.

Seemingly unperturbed, Smith approaches the outer edges of their territory. "Hey, Stace," he calls to the lacrosse girl who is clearly the leader. "What's going on?" Of course, he knows her. All the sporty people seem to live in their own special Gatorade-colored world.

I expect her to smile and flutter at him, a typical reaction to Smith. Instead she raises a curtain rod like a weapon. "Don't give me that look, Smith. I'm not letting you through."

"I don't wanna get through," he counters. "I just wondered what the deal is?"

"The deal!?" Stace shifts the curtain rod in her hands, as if she's so disgusted with his question that she's thinking of hitting him even though he's only standing there. "Don't tell me you're one of those dorks who immediately went into hiding?"

"No!" Smith's cool is shaken at the very suggestion that he might be part of the hidden dorks. "Lennie and I got here a few minutes ago."

"Lennie." Stace's gaze swings past Smith to land on me.

I waggle my fingers sort of lamely. "Hey."

The tip of Stace's curtain rod jabs me in the chest. "Why?" Another jab. "I wanna know why?" A quick tap-tap this time. For variety, I guess. "Fuck with all these other assholes. I don't care. But my sister was a nobody. Why mess with her?" The rod comes at me again and this time I'm pretty sure she's aiming to put it straight through my heart.

Smith swats it away. "Are you crazy, Stace? You don't even have a sister."

Stace goes white. Then she stumbles back a few steps. "I do have a sister." Her voice is low and suddenly full of tears. "She'll be a freshman this year. I never let her hang with me, I was—" She breaks off, unable to say any more as her whole body is racked with sobs.

Another girl leads her away, while a third one leans in to me and Smith. "Her sister was fat. Like really—" The girl blows out her cheeks and spreads her arms out to illustrate the amount of girth we should imagine. "She made a wish, I guess. To be small, we figure, because one second she was there, and the next . . . she just, like, shrunk right before our eyes. Stace put her on a shelf over there to keep her out of trouble, but she's not there anymore, because the shelf isn't there anymore." Smith and I both follow her gesture to an empty, oddly orange-colored space on the wall. The girl shakes her head. "The problem is there's no safe place in this house of horrors."

I know exactly who they're talking about. She'd squeezed in behind me while I was opening the third jar. I'd spun around and there she was, completely blocking my way. She had the biggest bluest eyes I'd ever seen and the look in them was wild and a little bit desperate. I recognized that look. That feeling. So I didn't even wait for her to ask.

"Make a wish," I said, holding the jar out.

She took it gingerly. Her hands were shaking as someone jeered, "She'll drink it all!" Those on the bottom rungs, like myself, generally decide on a defense strategy and stick with it. Me, I've always used my mouth, which is why I told that guy where to shove it. This girl, though, went still and then curled inward, her shoulders hunching and head sinking as if she wanted to disappear completely.

Her wish trembled at the tip of her lips, and she swallowed a few times, as if even her voice was in hiding. Then finally she spoke. "I wish I was small. No, tiny. Petite. The type of girl who looks like she could fit in a guy's pocket. That's what I wish more than anything."

I repeated her wish back word for word. Granting it, although I didn't know that then. Except . . . I can sort of remember thinking that I wanted to make it true for her.

Now, though . . . now I wish she'd stayed away from me. Or that I'd stayed away from her and the rest of this party.

I reach out and grab the third girl before she walks away. "Have you seen Larry Carver?" Her forehead scrunches as if trying to remember who that might be. I help her out. "Tall guy. Kinda dopey-looking. Dark hair, cut short. Looks like his mom dresses him. Says things like, 'Oh, gosh, sorry' a lot."

"Oh, yeah." She nods. "Sorry, haven't seen him."

Damn. It couldn't be easy. Of course not.

"What about Michaela?" Smith calls after the girl.

Her ponytail swings as she looks back over her shoulder. "Locked away with her lover boy."

"Lover boy?" Smith asks, but a shout from her team-mates pulls the girl back into guard duty.

I pull out my cell and text Larry that we're here and searching for him, when a guy runs by and presses a fist-ful of dollars into my hand. He then gives another pile of them to Smith.

"Enjoy!" he hollers before running along. Two seconds later, a bug-eyed boy stops in front of us.

"Show me the money!" he demands. "Show me the money!"

After Smith and I exchange puzzled looks, we both shrug and obligingly hold out our crumpled . . . our eyes meet in disbelief.

We are each clutching hundred-dollar bills.

The boy gazes at the money adoringly as if trying to fill his line of vision with nothing but green, and then he's gone, dashing after the first boy, who is still handing out the crazy amounts of cash.

I count the dollars in my hand. Eight hundred. I laugh in delight; if I survive this day I am gonna have a hell of a shopping spree. What a rare bit of good fortune that I granted a wish to someone so generous.

And then I remember the wish. "I wanna be rich. Like shitting-hundred-dollar-bills type of filthy rich."

I don't realize I've repeated his wish out loud until

Smith throws his pile of Benjamins to the floor. He stares at me in amazement when I quickly snatch his money up and add it to my own quickly growing bankroll. I return the look as he pulls a teensy bottle of hand sanitizer from his pocket and thoroughly coats his hands with the stuff.

"So what did the second guy with the crazy eyes wish for?" Smith asks as I shove my newfound wealth into my back pocket.

"Isn't it obvious?"

"'Show me the money' was his wish?"

I nod. "Yeah, I don't get it either, but he was so emphatic, I was just like, 'Okay, dude.'"

As we talk, Smith and I push our way through the house. At every turn there are fights, tears, and people running frantically from or to things that we can't see, but must be terrible judging by their reactions. I mostly stay tucked behind Smith and hide my face, because after Stace's reaction I realize that more than a few people might be able to connect the dots that lead straight to me.

Luckily, the chaos seems to be working in my favor, since few people register our presence at all. That is, until Larry pops out from under the dining room table and screams, "LENNIE! You came!"

The room becomes very quiet then. The group of people on top of the dining room table who'd been wrestling over the brass candlesticks—apparently wanting to use them as weapons—swivels my way. Another line of people who'd been stampeding past stop in their tracks. Three more people pop out from under the table, and I can't help but be amazed that so many would choose such an obviously lame hiding place.

With the exception of Larry, none of them look like they want to greet me with a squeezing-tight hug.

"Cash is here. *She* did this," someone says. Or maybe they all say it. My name is suddenly on everyone's lips, spreading and drawing more and more people into the room. It feels a lot like last night, actually, when they all wanted a sip of the shine. No doubt they are thinking the same thing as they close in.

Smith steps in front of me and somehow his voice is calm and friendly and confident when he speaks. "Everybody chill. I know this is a bad situation, but Lennie came here to fix it."

"More like she came to finish us all off!" a faceless girl in the crowd counters, and the mob roars its approval.

My stomach clenches. It doesn't matter what Smith or anyone else says. These people want blood. My blood, to be specific. And I don't really blame them.

Smith, though, seems to feel differently. The "hey, we're all friends here" smile has faded from his face and a new, more dangerous expression has taken its place. It reminds me of the wild, slightly dangerous, and totally sexy "I'm gonna kiss you 'cause you just saw something you shouldn't have" look. Except judging from the way his hands are curled into fists, I'm pretty sure he's not gonna make out with me or anyone else.

I'm not sure fighting is such a great idea, but since I don't have any better—or worse—ones, I take a deep breath and prepare to throw myself into the fray beside him.

WORSE
THAN WORST

S mith reaches behind his back and pulls a tire iron
out from underneath his T-shirt.

My first thought is: *Holy shit, how long has he had
that there?*

My second thought is: *Holy shit, why didn't he use that
sooner?*

My third thought is: *Holy shit, why not have a knife or gun
or something that is a tiny bit more effective?*

The third thought comes as the mob surges forward.
Instead of realizing how totally screwed he is, Smith takes
a step toward them, brandishing his tire iron like it's a
magic wand and he's Harry Fucking Potter.

It occurs to me that now would be a good time to run.
And that this may be my one shot at escaping.

And yet I don't move.

The tire iron goes flying from Smith's hand and as

luck would have it, lands directly at my feet. Smith flings a disgusted glare over his shoulder at me. I can't tell if he's upset that I'm just standing instead of helping him fight or if he can't believe I'm such an idiot that I haven't made a run for it yet.

Then he mouths the word, *"Run,"* finally settling it: he wants me to get away. This was an actual noble sacrifice.

In my life not many people have had my back. Not consistently. Not voluntarily. In response, I've tried to be a rock. I've tried to give zero fucks about anyone other than myself. Especially after Dyl. But let's be honest, if an idiot like Larry could sneak through my supposedly impenetrable hardened exterior, then it's really no tougher than the candy shell on an M&M. And yeah, I'm even ooey-gooier on the inside.

So, of course, I bend down and pick up that stupid tire iron. I'm dumb like that sometimes.

I had an English teacher sophomore year who liked to say cutting things as she passed papers back. One of her favorite lines was, "The difference between genius and stupidity is that genius has limits."

Here's to being limitless, I think, as I lift the tire iron over my head, take one last breath, and throw myself into the fight. But before I can whack anyone, a thundering crash makes the room go still. The gigantic china cabinet falls forward, slamming against the dining room table and spilling its no-doubt priceless crystal. I spot Larry standing in the spot where the china cabinet had been. He is red with exertion but grinning like an idiot.

"Go," he yells, pointing to the doorway behind us. "Basement. We come in peace."

The crowd surges forward again, a bit more slowly and carefully now as they try to avoid the bits of glass scattered everywhere. Larry disappears from view and Smith grabs my upper arm and unapologetically manhandles me out of the dining room.

I struggle to get loose. "We can't leave him!"

Smith ignores my protests and drags me away, through more rooms and hallways, until we reach a closed door that Smith pounds with his fist.

It opens a crack and an urgent yet low voice demands, "Password?"

"Um . . . we come in peace?" Smith says, and I realized this must be the basement Larry told us to head for.

The door closes again and I'm pretty sure we're screwed, which is exactly what we deserve for leaving Larry behind. But then there is the rattle of a chain and the door opens once more, this time wide enough to let us slip inside.

The door quickly closes and locks behind us while we blink and take in our new surroundings. We are at the top of a blue staircase that leads into what is apparently an aquatic-themed basement. As we walk down the stairs, it feels like heading underwater. Everything is blue from the ceiling to the floor to the lighting that swirls around casting flickering wave shapes onto the walls lined with—what else—fish tanks, stacked one upon another.

An old man calls out a crackly, "Namaste."

I turn toward the voice and see a supersize waterbed at the center of the room with a group of people propped in the center of its gently rolling surface. There is a wizened old man in the middle of them wearing a hat that Smith and I immediately recognize.

Anyone in our school would. A metal bowl with a brim, which Michael Turlington has worn since the end of freshman year when he brought it to school as part of an English project on Don Quixote. He calls it his Mambrino.

Every person in the school knows the story of the Mambrino, just like everyone knows Turlington. He's a senior notorious for living the high life. The very high life, if you know what I mean. We've had a few classes together over the years and he's always been cool to me, but that's probably because he has no idea who I am. Oh, I'm sure he's heard about my father. The thing is that Turlington's usually too stoned to remember those sorts of little details.

He usually doesn't even know what day of the week it is.

So the idea of him being the leader of this undersea basement group seems a little strange.

"Whoa!" Old Man Turlington calls as he squints at us. "Who do we have here? Come closer so I can see you."

Unsure of how welcome I'll be here once he recognizes me, I desperately try to remember his wish. He was there. I clearly remember his signature "Whoa" as I walked into the party and began pulling the mason jars from my bag.

Smith nudges me forward and now I get the full view of Turlington. Nearly unrecognizably wrinkled and ancient, he's propped up by pillows all around him, like he's a baby who might topple over without them. Following the baby theme, he's wearing some sort of loincloth or diaper—I honestly try not to look too closely—which makes his bony little shoulders, concave chest, and overall shrunken and withered appearance all too obvious. If I didn't know better, I'd swear he was at least a hundred years old.

A hundred years old. Aw, shit, now I remember his wish.

"Lennie, I wanna live to be old, like more than a hundred years kinda old, ya know what I mean? But I wanna still be cool at one hundred, like super cool so that all the chicks still want me and the dudes are like 'yeeeahhh-aahh, Turlington.'"

I nodded at him throughout this whole speech and

then, as I'd quickly fallen into the habit of doing, swiftly summed up his wish. "To being really super old and also amazingly irresistible. May all your wishes come true, or at least just this one!"

Cheers.

Unable to continue looking at the results of my sloppy wish granting, I scan the room. Oof. It's as bad as looking at Turlington. All those wishes so thoughtlessly recited while my head spun with the moonshine are coming back to me with a vengeance.

A girl with six—no, eight arms. She'd complained about not having enough time for work and sports and school and friends. I'd cut her off before she could go on any longer. "To having enough hands to do it all!"

Two boys wearing teeny bikinis, and looking good in them too . . . except for the fact that they seem more than a little uncomfortable. They'd wished for girls from the *Sports Illustrated* swimsuit edition, but I'd paraphrased their wish: "To both of you getting some hot bikini bodies!"

A trio of girls literally connected at the hip. "To being inseparable!" I think their wish had been to remain friends forever and not let anything break them apart. Again, I'd given it my own spin and the stormy looks on their faces suggest that their friendship might be worse off because of it.

"Greetings, friends," Turlington calls, drawing my attention to him and the girls curled up on his right and left sides. One has a mermaid tail but the other looks normal, except the way she's glaring tells me that I must have granted one of her wishes too.

"Hey, Turlington," I say weakly. "You're looking . . ." I pause, searching for the right word. Ancient? Mature? Well aged? I finally settle on, "spry."

Amazingly, he laughs at this.

"Good to see you, man," Smith says, leaning forward and exchanging one of those complicated dude-to-dude handshakes with Turlington that ends with both of them bumping a fist over their own hearts.

Settling back onto his pillows, Turlington gives us both a warm smile. "What can I do for you, my friends?"

"Um, we were really just running a—"

Smith kicks my ankle. "Dude, we only want to grab Lennie's friend Larry and get out of here. No offense, but this scene's a little crazy."

"Hmm. Yes." Turlington nods in this thoughtful way. "I get it. I do. You wanna be gone. Problem is, nobody who was here past dawn can get out without . . ." he trails off, seemingly lost in thought. Then he turns toward a dark corner of the room. "Ginny, come over here."

Turlington lifts a finger, beckoning, and the crowd in

that dark corner parts to reveal a scantily clad girl slowly slinking her way toward us. It is only when I notice the pointy ears on top of her head, the tail undulating behind her, and the sleek fur disappearing into the deep V of her cleavage that I realize I've found the girl who wished to be a sexy cat. Although, now that I think of it, she might have wished to be sexy *like* a cat. In my defense, that still makes no damn sense, so I don't feel too guilty about messing it up.

"Tell them," Turlington says as Ginny sinks onto the bed and curls up beside him with a sulky purr. "Tell them about how you tried to get out."

She ignores us for several long moments, licking her paw/hand in a way that is both gross and mesmerizing. I sneak a glance at Smith and notice that he is even more transfixed than me. I bet if she rolled onto her back and asked him to rub her belly he wouldn't hesitate to comply.

"C'mon, Ginny," Turlington coaxes in his creaky old-man voice.

With a hiss of annoyance, Ginny ceases grooming and turns her cat eyes toward me. "Lots of people ran for it this morning and they all came back so scared I didn't bother attempting my own escape," Ginny finally says in this low husky voice totally different from her previous high-pitched squeak. "But when I was getting some fresh air that bat came swooping down and I took off until I hit the edge of the driveway and then—" Her back arches up as in memory of that moment and I can see her fur standing on end. "It was like electricity. I was thrown backward. I think I even blacked out for a few minutes."

"Has anyone tried to drive through it?" I ask.

She shrugs, clearly disinterested. "All I know is, I'm not going out there again." With that she uncurls herself from the bed and stalks across the room.

"So you see"—Turlington spreads out his trembling hands—"there's nothing to be done but sit tight until Lennie here can reverse all the wishes. That is why you came back, right?"

"Well . . ." I start to say, and Smith kicks me again.

"I think you're right, Turlington," Smith says.

"Yep," Turlington agrees. "I've been given the wisdom of the ages, dude."

Smith nods. "I can tell. So look, we need to get some moonshine so Lennie can start making all those wishes unwished, if you know what I mean. Think you could help us get out of here?"

Feet begin to pound against the floor over our heads, almost like a stampede has broken out. As if on cue, everyone in our watery den looks up with fearful expressions. Moments later we hear multiple fists hitting the basement door and just as many voices raised in supplication, begging to be let in. Screams begin to filter through, and in them we can hear a name. I am relieved to realize it's not my own, but that quickly fades when I hear the gasps around me. Then that same name spreads around the basement.

Zinkowski.

I have never in my life seen so many people lose their shit so fast. It's sheer panic. At least fifteen people try to cram themselves into a cedar closet, until one of them asks, "What if it gets Cheetos'd?" and then they all fight to be the first to wriggle back out.

"Easy with the merchandise!" Turlington cries out in his old man's warble, as he's lifted from the bed at the same time that another group of his followers begin to pull the pillows away.

"Turlington!" I call as he's carried past me. "What's up with Zinkowski? I thought he'd be here with you!"

Turlington shakes his head sadly. "Zinkowski has gone to the dark side."

I can't believe it. Turlington and Zinkowski are best friends in a totally bromantic way. They fling their arms around each other's shoulders when they laugh. They finish each other's sentences. They leave graffiti all over school that reads Turl + Zinc. They seemed like the type who would be together eighty years from now, two old men sitting on the front porch chuckling at some lame joke only they understood.

"Come on." Smith ends my gloomy reverie on Turl + Zinc's lost love with a sharp shove. "We gotta get out before they block the door."

The freaked-out citizens of Turlington's underwater world have pulled themselves together and are now working toward the common goal of carrying several sheets of plywood up the stairs to blockade the entrance.

Smith gives me another push, but I am already moving. Although I have to wonder if now is the best time to escape. You don't have to be a survival expert to know that when all the gazelles start running away, you should follow them and not go in the opposite direction to find out what's hunting them.

And yet, here I am undoing the chain, while Smith holds back the guy who let us in. "You said you came in peace!" he hollers, clearly feeling a bit betrayed.

"Sorry," Smith replies, just as the door flies open. A sea of people comes flowing in, nearly pushing us down the stairs. Snagging my wrist, Smith fights against the tide and tugs me along beside him, until we pop back out again.

Seconds later, the door snaps shut behind us.

Outside of Turlingtown, the hall is quiet and empty.

"I'm freaked out," I whisper.

"What did Zinkowski wish for, do you remember?" Smith asks.

I close my eyes trying to remember. Turlington and Zinkowski were always together, so after Turlington made his wish . . .

Zinkowski stepped up and grinned at me with his blank stoner smile.

"Make a wish?" I asked, holding up the jar of shine.

"Wish." He laughed like he'd never heard of such a crazy thing, although he'd been standing right there while Turlington went through this exact same ritual. "Well, oookay." Then he squeezed his eyes closed, like a little kid getting ready to blow out his birthday candles. His eyes opened and he startled as if surprised to see me standing there.

"What's your wish?" I asked.

"Can't tell ya."

"You have to tell me. That's how it works."

"Well, ookay." He blinked at me and then swung his head in Turlington's direction. "Whadda I wish for?"

Turlington thinks for a second then says, "Midas touch. That's a wish." He turns to me for confirmation. "Right? That's like, totally a wish."

"Yeeee-ahhh," I answered slowly. I think their whole baked vibe was getting into my head too. "That's like when everything you touch turns to gold. That's like, a big wish."

"Suh-weet!" Turlington and Zinkowski said as one.

I raised the jar of moonshine once more. "To everything you touch turning to—"

"Wait, wait," Zinkowski broke in with a giggle. "Not gold. I want everything I touch to turn to Cheetos—" A snort of laughter made it impossible for him to speak and the hilarity was so contagious that all three of us cracked up so hard we had to lean on one another to keep standing. Eventually, we got ahold of ourselves and Zinkowski finished. "The Cheetos touch. That's what I want!"

And that's the wish I granted.

Oh, hell. Now I understand the panic.

I quickly fill Smith in.

I guess it's a sign of the human ability to adapt that he is barely fazed by the information. In fact, like me, he seems more bummed by the apparent dissolution of Turl + Zinc.

"Wow, that sucks," Smith whispers as we creep down the hallway. "You think Zinkowski's mad at Turlington for giving him the idea for the wish?" He jerks a thumb back in the direction we just came. "They certainly seem to think he's coming for them."

I shrug. "I don't—"

Abruptly, I fall silent as the sound of pounding footsteps approaches behind us.

"Go," Smith whisper-yells as he starts to run, and I take off behind him. When we reach the dining room where we left Larry, all the furniture is gone. Most of the shattered glass too. Instead, piles and piles of Cheetos fill the room. Orange cheese dust fills my mouth as it falls open in shock. This was clearly the center of whatever was happening overhead. I cough and gag, wondering if some of these Cheetos might have been people.

"Come on," Smith urges, glancing back to make sure I haven't fallen too far behind.

Panicked again, I break into a run, but instead of gracefully catching up with Smith, my feet slip and I crash into the center of a mini Cheetos mountain.

They spray up around me. Lying on the ground, half-buried in Cheetos, I decide not to call after Smith. Without me slowing him down he'll have a greater chance of getting the hell out of this nightmare. I owe him at least this for taking on that crazy mob armed with nothing but a tire iron.

Of course, at the exact instant that I decide to give Smith up, he reenters the room. "What are you doing?"

"I'm okay," I answer. "Just go. I'm right behind you."

Smith looks over his shoulder, as if assessing the danger. Then his gaze returns to where I am still gasping for air on the floor, surrounded by Cheetos dust. I make a move, like I'm getting up, so he'll feel free to move on, but instead it has the opposite effect. Smith launches himself toward me and in one fluid motion, grabs hold of my hand and pulls me to my feet.

"You set the pace," he says, no doubt noticing the way I'm huffing and puffing for breath. Distant shrieks send chills down my spine and I leap forward, only to be quickly jerked back like a yo-yo at the end of its string.

As I stumble toward Smith he tries to pull away, but our hands are firmly stuck together and the move sends me further off balance so that in a panic I grab for him and we become even more tangled until gravity has its way with us and we both end up on the floor.

Well, to be more specific, Smith is on the floor and I am on Smith.

It is not the worst place to be. Except for the fact that the room is covered with Cheetos dust and the boy who caused this destruction may return here at any moment.

Smith stares up at me in horror, hopefully because of the Zinkowski thing and not because he is realizing that he may now be stuck with me for good.

His free hand comes up and one finger gently traces a line across my cheek. "You got a little something right there," he says with one of those crooked Smith smiles. And then while I am frozen in this gootastic state, Smith lifts his head just enough to flick his tongue across the tip of my nose. "And there too," he adds.

I can feel myself go red as the furnace of longing flares up inside me. Embarrassed and afraid that Smith is messing with me, I force out a laugh. "Ha, funny," I say, the way a robot who is still trying to understand the concept of humor might.

Before Smith can laugh or lick me again, I scramble off him.

Or I try to scramble off.

Actually I do more than try, I fight for it. But every time I make a little progress, he pulls his hand—and mine along with it—causing me to topple over again. It's possible that he might be feeling equally frustrated as I do the same thing to him. A new and intense sympathy for the plight of conjoined twins fills me as we both become increasingly orange colored with the amount of Cheetos grit covering our bodies.

Finally, by unspoken mutual agreement, we stop and simply lie side by side, catching our breath.

"I didn't mean to get us stuck together," Smith says.

"I know."

"I wasn't thinking."

"I know."

"I'm—"

I hold my breath, wondering if that long withheld word of apology might finally exit Smith's mouth.

"You think this was Cheetos's last stand?" he asks instead.

I laugh despite myself and Smith joins in.

Everything is as awful as it can be . . . except there are worse people I can imagine being stuck with. In the grand scope of things, this is a tiny setback and one that can—with a bit of elbow grease—be reversed.

"We got unstuck the last time," I say. "I'm sure we can do it again."

So we pull and pull and pull. Nada. Smith pulls a credit card out of his wallet and gets a tiny corner of it wedged between our hands, but when he tries to force it further, it snaps in half.

Smith's face is white. Blood drips from where the plastic sliced across his hand. And we are stuck.

"I couldn't," Smith says in a tight voice.

"Hey." I give him an awkward pat on the shoulder. "We can try again later, right?"

Smith, like all people not used to losing, shakes his head. Playing cheerleader is just as foreign to me, but I give it a try anyway.

"C'mon Smith. Time to get up and get out of here. Be a fighter. Or a runner! Like at a track meet, except if we lose we might die."

Okay, so no one's gonna be hiring me to give motivational speeches anytime soon. And yet somehow it does the trick. Smith nods. Slowly, each of us checking with the other before making a move, we sit up and at last make it to our feet.

If our hands weren't already attached it would be a perfect moment for a celebratory hug.

Instead we start moving. Fast. Yet quietly. Tippy tippy toe. Quick. Quick. Quick. After all the people running around earlier, the quiet and emptiness now seems ominous.

We are almost at the front door and I am about to tell Smith that I can't leave without Larry, when a long curtain twitches and Larry bounds out. It's amazing he's lasted this long in here when he thinks under a table and behind a curtain are good hiding places.

"Lennie!" he yells, having apparently learned nothing

from the last time we did this. But no, he quickly slaps a hand over his mouth, before whispering from behind it, "Sorry."

I'm not about to wait and see if the mob comes after us again. I grab hold of Larry with my free hand. "Let's get out of here," I say, and then lead the charge to the front door.

MOSTLY
SCREWED

Perhaps it is a bit of an exaggeration to say we run for our lives.

We run as if we believe we can leave the insanity behind us, as if the insanity isn't clasping our hands together. As if I am not the very person who unleashed all of it in the first place.

Once we reach the Cherokee, Larry slips into the backseat while Smith and I fumble around a bit, trying to figure out how we can get in while holding hands. Finally, Smith shoves me inside and I clamber over the center console and settle myself in the passenger seat. As he starts the car, Smith glances over his shoulder. And then continues to stare. And somehow I just know.

"She's gone, isn't she?"

"Yes." Smith grinds the word out between his teeth.

Luckily (if such a word can even apply in this instance),

he spots her almost immediately, playing some one-on-one with Seanie, who apparently survived his run-in with Bat Boy.

Stomping on the gas, Smith sends us rumbling over the grass. Chunks of lawn go flying into the air as we skid to a stop by the basketball court.

"Time to go, Dyl," Smith calls out the window in this pleasant sort of way.

"Umm..." Larry stutters from behind me. "Isn't she—"

I spin around and give him a hard look. "No. Now, ssshhhh."

I look back out the window to see Dyl toss the ball to Seanie. She says something I can't make out, then jogs over and hops into the backseat. Before the door is fully closed, Smith is rocketing across the lawn once more—this time headed toward the street.

As the brick columns flanking the end of the driveway get closer, I twist in my seat to face Larry, who looks nervous.

"It's gonna be okay," I tell him. "We're getting you out of here."

He bites his lip. "They said it would hurt. They said—"

I never find out what else they said because at that minute we hit the edge of Michaela's property and Larry shrieks. It is this horrible high-pitched sound of agony that is its own type of painful just listening to it. On the bright side, it lasts only a few seconds. On the less bright side, this is because Larry begins to violently convulse.

Dyl reaches for Larry, while I scream, "Back up! Back up!"

Smith has already reversed by then, but is so shaken by hearing Larry that he slams us into one of the brick columns.

Foam drips from Larry's mouth as I yell at Smith, "Go! Go! Go!"

Smith manages to get us away from the column, and then backs up again until we are once again parked on Michaela's rolling green lawn.

The convulsions stop immediately. Larry's eyes roll up into his head and a second later he goes limp.

Throwing my door open, I jump out of the car—only to be yanked back by Smith's hand glued to mine. "Let me go!" The words come out shrill and full of unshed tears. Using all my weight, I jerk my body away from Smith's again and again, but our hands might as well be welded together. I slump back into my seat, curling into myself and finally giving in to tears.

After several long moments of my silent sobbing, Dyl's hand lands on my shoulder. "He's okay. Still breathing. Heart beating. All the good stuff."

That should make me feel better. It doesn't, though.

I did this to him. I brought him to Michaela's party and told him it would be fine. I made him drink and make a wish. I called him names because I was stupid and drunk and angry. And when he needed my help, I promised him it would be okay. I told him I would fix everything and nearly killed him instead.

I hear the car door open and the sound of Seanie's voice. "He okay?"

"Yeah," Smith answers. "Can you get him back up to the house?"

"No!" Swiping away tears with the back of my hand, I turn to face Larry once more. His expression is so peaceful I could almost believe he's sleeping. Except his skin is scary white and the breaths coming from between his parted lips are thin and raspy.

"We can't leave him here," I protest.

Smith gives my hand a tug. He looks almost as freaked out as I feel. "If you want to stay, I'll stay with you. I mean"—he holds up our attached hands with a caustic smile—"I go where you go, right?"

I blink at Smith, wondering if I've had a full mental breakdown and am imagining him saying these things. Reaching out with my free hand, I pinch his arm. It feels solid and real. The despair that had been crushing me lifts just a bit.

"Focus, Lennie," Smith says, bringing my gaze back up to his face. "We can stay, but I've been thinking. . . . You know how I told Turlington you needed to go home and get some shine to grant more wishes?"

"Yeah." I nod and then force a watery smile. "You're so full of shit."

"But what if I wasn't?" Smith replies. "Couldn't you get someone to wish that all the wishes from last night were unwished or something? You could at least try. Or, I don't know, maybe you should ask your uncles what to do."

"I thought you didn't trust them to not lock us all in the basement?"

"That was before I saw this." He sweeps a hand out indicating Michaela's house. "It's bigger than I thought. There's no way you can fit all of this in your basement. Your uncles are our only move at this point."

He's right. Of course, he's right. And I probably shouldn't have left my house until I fully understood this thing.

"That might be the best way to help Larry . . . and everyone else." Smith adds softly, pushing his advantage.

"Okay," I nod. "Okay."

Awkwardly I contort until I can place my free hand against Larry's cheek. He feels hot to the touch. I look up at Seanie. "Let him lie down somewhere. Get him something cold to drink. Maybe a cool washcloth too. Or a warm one. I don't know. Ask someone. Tell everyone to be nice to him and if anyone tries to mess with him, well, tell them I'll wish 'em an endless lifetime of gym classes with Mr. Proler. Got it?"

Seanie nods.

I nod back and it feels official. Like an oath.

I keep my hand pressed against Larry. "It'll be okay," I promise him, even though he's unconscious and can't hear me. As Seanie grabs Larry beneath the armpits and pulls him from the car, I make another promise, this one to myself: I will do everything in my power to make sure it isn't a lie.

Next time everything will really and truly be okay.

WON'T GO WELL

We ride in shell-shocked silence. The dashboard clock says it's 12:46 p.m. It seems unbelievable that this day still has so many hours left in it. I close my eyes, exhausted. I want nothing more than to go home and crawl under my covers.

"So," Dyl pipes up from the backseat. "I was dead, huh?"

From our connected hands I feel a tremor go through Smith. I stare out my window, unable to look at him or Dylan.

"Yeah," Smith finally answers after clearing his throat a few times. "You were . . ."

"Dead," Dyl helpfully finishes for him. "Seanie said it was a few months ago."

"Helpful of him," Smith mutters.

Dyl ignores this.

"Seems like a long time to be dead and then, ta-da, be somehow back alive again. I mean, I guess anytime you're dead it's weird to suddenly not be dead, but you'd think it'd be better for it to happen closer to the time of death so you're not, like, a rotting stinking decaying zombie."

"You're not a zombie and you're not decaying," Smith snaps at her.

"No," she agrees in a soft voice, which immediately makes the hairs on the back of my neck stand on end. The soft voice is almost always a precursor to the screeching loud voice. "But I do have these weird lines all over me and I feel kind of achy. What happened to me?"

I expect Smith to dodge the question. Instead he goes with a blatant lie. "Car accident. Bad one."

I stifle a groan, but Smith must know what I'm thinking 'cause he glares at me, making it clear he wants me to keep my mouth shut.

Dyl, meanwhile, keeps asking questions. "Was I driving or was it someone else? Was it a drinking thing? Were you or Lennie in the car? What—"

Smith cuts her off. "You were alone. It wasn't your fault. The other guy . . ." Smith stops and sighs. "It's hard to talk about, Dyl. Could you just . . . You're here, okay? You're alive. Let's focus on that."

Dyl was always quick to argue and never hesitated to

push back against Smith when she felt he was bossy or full of shit. To my surprise, though, she says nothing, and a strained silence fills the entire car.

It's a relief when we pull up in front of my house. I don't care if my uncles yell at me. Hell, at this point I'd welcome it. Anything to break this terrible quiet tension.

As I climb over the middle console and exit the driver's side door behind Smith, I hear off-key singing emanating from the house. *That's not a good sign*, I think, at the same time that Smith asks, "What is that noise?"

I don't blame him for not being able to recognize the loud caterwauling as that of human voices. My uncles only sing when they're so deep in their cups they can barely speak. It's like something in their brains says speech is nearly impossible so the only choice is to try and harmonize.

It sounds like they've chosen "Whiskey in the Jar," which is one of a handful of Irish drinking songs in their repertoire. Usually they're too far gone to remember the verses, so they repeat the chorus on an endless loop, in this case, *"Whack for the daddy-o, there's whiskey in the jar."*

As I push the front door open, I turn back to Smith and Dyl. "Let me handle them, okay?"

"Wait." Dyl grabs hold of Smith and my connected hands. "First I want to know what's up with this."

This time, instead of a stupid lie, Smith tries to evade the question. "It's a wish thing, Dyl. We'll explain everything later."

"I want to know now," Dyl stubbornly insists. "Seanie explained about Lennie and the shine and the wishes. So what I want to know is, what wish caused this night-of-the-living-dead thing I've got going on?"

"Dyl, we got bigger things to worry about right now, so maybe we could wait to play catch up later." Smith brushes her off so easily, as if he's already forgotten what it felt like to lose her forever.

In response, Dyl makes this sound in the back of her throat that I instantly recognize as her super-pissed-off growl. Trying to head off a full-on sibling explosion, I say something—*anything*—to try and break the tension. "What wish caused this? That's a tongue twister, huh? Betcha can't say that ten times fast."

This earns twin sighs of disgust. They're back on the same page, but not for long, because Dyl quickly turns her attention to me. "I'm gone for a few months and you team up with Smith? That's low, Lennie. I hope you used protection and didn't believe Smith when he told you not to worry about stuff like STDs and birth control, 'cause his magic penis would take care of everything."

"His what?! No! Smith and I are not— We

didn't— No. No. No. That's not what happened. Or will ever happen." I am incoherent while beside me Smith is suspiciously silent. No sighs. No snorts. No nothing. Realizing I should follow his example, I shut my mouth and refuse to let any more words tumble out of it.

"Oooooo-kay," Dyl responds at last. "Chill. That was a test. You passed when you turned red at the very mention of Smith's penis. I think you'd hyperventilate if you actually saw it."

"Ha ha ha. You're so funny," I reply, trying to hold on to the last shred of my dignity.

Dyl grins. Clearly my discomfort has put her in a better mood. "I am pretty funn—" The color drains from her face and she stumbles forward. I grab her arm, holding her up. A moment later she pulls away.

"Are you okay?" I ask, even though from the way she's still swaying the answer is obviously no.

"Fine," she answers, shaking me off. "What are we waiting for anyway? Let's go inside."

I almost tell Dyl that we're standing here because she stopped us, but it's never worth it to argue over tiny points with her. Like Smith, she rarely concedes anything.

Still avoiding Smith's eyes, I shove the front door open and step inside. "Hello?" I yell. "I'm back." Either my uncles don't hear me or they are not talking to me, because they go on singing without a pause. Walking farther into the house, I am surprised to see my mother sitting at the bottom of the stairs.

"Hey, Mom." As usual she seems oblivious to my voice as she stares into outer space and sucks on her cigarette.

With a shrug, I continue toward the TV room where my singing uncles stand with their arms slung around one another's shoulders, their chests puffed out, and all three mouths open wide enough to get a good look at their tonsils.

The moment they see me, though, it's like someone pulled the power plug—the drunken concert ends and is replaced by a steely silence.

"So you came back, huh?" Uncle Jet slurs. He squints as if trying to see me more clearly. "You make a wish to turn yourself orange?" His gaze flicks toward Smith, while at the same time he sniffs the air. "You're both orange and you smell . . ." Uncle Jet looks at Uncle Dune and Uncle Rod. "What's that smell? It's sorta—"

"Cheesy," Uncle Rod announces. "Like you wished to be a mac and cheese girl."

"Why the hell did you wish for that?" Uncle Jet roars.

"I didn't!" I quickly say, since I can tell he's getting ready to lose it. "I haven't done any more wishing." I don't mention that I'm here to ask about making more wishes to get everyone out of this mess. Coming clean and telling them the whole dirty truth is not the way to handle them right now. When they get like this there's only one way I can make them stop bellowing and actually listen to me.

I need to get on my belly and grovel.

I let my head hang low in obvious shame, before slowly lifting my eyes. "I'm sorry. I did a terrible thing and I know you can never forgive me, but I really need your help right now." I let a single tear trickle down my cheek. It's not hard to turn on the waterworks. At this point it's actually harder to keep them off, but getting too weepy would send my uncles running, so I only allow that one to squeeze through and then my head falls again while I struggle to hold the rest of them in.

Uncle Jet lets loose with this huge groan/sigh combo and flops onto the couch. "Okay," he says. "Tell us the worst of it."

"Well . . ." I hesitate, trying to think of the best way to tell them everything in a way that won't totally freak them out.

"She granted the wishes of all the jackasses, bitches, and douchebags from school and now they're all trapped at Michaela Gordon's house," Dyl jumps in. After she died, Dyl's constant need to charge into situations without a second thought seemed like an admirable quality, but now that she's alive again, I remember how often I found it incredibly irritating.

"Not *all* of them," I interject. I should've saved my breath because Dyl doesn't even acknowledge the point.

"It's pretty bad over there," Dyl continues. "And Smith's hand is stuck to Lennie's—I'm not sure why. I guess that was her wish or something. And my brother made a wish to bring me back from the dead, and hey, look"—she spreads her arms wide—"here I am!"

My gaze snaps toward Smith and I see that he looks as surprised as I am by Dyl's interpretation of events. And guilty too. I give a quick shake of my head, trying to let him know that I have no intention of correcting her.

Anyway, it doesn't matter, because Uncle Jet is back on his feet and roaring, "Don't talk nonsense. You can't bring people back from the dead with a wish. That goes against the natural order of things and none of us has got that kind of power. Tell 'em, Dune. Rod. Tell 'em."

Uncle Dune and Uncle Rod quickly jump in shouting how we must be crazy and that telling lies isn't gonna make it any easier to sort this all out.

Dyl puts her chin up in this way that says she's ready to go to war. She never did like being yelled at. And finally we get the shrill voice that I'd been dreading. "You wanna read about it? Google it. I already did. It was front-page news."

For once, Smith and I are on the same wavelength. As Uncle Jet's face goes white, we grab Dylan and drag her into the kitchen. As we do so Smith mouths the word *front page* at me. I nod grimly, knowing exactly what he means. If Dyl read the news articles, she already knew how she died and was just testing us with the questions. And Smith, with his lies about car accidents, failed. Big time.

"Dyl, stop," I tell her once we are out view of my uncles. "We need their help."

"I'm alive," she snarls back at me, still looking for a fight. "I'm alive and I'm here and I'm real and I'm not going away." Tears glitter in her eyes as she reaches the end of this speech, and my own anger vanishes.

"Dyl." I reach toward her, but she jerks back. "C'mon, Dyl. You're alive. They may not understand it or believe it, but you are. We can all see that."

"Five months later, Lennie, and you're more full of shit than ever. Don't tell me they're wrong and you're right when the only thing we know for sure is that, as usual, you don't have a fucking clue." Dylan spits one hurtful word after another and then spins around to escape out the back door.

When I move to run after her, Smith refuses to budge. "Maybe give her a few minutes."

I hesitate, listening to the dogs barking like crazy. Dylan

always loved my uncles' pack of mongrels. She'd bury herself in the midst of their furry bodies and become half animal herself as she rolled around and wrestled with them.

"Okay," I say to Smith. "Let's talk with my uncles while she cools off."

But when we walk back into the TV room, my uncles are gone. "Shit," I swear softly.

Pulling Smith behind me, I run to the front door, hoping they're just out on the front stoop having a smoke. But again, there's no sign of them. Or their truck.

Cursing my uncles for never being there when I need them, I go back inside and slam the door shut behind me.

"Leave it open," Mom says from where she's still perched on the bottom step. "Nice to get some air in here."

I stare at her, a little shocked to hear her speak without prompting.

"Hey, Mom," I say gently, the way you'd talk to someone who spooks easily. "Did ya see where the uncs went?"

She shrugs. "Heard them on the phone with Old Bill asking for a ride."

Old Bill's our next door neighbor who is passionate about the state of his lawn. In exchange for making sure the dogs never bend so much as a blade of his grass (much less whiz on it) he is my uncles' on-call designated driver.

"That was it? Nothing else?" I can't help but hope that

they might have left some additional crumb of information behind.

Mom shakes her head, crushing any such ideas. Then she holds up a single finger and says, "Wait."

I wait.

"They said . . ."

I lean forward, no longer hoping, but physically needing a way out of this before the burning pit of anxiety inside me explodes. I don't care how impossible the solution is. A magic potion we cook up by retrieving an insanely rare flower from the world's highest mountain. An incantation spoken in a dead language that only five people on the planet know. True love's kiss from a prince without any lips.

Just something, anything that might lead to things getting better instead of worse.

"I got it now," Mom says, her long-suspended finger finally falling. "You're fucked. Totally fucked. That's what they said."

I groan, but Mom ignores me and keeps going. "But they were gonna try to clean up your mess anyway. And you're to stay here, no matter what . . ." She sucks deeply on her cigarette and then exhales her next words along with a lungful of smoke. "Or else."

It's amazing that I remain standing. That I nod and

say, "Of course," while my chest squeezes so hard I feel like I'm dying and a part of me even wishes that I would.

"Let's get Dyl," I say to Smith in a flat voice. "And after that we'll . . ." I trail off, having no idea what we should do next. My first instinct is to track my uncles down. I assume they'll go looking for the epicenter of crazy, also known as Michaela's house. But I never mentioned her name to them, much less her address. No matter how legendary Michaela's parties may be, I don't think news of them has made it to the forty-plus crowd. With any luck they'll drive around for a while, blow off some steam, sober up, and then come back home so we can finally talk and I can get some answers. Which means that my grand plan is to sit on my butt and wait.

"Hide." Mom interjects with another option. "Or run. Tried to keep you from him, hoped you wouldn't get into the shine. No fixing it or fighting it now. Try and avoid him. Won't go well, he'll get you regardless, but if you're fast it might be later instead of sooner."

"What?" I gasp, trying to make sense of all these words flowing from her. I might as well have saved my breath. Mom's already grabbed her Niagara Falls mug, nearly filled to the rim with ashes, and is turning away. Still, I can't keep myself from calling after her, "Mom, I don't even know who you're talking about."

This stops her. "Your father, of course. Who else? The one who brought you into this world, and nearly took you right out of it again."

I can't believe Mom is talking about Dad for the second time in as many days. This time, I'm not gonna let the opportunity slip away. "You're talking about when he kidnapped me, right?"

"No." She shakes her head so adamantly that she wobbles, and Smith, who's been hanging back, reaches forward as if to grab her. Somehow, though, she manages to right herself. And then she kicks me in the teeth. "I'm talking about when your father tried to kill you."

Okay, she doesn't *literally* kick me. But the effect is nearly the same. I stumble, and for the first time, I am glad to have Smith attached to me, because he is immediately there holding me steady.

I take a deep breath and remind myself that my mom isn't the most reliable source. But she keeps talking, making it impossible for me to shrug it off as typical Mom craziness. "Of course, your father did it to force my hand. He had a pillow pressed against your little baby face and I had minutes to decide whether to save you. So I did, and in doing so, I lost myself."

"You what?"

Just like that, her back is to me and she's moving up the

stairs. Once again I have ceased to exist. Funny, it's always been like this, but now after being given that little bit of knowledge, I am desperate for more. Scrambling up the stairs behind her, I grab hold of her arm, forcing her to swing around and face me. "Mom. Come on already. You owe me a little more information than that."

Beneath my fingers I can feel her trembling bone covered with only the thinnest layer of flesh, and it makes me surprised she even has the strength to hold her cigarettes. Immediately guilty, I loosen my hold and soften my tone. "Please, Mom. I only want—"

The Niagara Falls mug smashes into my chest, cutting me off. She hits me with it a second time and instinctively I swat it away. The mug tumbles down, hits the stairs, and an instant later the ashes inside explode upward.

A black cloud surrounds us as she leans in and stares at me in this horribly bleak way. "You want. You always want, but I've given you everything I've got, Lennie. Everything. There's nothing left in me to give. You got it all."

I stumble back down the steps, wishing I'd never pushed her. Learning once again that if you never reach your hand out, you never have to worry about it being slapped away.

Meanwhile, Mom scoops her mug back up before spinning around to disappear in a cloud of her own smoke.

I stand there, stunned. And deserted by my entire family, at what I think can be classified, without hyperbole, as the worst moment of my life. If you'd asked me yesterday, I woulda told you that I didn't count on one of them for a single thing. And I didn't. Except. I guess I sorta thought if I really needed them, they'd pull their shit together, load the guns, put on their best camo and some Kevlar vests—that'd fallen off the back of a truck—and they'd charge in to the rescue. Instead, they left me here. Alone.

"Hey," Smith says softly, giving my hand a little shake. Well, almost alone.

"Gimme a minute," I mutter, now even more mortified. I'd somehow forgotten he was there, attached to me, and witnessing the whole horrible thing.

Smith sighs. Then, in a whisper-soft voice meant only for my ears, he says, "I know that you already know Teena's not winning any Mom of the Year awards, so I'm not gonna tell you that, but . . ." I wait, shocked that he's—even obliquely—referring to the weird mother-son kiss I witnessed. "Some parents are worse than others and ours are, well . . . the worst of the worst." Smith's hand squeezes mine, and this time I am glad to feel his fingers interlocked with my own. If anyone had to witness that terrible scene, I'm glad it was him.

My throat is too tight with unshed tears to say

anything, so I simply squeeze his hand back.

Another moment passes. Smith clears his throat. Loudly. "I know you're having a moment," he says. "But I'm starving. And I'm guessing you are too." He takes a step away from the stairs, tugging me along with him. "Let's get Dyl and then figure out what comes next."

I resist, for just a few more seconds, and then I lift my chin and swallow it all down—the same way I've always done.

"Okay," I say. "Let's go."

(NOT THE) BEST DAY EVER

We can't find Dyl.

We spend half an hour hunting through the garage, which is basically a junkyard for broken TVs, microwaves, fridges, and even a few toilets. When it's clear she's not hiding behind or inside any of these things, Smith suggests letting the dogs out to find her scent.

Before I can say, "Worst idea ever," he swings the fence open and encourages the dogs by saying, "Go get her, boys."

Smith apparently has only experienced dogs via TV and movies where they're all Lassie save-and-rescue types. Witnessing the shock on Smith's face when the dogs don't immediately rush off in search of Dyl and instead knock him to the ground is a rare moment of actual non-suckage. Of course, two seconds later they knock me down too.

And then they lick us. Not in a sweet loving way. No, they want the cheese that is still all over us, and they don't stop until we are good and slobbery.

Then, as we peel ourselves off the ground, they go running in ten different directions, which is pretty impressive, 'cause my uncles only have five dogs. We finally convince them to return to the backyard by waggling hot dogs at them—the only treat enticing enough to make them give up their freedom.

Smith and I celebrate recapturing the dogs by spraying each other with my uncles' hose. We even bring down some shampoo and soap, and get all sudsy right there in the front yard with our clothes on and everything. This is followed by an awkward trip to the bathroom that involves humming and closed eyes.

Finally, we sit on the front stoop drying out our clothes, eating Dinty Moore straight from the can, and hoping Dyl will wander back on her own. Smith also intermittently hollers her name and various neighbors curse back at him and offer many anatomically impossible threats of what they'll to do him if he doesn't shut up.

I grow increasingly tense as my uncles' souped up truck doesn't come roaring down the street to deposit them back at home. If they somehow found their way to Michaela's, it's easy to imagine at least twenty different terrible things that could happen to them.

In short, it's not the best afternoon ever.

"Maybe she's back at my house," Smith finally says, but in a way that makes it sound like he doesn't really believe it. I don't think it's likely either, so I shrug. "Or maybe," Smith continues, "she's hooking up with a great guy she met on the internet."

"Wow," I say. "Waaaay too soon to be making jokes about that."

"Who's joking? Anyone dumb enough to do that once—"

I interrupt, talking over him as loudly as possible, just to make him shut up. "Dyl made a mistake, you moron. She wasn't trying to get killed. Someone lied to her and she fell for it. She dared to have feelings and some shitbag used them against her. How is any of that her fault? Why is it stupid to trust someone? To like someone and want them to like you too?"

I stop there, since it is obvious from his smoldering glare that Smith doesn't want to hear any of this. Clearly, anger is Smith's comfort zone. I can see it on his face, the way he blames me and blames Dyl and is so fucking furious with everyone and everything. This is the exact type of look that used to make my heart leap into my throat, because even though it was sorta scary to see this black core inside of him bubbling up and threatening to spill over, it was also sorta hot. I guess the fact that I thought this was hot says a lot about what's inside of me as well.

But at this moment, I am too worn out to feel anything.

"Stomach bothering you, Smith? 'Cause you look a little . . ." I make a face indicating distress. "Sometimes the Dinty Moore can hit ya that way."

He closes his eyes, no doubt disgusted by my puerile sense of humor and wishing he could be stuck to anyone in the world but me. . . .

And then he laughs. It's a choked sort of laugh, like he doesn't want to give in to it.

"Come on," I say, before we can get into it again. The two of us seem to do best when we keep moving; it's only when we stop that we dwell on things that are probably better left alone.

Tugging at his hand, I draw Smith back inside the house. He follows without resistance as I lead him into the kitchen, pull out the coffeemaker, and begin the process of brewing up a big pot of caffeinated sludge.

"You're making that kind of strong," Smith notes as I fill the filter to the brim with grounds.

"Yep," I reply. "That's kinda the point. It's only"—I

twist around to get a peek at the clock on the microwave—
"two thirty and my spine is already getting that liquidy
feeling, like it's not gonna hold me up much longer."

"So you want me to pour it down your back when it's
done brewing?"

I smirk. "Maybe. Anything to stay awake."

"Or," Smith says, "we could stretch out on those big
couches and take a little nap while we wait for your uncles
to show up and Dyl to wander back."

I turn to stare at Smith in disbelief. "One doesn't nap
in the middle of a shit storm."

Smith laughs, which I think is a concession, but no,
Smith never concedes. "No, the shit storm has passed.
We are now up shit creek without a paddle. Which means
we're stuck and might as well go gently down the stream.
Think about it," he says, pulling me back into the living
room toward my uncles' admittedly super-comfy couches.
"A power nap. Fifteen minutes, tops. We rest our eyes
and wake up refreshed with a big pot of coffee ready to be
slurped down for an extra boost."

He flops onto the couch, taking me with him. I'd like
to say I put up a fight. Instead, a little sigh escapes me.
Smith leans into me and I lean right back, letting my head
rest on his shoulder. "Gently down the stream," I murmur

softly as my eyes start to drift closed. "Life is but a dream." Then I have a sudden and terrifying vision of Larry with foam dribbling out between his lips. I jerk back up.

"Yeah, no, not tired," I lie.

"Lennie, you just yawned like ten times."

"Not 'cause I'm tired." I pause to disguise a yawn as an annoyed sigh. "I'm bored, actually. It's been nonstop action all day and now this is . . . well, it's kinda boring sitting here."

"Okay, I got a better idea," Smith says. He reaches forward and after digging around a little pulls a little blue ukulele out from under the pile of stuff that lives under the coffee table.

"How'd you even see that under there?" I ask. "Uncle Rod got that a few years ago to impress one of his lady friends. When it failed I think he blamed the ukulele and banished it."

"I have good eyes," he replies with a grin. "And now for some bedtime, er, power nap music." I open my mouth to argue, but Smith is already positioning the ukulele so that the neck is in his free hand while the body rests between our two legs. "I'm gonna need some help from you."

"Sorry." I tuck my free hand behind my back. "I'm not musical. I'd probably break it."

"Come on, Lennie." He gives the baby guitar a little jiggle as if to show it won't bite. "All you gotta do is strum when I give your hand a squeeze." His fingers, locked around mine, tighten, demonstrating how it works.

Reluctantly, I squeeze back. "Fine. But don't blame me if it sucks."

Ignoring my whining, Smith begins to pluck at the strings and then reaches up to twist the tuning knobs until, I guess, it sounds the way it should. Then he looks at me. "Ready?"

I shrug. "Yes?"

Smith grins in response. "Okay, let's practice your strumming first. Just run your fingers—"

I cut him off. "I'm not a complete idiot. I know how to strum a guitar." To prove my lack of idiocy, I do exactly that. Or I try to. It's actually harder than it looks to gauge the right pressure to apply in order to hit all the strings in one smooth movement. But after a few minutes I get the hang of it and start to feel pretty confident that I'll be able to handle my end of things.

Then Smith begins forming chords. He goes slowly at first, while we both get the hang of him squeezing my hand and me responding with a strum. Amazingly, when Smith picks up the speed, I find myself falling into a rhythm and even anticipating the hand squeezes.

At first the music coming from the guitar seems like random sounds. Nice random sounds, but not a song. Until something changes and it begins to sound familiar. I can't quite place exactly what the song is until we reach the chorus and Smith begins to softly sing along.

"*I wanna hold your ha-a-a-and. I wanna hold your hand.*"

I stop strumming, caught between laughter and . . . something else.

Smith stops singing and looks up at me with his too-intense eyes. "Bad song choice?"

I swallow. Shake my head. Try to say something else. Try to break eye contact. Try to keep pulling air into my lungs.

And fail on all counts.

I remember Uncle Rod struggling to play this ukulele and how ridiculously small it had looked in his giant hands. Still, he'd stayed at it longer than I had expected him to, and when I asked why, he'd grinned and said, "The ladies can't resist being serenaded with a love song, Lennie."

I'd snorted my derision. "Please," I'd said to him. "I would never fall for that."

But, of course, I'm sucked in after only one line of the song.

Smith's free arm comes around me, drawing me closer while our eyes lock. A kiss is coming. It's a foregone conclusion at this point, but we both draw out the moment, letting the anticipation build.

And it turns out I was right.

We weren't really that tired after all.

A HIGH POINT

"Lennie," Smith murmurs against our nearly joined lips.

"Present," I whisper back, fully complicit in stretching this moment out like taffy.

Our joined hands are trapped between our bodies and I swear I can feel his heart's mad thumping against my knuckles. Meanwhile, his free hand travels up my spine, pressing me closer. Unsure what to do with my own hand, I wrap it around Smith's bicep, which I've admired more than once. His fingers curl around the back of my skull, tilting my head and tangling into my hair.

And then Smith freezes. His mouth goes still and he jerks his hand from my head so quickly that he yanks a chunk of my hair with it, while making this noise in the back of his throat that sorta sounds like *blech*.

"Ouch!" Rubbing at my aching skull, I pull away from Smith.

"Sorry," he says quickly, reaching up to pull me back toward him.

I press my hand against his chest, stopping him. "What was that?"

"What was what?"

"The thing with my hair just now."

"It was nothing." He reaches toward my hair as if to reassure me, but then stops and lets his thumb trail across my lips instead. "Forget it, okay?" He uses our linked hands to coax me back toward him until we are close enough for his lips to brush against mine and continue right where we left off.

Except. I can't.

"Touch my hair again," I murmur.

Smith pauses and with a sigh, touches one finger to a strand curled against my shoulder. As he does so an unmistakable shudder goes through him.

Grabbing hold of his wrist, I yank his hand up and press it to my skull. He immediately tears it away and springs up into a sitting position.

"It's the Cheetos. Okay?" He wipes his hand against his leg. "Don't be offended, but when we were shampooing our hair outside, you weren't really scrubbing the way you need to do when—"

"Hold up," I interrupt. "Are you seriously giving me a lecture on how to wash my hair?"

Smith pauses, no doubt considering if this might finally be a time when he should suck it up and apologize. But no. "When you get something like that in your hair, you can't just do your usual wash technique. At your scalp it's still kind of gritty and . . ."

"Gross?" I fill in for him.

"No, not . . ." Smith hesitates as my eyes narrow. "Okay, yes. A little gross. When I touch it, a faint wet cheese smell sorta drifts out. . . . It's not that bad, really."

"Oh, clearly. You're practically gagging."

"It's not you. I'm sort of a hair freak. It's a thing—"

"I know. I've seen your hair-care collection in your bathroom." I roll my eyes, trying not to feel crushed. Even though I am.

"Well." Smith clears his throat, "Do you have any dry shampoo? I could help you comb it in."

"Oh, no, I wouldn't dream of asking you to touch my disgusting hair again, Smith."

"Come on, Lennie. Don't be like this. We were having a good time and—"

And that's when I lose it. We were having a good time? *That's it?* "You know what a good time would really be?" I demand. "Almost kissing someone who isn't a shallow ass-hole. You know some guys would be like 'Ooh, is that new perfume? I like it.' Not because they think wet Cheetos smell good, but because they like me enough to lie."

"Yeah," Smith spits right back at me. "All the best guys lie to get into a girl's pants. That's how you know you got a winner."

"I'd rather have someone who tells me nice lies instead of being cruelly honest," I throw back at him, even though it's not even true. But it sounds good and pisses Smith off, which is what I really wanted.

He mows a hand through his own perfect cheese-dust-free hair, probably intentionally trying to rub my nose in it. "That must be why you like Larry. He seems like a guy who could sell that type of bullshit."

"Ugh. Newsflash, Smith. Larry and I are not a couple! Or friends with benefits. Or benefits with friendship. Or anything else." I close my eyes, feeling more exhausted than ever, while Smith says nothing.

"Let's just do your power nap thing, Smith. I mean, if you can stand having my disgusting hair so close to yours. If not, give me a plastic bag or something to wrap around my head. Okay?"

I can actually feel him staring at me in that intense way he has. Then the couch shifts as he leans back beside me.

I do the same, although now I'm so tense it's hard to relax.

Thank goodness the couch is huge. I scooch as far away from Smith as I can.

Distantly, I hear the coffeepot dinging, letting me know the caffeine is ready. My eyes drift closed, though, and I decide to give myself a few minutes. Five, tops. Then I'll get up.

"Hey, Lennie," Smith says. I am already half asleep and his voice seems to come through a long, echoing tunnel before reaching me. "You know what the craziest thing about today was?"

My limbs are heavy and my tongue is thick with sleep. Still, I am curious enough to make my lips form the word, "What?"

"Not one person made a genie in a bottle joke. Not one."

I am too mad to give Smith my laughter. And too tired to argue that moonshine comes in jars.

A moment later, though, when he whispers, "Good nap, Lennie," I find the strength to murmur back, "Good nap, Smith."

And seconds later when I fall asleep, I am pretty sure I do so with a smile on my lips.

ON THE LESS BRIGHT SIDE

I wake with a sudden jolt. The cable box clock tells me it's 3:23. Which means I've been out five minutes, tops. Beside me, Smith groans.

"What was that?" I ask at the same time someone goes *BAM BAM BAM* on the front door.

Oh, no. This is how the day began. And the day began badly.

"Why is it always three knocks?" I ask aloud. At the same time I remember who was knocking this morning: W2. I hadn't given him another thought after he got locked up in the basement. Did my uncles set him loose? Is he here looking for revenge?

Smith rubs at his eyes sleepily. "I dunno. How many times do you want people to knock?"

"How about not at all?" I snap at him.

"So you're one of those types who wakes up grumpy,

huh?" He asks the question while in the middle of a huge yawn, with his eyes at half-mast. His bruising has, if anything, only gotten worse as the day's gone on, and yet for some reason he keeps looking better and better. Damn him.

I glare and resist the urge to slam him with, "And you wake up sexy," 'cause that's not actually an insult. "Let's just go see who it is and what they want before they knock the door down."

We pull ourselves from the couch's cushiony embrace and go to answer the door. But it turns out we don't have to, because at that moment it flies open and a big dude with an eye patch plows his way into the house.

"We're here for Lennie," the pirate man announces while his hard gaze darts back and forth examining us both. The guy is only a few inches taller than me, but what he lacks in vertical stature he more than makes up for in width. Every inch of his body is packed with muscle.

"I'm Lennie," Smith immediately answers.

"No," I say, at the same time the big dude says the same thing. Then he adds, "What you are is in the way."

Then he very calmly jabs a short little syringe into Smith's upper arm.

"What the—" Smith reaches for the syringe, pulls it out, and then his eyes roll up into his head and he falls to the floor, bringing me down beside him.

"What the hell did you do that for?" I yell as I struggle to sit up.

Something darts out from behind the big guy and slams into me. My head hits the hardwood floor and I close my eyes, feeling dazed.

"Damn it, Jules," Pirate Man says.

Jules doesn't reply. She's a bit busy, I guess, grabbing hold of my shirt with her two tiny fists and shaking me so hard my teeth rattle.

At last she stops and makes this deep growling noise. I stare at her, speechless. Jules looks like Tinkerbell gone bad, complete with a bleached pixie haircut and lips painted an otherworldly shade of blue.

Being the sensitive person that I am, I say the only thing possible in such a circumstance.

"Arrgghh. The pirates get ya, Tink?"

Her fist slams into my face, causing some tinkerbells to go off in my head. I open my eyes in time to see good old Pirate Man reaching in to pull her off.

Tinkerbell growls at him, while I sigh in relief. Until I realize that now I have to deal with Pirate Man— aw, hell, I'll just call him Captain Hook to keep things consistent—instead.

But no, he turns away from me to argue with Tinkerbell

again. "Come on, we talked about this. No roughing her up. Delivery only."

She shrugs, crosses her arms over her chest, and turns away.

Captain Hook throws up his hands. "Fine. You want revenge? Go ahead and cut out her tongue. But you get to explain to Cash why she can't say, 'I love you, Daddy' anymore."

Tinkerbell spins back around and points at her eye, then shows four fingers and finally jerks her finger toward Captain Hook's eye patch. He nods. "Eye for an eye. I get it. But Jules, you know this isn't gonna change anything, right?"

She looks up at him with these big, pleading eyes.

By this point I've scrambled to a half-crouched position, which is as high as I can get with Smith still passed out on the floor. I swallow, realizing it's up to me to keep the two of us safe. And apparently away from my father, who after all this time seems to be looking for me.

Balling my free hand into a fist, I wait until Tinkerbell stops in front of me and pulls out a syringe that looks exactly like the one that just took down Smith. She hesitates for a moment to remove a stubborn plastic cap from the tip of the dart, and I take my chance.

I throw myself at Tinkerbell and am pleasantly

surprised when my fist connects with one of her delicate cheekbones.

Boom goes the dynamite. I have to admit there is a certain amount of satisfaction in watching her stumble sideways. Sadly, it's short lived, as Tinkerbell quickly recovers, using the wall to bounce back toward me.

Damn. It's gonna take more than one hit to bring her down, which is not great since my whole hand is still throbbing from the first one. Still, I curl my aching fingers into a fist once more, ready to hit her as many times as it takes, when Tinkerbell suddenly sags and hits the floor.

"Holy shit," I say, shaking out my hand and fighting off tears of relief that I won't have to hit her again. "I knocked her out."

Captain Hook, who I'd stupidly forgotten about, laughs. Then he leans down and plucks the syringe from where it is stuck in Tinkerbell's leg. Pinching it between two fingers, he holds it out to me. "Not exactly."

I take the needle from him. "I'm guessing this is a one-use-only thing, or you wouldn't have just handed it over."

"That's right," he says as he folds his arms over his chest and stares at me. It's not exactly a nice look, but at least he's not advancing, because if Tinkerbell's tiny face bruised my knuckles, his would definitely break them.

"Soo," I say. I attempt a smile. "What do you say we call this a draw? We each have a friend down for the count. Why keep going? I've got better things to do, and I bet you have a pretty busy schedule. Right? So let's call it a day. It's been nice to meet you and I'd show you to the door, but, you know, I'm attached to an unconscious person."

His face is impassive. His lips don't twitch. His eyes don't blink. He is either frozen or built from stone or perhaps simply unfazed by my attempt to make him go away. Yeah, it's probably that last one.

I try a different tactic. "Hey, you hungry?"

And finally this gets a reaction. His eyebrows shift upward, slightly but unmistakably, before quickly slamming back down as Captain Hook realizes he's given himself away.

"There's pizza bagels in the freezer," I tell him, and then to sweeten the pot, I add, "a family-sized box of them, not even opened yet."

Captain Hook blinks. Aha! I've got him. He picks up Tinkerbell like she's a feather pillow and heads toward the kitchen. As I sit there in shock, Captain Hook strolls back in and lifts Smith with as little effort as he used to grab

Tinkerbell. Having no other choice, I trail behind him to the kitchen.

After he settles Smith onto a chair next to the one that Tinkerbell's slumped over in, he microwaves a plate of frozen pizza bagels and sets them on the table between us.

I push the plate toward him. "They're all yours, big guy."

He accepts with a nod and starts eating. Less than five minutes later, every last one of them is gone.

"Now you want to leave?" I try.

Captain Hook shakes his head. "Sorry, kid, it's time to go have a daddy-daughter reunion."

"So you work for my dad?" I ask, trying to stall. "Like that Rabbit guy?"

"That weasel? Are you kidding?" This comparison seems to bother Captain Hook, for reasons I don't understand. "I'm not a bad guy."

"Really? Because my unconscious friend and your stated intent to kidnap me say otherwise."

He sits there mulling something over, while I sweat and curse myself out for being unable to resist back-talking someone who is in the position to quite literally crush me. Finally, Captain Hook leans forward and says, "If your eye causes you to stumble, pluck it out and throw it from you. It is better for you to enter life with one eye, than to have two eyes and be cast into the fiery hell."

"Um," I say, because what kind of answer is that even?

Luckily, Captain Hook fills me in. "That's the bible passage your father quoted while removing my eye."

My stomach clenches. My father. Of course. "Oh."

Captain Hook nods. "Yeah."

I gulp. "So what did you do to piss him off?"

He pauses, giving me another one of those assessing stares before answering, "I failed to find you."

"You . . . you . . . what?" I stutter.

"I failed to find you," Captain Hook calmly repeats. When I continue to gawk at him, he takes pity on me. "You're not the only special person in the world, you know."

"I'm not special," I blurt out automatically.

The Captain impatiently waves this away with one massive hand. "You have special abilities. While your specific powers are rare, there are people all over the world with equally strange abilities." He pauses significantly.

"Like you?" I guess.

"Yes," he confirms. "Like me. And like Jules. And many, many others who your father keeps as pets. There are even more who your father is simply content to keep tabs on from a distance. And then there are his obsessions. The ones he knows of, but can't find. A girl who has stayed forever seventeen by stealing other girls' bodies and lives.

A boy with the power to absorb bullets and magically heal. And . . . you. A girl who can grant wishes through moonshine."

"No," I say, shaking my head. "That's not right. This is the house where I was born. He knows where I live. I've been here the whole time. Not hiding at all."

"You haven't been hiding, because you didn't need to," Captain Hook corrects me. "Someone put a very powerful protective spell over you."

By this point I'm sure the Captain is just as sick of my gape-mouthed confusion as I am. His eyes narrow and he leans across the table. "You can't be this clueless. You've granted too many powerful wishes to be innocent."

"I am that clueless!" I say. "Really! I didn't even know I was granting wishes. It was all a big stupid accident."

Captain Hook shakes his head. "That's impossible. There's a ritual that must be completed. How would one know the ritual without understanding the consequences?"

You'd be surprised, I think.

"Besides," Captain Hook continues. "It's clear these wishes were granted by someone with experience and . . ."

"And what?" I demand.

He sighs, clearly annoyed by my constant interruptions,

and I think he's not gonna tell me anything more, but then he finishes, "By someone with too much experience and too much power to be innocent."

"What does that even mean?" I slam my hand on the table, feeling agitated by his words even while I don't fully understand them. "Stop with the cryptic bullshit already."

"Cryptic!" Captain Hook's mouth purses in disapproval. "All right, then. How about this? A normal wish maker can't raise the dead. Nor can they grant more than a few wishes in the span of a single evening. There's only one way for a wish maker to gain that sort of power and that's by taking it from another wish maker. And a wish maker, once stripped of their powers, is a shattered person, unfit for anyplace other than a mental hospital." With every word Captain Hook leans in closer. I'm not bothered by his imposing physical presence at that moment; instead, it's his little speech that's slamming into me, making me cringe as I absorb the not-so-subtle subtext: the person who granted those wishes is a monster.

I am a monster.

Suddenly, my mother's words from earlier come back to me. "*I gave you everything.*"

Oh, please, someone tell me that what I'm thinking is

not possible. That I didn't take my mother's powers. That I'm not the reason she's a total nutcase. And yet all the pieces fit.

Well, except for the one where I remember actually doing something to Mom.

"So what do you and Tinkerbell have to do with this?" I ask.

"Tinkerbell?" he asks, looking amused for a moment. Then he glances her way and sobers up once more. "I wouldn't let her hear you say that. And I'm Benji, by the way, so you can forget whatever cute little nickname you've given me."

"Captain Hook," I admit.

"Hmmph," is his reply, but again he struggles to suppress a smile. Then he shifts back into business mode. "As I've already mentioned, Jules and I were two of your father's pets, kept for our abilities. We both have the ability to find people, specifically people with powers. When we failed again and again and again to track you down . . . Well, he took my eye and her tongue as a sort of motivation. And when that didn't deliver the results he wanted, he threatened to take our lives. Then you resurfaced with a veritable tsunami of wishes granted all in one evening. Suddenly our task became much easier. Cash sent us to fetch you with the promise of our freedom as payment." He says this last bit somewhat apologetically. And I get it.

It's them or me. And they think I'm a monster exactly like my father.

"What if"—I stop and take a deep breath and then make myself push on—"What if I didn't do any of it on purpose? What if I'm trying to make up for all those crazy wishes? To fix them somehow? You think then that maybe you could take your friend and get outta here? Just take off running in the opposite direction of wherever Cash is?"

"Can't," Benji answers, instantly crushing the slightest glimmer of hope. For a long moment he stares off into the distance as if lost in his own thoughts. When he speaks again, it's in the low voice reserved for confessions. "I'm sorry. If it was only me . . . " His gaze drifts toward Jules and the picture becomes clearer. He's got a thing for her and there's no way he's risking Cash refusing to let her go.

He pushes his chair back and stands. "Come on," he says. "We've wasted enough time. It looks like Jules is starting to come around, and you'll want to be safely locked in the trunk before that happens."

As he reaches for Smith, I do the only thing I can think of. It's the same move I saw a two-year-old at the grocery store use the other day when her mother refused to buy the stuffed animal she had clutched in her chubby little hand.

I squeeze my eyes shut.

Open my mouth wide.

And scream.

TEN
DIFFERENT TYPES
OF CRAZY

othing happens.

I stop screaming and open one eye to see Benji staring at me in disbelief. If nothing else, I may have finally convinced him that I am definitely not a criminal mastermind. But before I can once again ask him to please let us go, five hundred things happen all at once.

The first is that a tennis ball hits Benji's forehead. Then three more tennis balls come shooting into the room. One hits Benji, the second goes wide right, and a third gets me in the back of the head.

"Lennie, get down," Dyl shouts. I immediately hit the floor, dragging Smith with me to relative safety beneath the kitchen table. Once secure, I glance over my shoulder to see not Dylan, but W2 of all people, coming to the rescue using the tennis-ball-spitting machine Uncle Rod bought years ago in yet another attempt to impress a potential lady friend.

I snap my head in the other direction to see Benji swinging his gigantic hands like rackets. He manages to bat most of the balls away while advancing toward W2.

Just when Benji's close enough to rip the machine from his hands, W2 chucks the whole thing at his head. Benji catches it, then tosses the machine aside and balls up his fists in a way that suggests he's decided to keep things straightforward and simply beat W2 into jelly. From across the room, I see Dyl slide into the kitchen through the back door, holding a gigantic can of Aqua Net in one hand and a Zippo lighter in the other.

"Hey, meathead," she shouts at Benji. He swivels to face her with a murderous look and suddenly I am incredibly afraid.

Not for Dyl, but for Benji.

Even though she doesn't smoke, Dyl always carries at least three lighters at all times. Papers that other people would throw out, she burns. Bugs that other people would squish, she burns. Old clothes, moldy leftovers, and anything else she can get her hands on—it all burns.

When she's bored, as she often is, her favorite thing in the world is to grab one of her Zippo lighters and a can of hair spray to create a DIY flamethrower. I usually keep as far away as possible during those times, while also making sure to have my phone ready to go in case I need to dial 911 when the hair spray explodes and takes half of Dyl with it.

With this thought in mind, I pull my cell from my pocket. A quick glance at the screen tells me the battery is two seconds from dead and I have a text message from Larry that simply reads: HELP.

Aw, crap. It's definitely a never-rains-but-it-pours type of day.

Unable to do anything about Larry, I shift my focus back to Dyl, who is advancing farther into the kitchen while fire shoots out in front of her. Maybe it's the way the flickering flames reflect on her face or the wide, maniacal grin, but she looks ten different types of crazy.

Behind Benji, W2 fires up his own homemade flame-thrower. The two of them quickly have poor Benji pressed up against the fridge with his hands held high in surrender. W2 falls back, but Dyl moves closer, apparently determined to barbecue him.

Without taking my eyes off Dyl, I begin to frantically shake Smith, wanting him to wake up now and tell his sister to take it down a few notches. At the same time, Dyl cranks it up a million notches. She swipes the flames across Benji's midsection once, twice, and then she laughs when his shirt catches fire.

"Dyl!" I scream. "Stop!"

I don't actually expect her to listen, but luckily—I really can't even believe I am saying this—W2 is there. He pulls her back a half step, allowing Benji to grab hold of a dishcloth to smother the flames. Meanwhile, Dyl shoots forward again.

"We'll go!" Benji yells, throwing his hands up once more. "Just let us go."

Dyl considers this for a moment, then nods. "Get out," she says, her voice hard and angry. "Now."

Benji doesn't waste any time taking Dyl up on her offer. Scooting around the edge of her flamethrower, he snags Jules and is out the back door before I can even count to ten.

"The cops are on their way," Dyl screams after them. "So don't even think of sticking around."

The door slams and I come crawling out from beneath the table, dragging Smith behind me. "What the hell? Stop with the fire already! And go lock the doors. Oh my God, what if they come back? Oh, shit. Oh, hell."

"Duuuuude," W2 says in response to my freak-out, while Dyl merely nods and says, "I'll go lock the doors."

As she leaves, W2 holds a hand out to me. "C'mon, let's get my boy Smith off the floor."

I eye him warily, wondering what's happened to him

since this morning when he was threatening to sue and basically ruin my whole family.

"Don't leave me hanging, Lennie," W2 says, giving his hand a shake.

"Umm," I say. "I need a minute down here to recover. Sooo . . ."

"Oh, I get it." W2 nods knowingly. "You think I'm still mad about the balls. But look, I don't hold grudges and also that whole wish thing worked out okay. Turns out all the equipment works the way it should, if you know what I mean."

"I know what you mean," I quickly answer, not wanting to hear anymore.

But W2 keeps going. "Yeah, I thought if the boys were steel, the piston wouldn't pump anymore, but Dylan was like, 'How do you know it's broken? Have you given it a test run?' And I was all, 'No, I haven't, but *you're* welcome to.' Foreplay, you know?" W2 winks at me and I try not to gag.

"You and Dyl did not hook up," I say, praying I'm right.

"Hey, hey, hey, that's personal," W2 protests, which immediately tells me that nothing worth bragging about happened between them or else he'd be doing so right now. "But I'll tell you this. Everything down here"—his hands draw a big round circle around his crotch—"is working the way it should. Seems like the boys are only encased in steel. Sorta like M&M's, you know? Melts in your—"

"Hey, look! Smith's waking up!" I announce in my loudest voice. This is finally enough to shut W2 up.

Even better, it's true. Smith is groaning softly. "Hey," I say quietly. He blinks a few times, as if trying to focus, and then his gaze settles on me. Our eyes meet and he sorta smiles, almost like he's relieved to see me.

"Lennie, hey." His voice is low and husky. That half smile already had my heart flip-floppin' around in my chest like some poor fish gasping for water. Hearing him say my name in that way only compounds the damage.

"You're awake," I say stupidly.

"Yeah," he agrees. Then his free hand finds mine and we simply hold hands. Both of them. One pair because we have no other choice. But the other . . .

"Dude!" W2 sticks his head under the table. Instantly the mood is shattered into pieces so small they disappear entirely. Our free hands slip apart. "You gonna hang out under there all day? You scared of the bad guys? No worries, bro, I chased them away."

I whirl to face W2. "*Dylan* chased them away."

"Dylan's back?" Smith sits up and looks around. "Where is she?"

"Right here." Dyl steps into the room as Smith and I

slide out from under the table. "Sorry for bailing. I needed some time to work stuff out."

"With W2?" Smith asks doubtfully.

Dyl shrugs and looks away. Smith opens his mouth as if to say something else and then closes it again. We stand there for several moments in awkward silence. Well, Smith, Dylan, and I stand there in awkward silence. W2, oblivious to anything that doesn't concern him, hums while hunting through the cupboards. Finally, he slams his hands on the counter.

"There's nothing to eat here, man. And I'm starving. Lennie, they better serve food at your dad's bar."

"What are you talking about?" I snap.

"What am I talking about?!" He rolls his head around in this really obnoxious way, like he can't believe what I'm saying. "Lennie, c'mon already. The dude wants to see you, and if he's got people like that working for him"—W2 jerks a thumb in the direction of the back door Benji and Jules just exited through—"he's probably gonna get his way eventually. It's time for a power move. You go to the man and say, 'Look, Pops, no need to send your minions, I came here alone to face you mano a mano.' Then he's looking at you like you've got some balls of steel. WHUT!?!" W2 swivels his hips so we can all hear the gentle *ting* of the metal between his legs. "That's my new catchphrase, by the way. Balls of steel. WHUT!? Awesome, right?" I open my mouth to answer in the negative, but W2 is clearly all amped up by his victory and there's no stopping him now. "Oh, and you're welcome, by the way, for the save. You owe me now. Big time. It's lucky Dylan and I heard those freaks when they came in and decided to lay low. And it's even luckier we are such badasses that we were able to scare them away."

"Dyl's a badass. You're an asshole," I correct him. "It's a small but subtle difference."

W2's ego is impossible to puncture, so my words bounce right off him. "But they're totally coming back. And somebody's gonna call the cops eventually, so you'll be dealing with them too. Anyway, the answer's obvious. Your family's a bunch of losers, except for your dad. He's the man. So now we go to your dad."

"No way," I say. "Weren't you eavesdropping? Didn't you hear about all the horrible things he's done? I'm not messing with him. No way. And if you had half a brain," I add, pointing to W2, "you'd want to stay far away from him too."

"Oh, c'mon, he's probably not that bad. People are always talking shit about me too, but I'm not the bad guy they make me out to be."

"No," I counter. "Actually you are."

Dyl impassively studies W2 for a moment before turning to me with a shrug. "He did help save you."

"I don't care. He's the worst. While you were gone just now he told me you helped get his junk working again."

That crazy look lights up Dyl's face again, confirming that it wasn't just the flames causing it earlier. "You know, Lennie, everything isn't always about you. And it's none of your damn business what I did or didn't do with W2."

I feel like I've been punched. Dyl and I were always united in our mutual scorn for Smith's fratty friends. For her to side with the very worst of them . . . I swallow hard, before finally answering. "Okay, fine, whatever. W2 can go meet my father. Tell him I said to stay the fuck away from me. I'm going back to Michaela's."

"Aw, yeah, party!" W2 throws his head back and howls. Then he grabs hold of Dyl's arm, dragging her with him as he races out of the kitchen while calling over his shoulder, "Race you guys! Last one there buys lunch!"

Smith and I don't even attempt to chase them. We simply stand in the kitchen and do nothing at all. I wait for him to say something about me or Dyl or W2 or anything that has happened. But he is silent. And still. And inscrutable.

"You're quiet," I observe at last, feeling the need to say something.

He shrugs. "I don't like being a dead weight."

I laugh, certain he's making a joke. Smith does not join in. It occurs to me that this might be one of those ridiculous male pride things. Trying to make it better, I point out the obvious. "Well, you were unconscious."

This makes it worse. Smith sighs in this dejected way, as if I'd instead said, "Well, you were useless."

It's amazing to see such a huge chink in his armor. Funny enough, it makes me like him more. Or like him in a different, fuzzier way. Not from afar, like he's some distant god that I'm hoping to brush up against, but in a way that makes my heart sort of swell. It's deeper than attraction.

And it scares the hell out of me.

So I don't tell him how right now he's the only thing keeping me from collapsing into a pile of defeat. And that having my hand stuck to his is—without a doubt—the best worst thing that's ever happened to me.

"Buck up, Smith," I instead say, more than a little roughly. "We're going to Michaela's, remember? I'm sure you'll have plenty of chances to prove your manhood there."

His shoulders go back, his chin comes up, and that little chink closes solid like it'd never been there at all. "Bring it," he says, sounding every bit as stupidly confident as W2. And if it's all just an act, at least it's a good one.

Deciding to borrow his self-assurance—even if it's totally fake—I parrot back at him, "Yeah, bring it."

Then, as prepared as we'll ever be, we march out the door, almost as if we truly believe we can leave all our fears behind us.

WORSE
THAN WORST

According to the clock on Smith's dashboard, it's 5:11 by the time we reach Michaela's. We roll up the driveway only to find that our spot's been stolen by my uncles' truck.

As we pull up beside it, I see Old Bill snoozing in the front seat. Rolling down my window, I reach across to tap on his. Old Bill jerks awake and blinks at me through the glass in this sleepy confused way before his eyes go wide. "Lennie!" he exclaims as his window comes down. "What are you doing here?"

"I was gonna ask you the same thing."

"Hmph," responds Old Bill, which is actually a pretty typical reply. He's not exactly a chatty guy. So I'm amazed when he decides to elaborate. "The boys said you'd caused some trouble at a party. Wanted to see the damage. Drove round with the police scanner. Heard some noise 'bout a flying boy or some such nonsense and Jet says, 'That's it.'" Old Bill shakes his head. "Flying boys. Hmph. They grow the weed too strong these days, that's the problem. So anyhow, we came here. Your uncles talked to the officers. Musta made nice 'cause the cops left and your uncles went inside. That's all I know."

It's probably the most Old Bill has ever spoken in one go. He looks exhausted.

"Thanks," I say, but he's already rolling his window back up and letting his eyes drift closed once more.

"Is this a good or bad thing?" Smith asks as he helps me climb over the center console.

"Don't know," I answer. "Good, I guess, that my uncles were here when the cops came. They've got this knack with them. Whenever they've gotten pulled over or a cop comes to the door 'cause they're making too much noise, all my uncles have to say is, 'What's the problem, Officer?' and bam, suddenly it's like they're best friends."

"Wow," Smith says as we finally get ourselves out of the Cherokee and start walking up to the house. "So your uncles totally made a wish that all cops would like them."

"No!" My response is automatic. But then I think about it. I always figured their way of charming cops was sorta like the stuff falling off the back of a truck thing, that my uncles simply happened to know people who were helpful. . . .

Holy crap. That was another wish. Of course. It all makes a crazy sort of sense. Uncle Jet said they had a lot of wishes, 'cause they could each grant for one another, and apparently they'd used their wishes a hell of a lot more wisely than me.

"Your uncles are smarter than they look," Smith quietly observes.

"Yeah," I agree, feeling my whole world being rocked. "I guess they are." As we reach the front door something else occurs to me. Maybe they're smart enough to have figured out how to fix this whole mess. Maybe we'll walk inside and everything will be back to normal.

Foolish hope swells inside of me as Smith swings the door open.

We step inside. And hope dies.

As I take in the destruction, my mouth falls open. Couches shredded and flipped. Streaks of color across the walls that might be blood or vomit. Red Solo cups littered everywhere. There's even one stuck to the ceiling.

The only thing that's missing from this scene is people. Stace and the lacrosse girls. The money guys. There's no sign of any of them. They're here, I know that for certain. Not just because none of them can leave, but because the place pulsates with a certain nervous energy. Twenty steps forward—I count them for courage—on legs stiff with fright, take me through the living room and into a room with a piano and . . .

I only have time to notice there are legs dangling out from beneath the half-closed piano lid before falling flat on my face.

Two seconds later, I'm being pulled to my feet, not by Smith but by a cooing Michaela Gordon. "Oh, Lennie, I'm so glad you could stop by again. So sorry I missed your last little visit. Are you okay? You really have to watch out around the doorways." She leans down and flicks what I now see is a thin wire strung across the doorway. It's crudely bolted into the wall on either side, making it not all that invisible really. I only missed it because I was distracted by the legs hanging out of the piano . . . which I can now see are a pair of pants that someone stuffed.

"What's with the booby trap? And the end times décor?" I ask.

Michaela looks around the room in this blasé way, as if everything is the way it's always been, furniture upended, piles of family pictures shattered and left in a corner, the chandelier hanging from a single frayed wire and dangling only a foot off the floor.

She turns back to me with a shrug. "Survival of the

fittest. Like *Lord of the Flies* or *American Idol*, ya know? I think that's pretty obvious. What I'm more interested in knowing is why you're here. Again. I heard all about how you were touring the place this morning checking out firsthand all the damage you'd caused. Then when the sightseeing was over, you flipped out and nearly killed your friend Larry in the process of making your escape."

"He's why I'm here," I say shortly. But then I also add, "And for my uncles."

"W2 and Dylan too," Smith adds.

"So another search and extract and fuck everyone else. Is that right?" Michaela asks. Her fake bitchy smile is now completely gone. It's obvious she's not playing anymore.

"What exactly do you want her to do, Kayla?" Smith asks. He steps forward a bit as if he wants to protect me.

Michaela smirks at me before focusing her attention on Smith.

"Really, Smith? Just 'cause Lennie's magic or whatever, that doesn't mean you aren't still slumming it." Her attention shifts back to me. "And to answer your question, I expect Lennie to get these fucking people out of my house."

"Go to hell," Smith replies, at the exact time that I say, "You're right. This is all my fault. And I'm really sorry about—"

"Nuh-uh," Smith interrupts. "She didn't mean to do it. She's trying to fix it. So I think we can skip the groveling."

"It's okay, Smith." I give him a little shove, letting him know I can handle a simple apology, even if he can't. "I *am* sorry. All right? Way more sorry than anyone can know. Even if I didn't know what I was doing. I wish I had some idea of how to undo it all . . . but I don't."

"So you're fucking useless as always," Michaela sums things up, and maybe it's low self-esteem or an inability to deny the truth, but it takes everything in me not to agree with her. "Have you even tried to undo any wishes?"

"Well . . . no," I admit.

Michaela rolls her eyes. "Typical. Well, I was talking with Jet, Rod, and Dune—"

"Whoa, *what?*" I interject. "You were talking to my uncles?"

This earns me another eye roll. "Yes, Lennie. Do you think there's another trio of people with those names? Try to keep up. Anyway—"

Michaela likes the sound of her own voice, so I know it's a mistake to keep stepping on her lines, but I can't help myself from interrupting once more. "What are they even doing here?"

"Lennie . . ." Michaela sighs deeply in this martyred way. "I am getting to that. If you would keep your mouth shut, we could get through this so much faster. It's not like I don't have better things to do than stand here explaining basic shit to you."

"Power freak," Smith mutters.

Michaela shoots a dagger-laden glare his way and then continues. "*Anyway*, your uncles showed up here and have—to my surprise—proven quite useful. First, they somehow convinced the police to go away. Then they offered to help me restore order around here, and having realized they weren't quite the ignorant white trash they appear to be, I was happy to join forces with them. While divvying up tasks, we had a good chat about what might be done to get this whole mess cleared up before my parents return tomorrow evening. Jet floated the idea of some carefully selected wishes being used to undo some of the damage. And I agreed that would be the best course of action."

I can't help it. I feel betrayed. While I was nearly kidnapped by Benji and Tinkerbell, my uncles were having a powwow and strategy session with Michaela. "Where are they now?" I demand.

"Upper floors. Working on containing Zinkowski. It's one of our top priorities," Michaela replies crisply.

"Zinkowski!" I gasp. "You're gonna let them get Cheetos'd while you stand by and do nothing?"

"Do nothing?" Michaela snaps back. "I've gone up against Zinkowski three times in the last hour alone. I am the reason the walls of this house aren't made of cheese at this point! So don't you dare talk to me about doing nothing, especially when you started this whole shit storm and have done fuck-all to fix it."

Before I can apologize for the second time, Michaela pulls a whistle from the front of her shirt and gives three quick tweets. Almost immediately, as if they'd been lying in wait, a group of about twelve girls and guys come marching into the room and line up behind Michaela straight and orderly like soldiers at attention. I recognize several of the freshmen from last night and a few sophomores. It makes sense. Most of my wishes went to the more senior partygoers, which would explain why these were the normal non-wishers left for Michaela to enlist.

"I need four volunteers to escort our visitors to the infirmary," Michaela announces in her new voice full of steel. It's a lot like her old voice, except the mean-girl bitchiness has been sharpened as if all this time it was waiting to be perfected for this very moment—when someone would need to step forward and lead.

"I think you're supposed to do the beating before patching us up, Kayla," Smith says. I look over at him and see he has this slight smile on his face, as if he finds this all amusing. Normally, I'd be totally convinced, but not after seeing that bit of vulnerability earlier. Now I'm tuned in and can feel the tension thrumming through him.

Michaela steps forward and gives Smith a sharp little slap across the cheek. "It's tempting. But I can't really waste manpower on beating your asses. So to keep you out of our way, I'm having you visit Lennie's friend Larry."

"Larry!" His name bursts out of my mouth. "Is he . . . okay?"

"He looks like shit. Feels like it too. But he's alive. No thanks to that stunt you pulled. Were you trying to kill him?"

She doesn't wait for our answer, but turns back to her troops and quietly confers with them, giving a series of orders that sends them running off in three different directions, leaving only five of them. As she spins to face us once more, the high-pitched screech of whistles blowing permeates the air.

"Come on, come on . . ." Michaela mutters under her breath.

"I got three upstairs and two from the media room," announces ones of Michaela's soldiers.

"Are you sure it was three?" Michaela asks.

"I heard it that way too," another troop member offers.

"That's what I thought." And then Michaela squeals with joy and pumps her fist in the air. "We've got him. I can feel it. We've finally caught him." She points to the two freshmen who'd spoken up. "You two go upstairs and find out what the message is."

"Is it Zinkowski?" I demand. "Are my uncles okay?"

I am ignored. It's like I didn't even speak.

"What about the other whistle?" another minion asks Michaela.

She waves a hand through the air. "How many shits do you think I give right now about a minor territory skirmish? Turlington doesn't own the basement. Let him and his followers work it out for themselves."

"Michaela." Smith grabs her arm and pulls her close. "Lennie asked if her uncles are okay. Wanna take two seconds to answer her?"

Michaela rips herself from his grasp. "You manhandle me again, Smith, and you'll be in solitary."

With a grin Smith holds up our connected hands. "I'd like to see you try that."

"Hmm, well I guess being stuck with Lennie is punishment enough." She smirks at her own wit before turning to me. "This has nothing to do with Zinkowski or your uncles. Now shut up and let me run my operation."

Before I can tell Michaela where to stick it, the two minions who'd left in response to the whistle come running back in.

"We got him!" the girl excitedly announces. "He tried to escape through the laundry shoot and got stuck. They're pulling him up right now."

"And is someone on the basement end in case he slips through?" Michaela asks.

"Yes, ma'am," the boy answers this time, clearly wanting his share of Michaela's oversized grin. "Both ends are secured. There's no way he's slipping away this time."

Michaela's fist closes over her heart at the same time her eyes close and two little tears squeeze from them and run down her cheeks. "Finally," she whispers. "Todd Wilkins, you are mine."

"Wee Willie Winkie?" Smith laughs in disbelief. I have to admit that my mouth falls open as well. "That's who you're hunting? The guy who has spent most of the past year practically stalking you? Are you serious?"

Michaela wheels on him, enraged. "Don't you call him that! Don't you dare! I can and will have you killed, Smith. So don't. Just don't."

The smile slides from Smith's face and confusion takes its place. "Kayla, you gave him that nickname."

"I know it," she answers, tears glittering in her eyes

once more. "And it kills me. All he wanted was my love and I ridiculed him for it. Never again, though. Once he stops running and I have him captured, I will spend the rest of my life begging his forgiveness. Not just for that terrible nickname, but for failing to recognize sooner how precious he truly is to me. From now on he will be my everything and he will never get away from me again."

"That's fucked up," Smith says quietly. Michaela makes a little annoyed *tsk*ing sound . . . but she doesn't disagree.

Meanwhile, the gears in my brain finally turn and I realize exactly why Michaela is suddenly so gonzo for Todd.

Todd Wilkins was one of my last wishes. He'd slipped in and whispered, "I want Michaela Gordon to want me. To want me so bad it hurts." As drunk as I was at that point, I still remember being taken aback. Of all the messed-up shit I'd heard so far, it was the worst. Because unlike the other silly, wistful, or just plain odd wishes, this was the only one that seemed mean. Of course, a few minutes later Smith walked into the room and his wish became the meanest, most messed-up shit I'd ever heard and I forgot all about Todd Wilkins.

"He wished for this, Michaela," I say softly.

"Of course he did," she snaps back at me. "And it's the only good thing that's come out of this mess. How else would my eyes have been opened?"

"But—"

"No. Don't you dare try to make this into something ugly and wrong. Those wings on Bat Boy out there"— Michaela points toward a nearby window—"that's screwed up and unnatural. But how I feel for Todd . . . It's right. I can feel it's right and soon he'll feel it too."

She stands there trembling with . . . passion? I have to look away because watching her feels almost intrusive. Luckily, after a way-too-long moment she shifts back into evil dictator mode.

"Take them upstairs," she orders two minions. "I can't have them underfoot right now. And make sure to watch out for Blobert, he keeps trying to start trouble. The rest of you fall in, we're going to personally oversee the Todd extraction." She turns to Smith and me. "I'll send your uncles to you once Zinkowski is fully secured."

"What's the deal with Blobert?" Smith asks, even though Michaela has essentially dismissed us. I'm pretty sure she's not gonna answer, but with one last long-suffering sigh, she replies, "I suppose you should know for your own safety. Robert Blouson, aka Blobert Boobson, apparently made a wish to be hotter than Brad Pitt."

"Oh, yeah," I murmur softly as I remember. Then I can't help but add, "You came up with that nickname too."

"Yes, I know. I regret it. Okay? So no more nicknames, even if I am rather brilliant at coming up with them," Michaela replies with an acid-tipped smile. "Anyway, Blob—I mean, Robert—is one of the few people who's actually happy with the way his wish turned out and has consequently caused quite a bit of trouble for us. Specifically, every time we get Zinkowski cornered or locked away, Blobert gets in the way. If you see him, don't trust a word he says."

With that, Michaela and her entourage march from the room in one direction while Smith and I are led in another.

It's another reminder of how upside down everything is that I'm actually sad to see her go. While Michaela was standing there, I felt safe, like someone was in charge who was gonna keep things under control no matter what kind of shit happened. It's kind of amazing, really. Instead of freaking out and hiding under her bed like any normal person would've done, Michaela has risen to the occasion.

I'd be jealous except, let's face it, some people are meant to rule the world and some are meant to ruin it.

At this point I don't think there's any doubt which category I fall into.

FALLING
HARD

Michaela's minions lead us through the ruins of her house. In some areas, the orange streaks on the walls combined with the cheese reek is brutal. Needing a distraction, I turn to Smith.

"So Michaela's sort of—"

"A crazy bitch?" Smith finishes.

"Yeah, of course. But in a way that's really—"

Again, Smith knows exactly what I'm trying to say. "Badass."

"And impressive," I add. "I mean, while I was twiddling my thumbs—well, no, I couldn't even be that useful because of our whole hand thing. I guess we were sorta twiddling together. . . ." My face burns as Smith starts cracking up.

"I think I'd remember if I'd twiddled you, Lennie." He says it in this low, sexy, laughing voice that makes me feel equally mortified and tantalized.

In front of us the two freshmen titter.

I decide to change the subject. "So Michaela Gordon and Todd Wilkins?"

Smith, still laughing, shakes his head in response. "Makes me feel pretty good about you only getting my hand."

I don't think he was aiming to hurt me, but . . . ouch. And I know I should laugh it off, but I can't. I just can't.

"Todd was the one who made the wish for Michaela to want him. As I'm sure you've already figured out since the whole school's been watching him drool over her for years." Even as the words are coming out of my mouth, I realize that this right here is why I'm upset. Maybe the whole school doesn't know it, but I've been hung up on Smith for at least as long as Todd's been dreaming of Michaela. This makes me less obvious, but just as pathetic.

Still, I'm not about to admit this to Smith—or to our guides, who are hanging on every word. "And I didn't wish for your hand, Smith. That was all your doing, remember?"

"Shit, Lennie, calm down. I didn't mean it like that." The smile has finally been wiped off his face.

"Then how did you mean it?" I demand.

No answer. Smith only looks away, with a guilty

expression upon his face. And almost instantly, I deflate. Funny how that works.

At the very moment when I'm about to give in, mostly because fighting with the person you're stuck to while in the middle of a house of horrors is a bad idea, Smith surprises me by breaking the silence first.

"Okay." He pauses, and then shockingly adds, "You're right."

"Wait, what?" I shake my head, trying to clear it. "Could you say that again?"

"Nope." Smith grins at me, looking almost relieved to be in my good graces again. "I never apologize more than once."

"Oh, no no no no." I laugh despite myself, feeling the last residual bits of anger drain away. "That was not an apology. An apology is two words, and those words are: I'm sorry."

As soon as it's out of my mouth, I know exactly what Smith's response will be, and he doesn't disappoint. "I accept your apology."

He busts a gut laughing and the freshmen join in too.

Just as I'm about to tell all three of them where to stick it, we walk into a small bedroom and there is Larry, tucked into a tiny twin bed with a ruffled pink comforter on it. I race over, dragging Smith behind me, not bothering to hide how happy I am to see him. He has an old Nintendo 3DS clutched in his giant paws and a huge grin on his face. "Lennie, look!" he says, holding it out to me. "Michaela has *Donkey Kong!*"

"Awesome," I say, and then unable to resist anymore, I reach in for a big hug. Smith sighs, but doesn't physically resist as he gets half pulled in as well.

Larry, of course, hugs me back immediately. Like everything else he does, Larry hugs with his whole heart. Still, that grasp also reveals how weak he is. The few times I've been caught in one of his hugs he squeezed me so hard I was afraid my ribs would snap. This hug doesn't constrict my breathing at all.

I gently pull away, not wanting to use up any more of Larry's obviously depleted strength.

"You okay?" I ask now. "I got your text asking for help, but then my phone died."

"Help?" Larry's brow furrows in confusion . . . but then suddenly clears again. "Oooh, right. I couldn't get past this one board, and I wanted to know if you'd ever beaten it. But don't worry, I figured it out."

"Great," I say, and Larry nods, totally missing the sarcasm. But even knowing Larry didn't need me to return to Michaela's, I'm glad I did. Seeing him, alive, healthy, and oh so very Larry has given my lagging spirits a little lift.

It's like standing on a teensy ice floe of happiness—even though I know it's melting beneath me, I'm still glad to be there anyway. I can't blame global warming that only two seconds later, the feeling is completely gone.

Whistles once again sound from everywhere all at once, followed by feet pounding past our doorway. I whip around in time to see an unmistakable flannel pattern fly past. "My uncles," I say to Larry.

"Go." He flaps a hand at me. "I get it. Michaela says you're gonna find a way to wish us all back to normal. That you'll fix it."

Larry says it like it's a foregone conclusion. Like, of course I'll make everything all better. Easy-peasy.

The sound of the chase is growing more distant, but I feel like I need to say something to Larry. Either set him straight or tell him more lies about how of course I'm going to fix things.

"Yeah. No," I reply, somewhat nonsensically as I waffle. "Of course, I'll . . . I'm gonna make sure—" I stop, unable to think of any promise I'm not sure to break. At last I settle on, "You look tired. Get some sleep, Larry. I'll be back soon."

I don't wait for him to answer with more of his "gosh, gee whiz, Lennie, I sure am lucky to have a friend like you" crap, which right now would feel like someone taking a weed whacker to my guts.

Smith and I zip out the door and run in near-perfect sync down the hallway, up the stairs, and through the endless rooms of Michaela's house.

We lose my uncles anyway.

Without a word we turn and start to retrace our steps, hoping they might have peeled off into one of the rooms. We hit pay dirt on the second floor. From behind a half-closed door we hear a soft whining voice.

Smith, having apparently overcome his belief that one should always knock first, pushes the door open and we enter an enormous bedroom done entirely in shades of gold. I think the color scheme is meant to play off the shelves overflowing with trophies for various clubs, events, sports, and activities.

This is, of course, Michaela's room.

And she stands at the center of it. No longer calm and put together, but looking strangely vulnerable and un-Michaela like with huge tears streaming down her face as she confronts her one true love: Todd Wilkins.

For his part, Todd stands trembling at the other end of the room, his hand on a door leading who knows where. His darting eyes take us in for a moment before quickly focusing back on Michaela, who he watches the same way you might a lion or some other carnivorous animal with the power to rip the flesh from your bones.

"So-so-so," Todd stutters at last. "I can really go?" His voice breaks at the end and I wish Michaela could wake from this spell and tell Todd to take his whimpering far, far away from her.

Instead, she simply smiles through the tears.

"Yes. I told you, Todd, I love you too much to keep you, too much to hold you when you want to be free. Just please know that I'll wait until the end of time, if that's how long it takes for you to pull your head out of your adorable ass. And when you do, I will be right there ready to blow your fucking mind."

At that moment I fall a little bit in love with Michaela, because even pathetically, desperately, and—worst of all—unwillingly in love, she manages to be certain of her own worth. But even more, she is generous. She loves Todd to the point of insanity, but is still willing to let him go. One might argue that love—even this totally messed-up version of it—has made Michaela a better person.

Todd, though, is an idiot ten times over and doesn't seem to notice any of this. Instead he continues to stare at her like he can't decide whether to make a run for it or lie down and play dead. Then something in him breaks. He flings the door open, then moves to charge through it and out of Michaela's life—when Zinkowski comes stumbling in instead.

Todd trips over his own feet as he backpedals and lands in a heap on the floor. Zinkowski, looking more dazed and confused than I've ever seen him, keeps walking straight forward, putting him and Todd on a direct collision course.

"Todd!" Michaela screams as she leaps forward to the rescue. Seeing her coming toward him, Todd frantically half crawls, half butt scoots away from her. He's so focused on getting away from Michaela's outstretched arms, he seems to have forgotten Zinkowski.

Todd hits Zinkowski's legs, then does this weird yodel of terror as Zinkowski tumbles forward, arms outstretched—

Michaela leaps, like her insane love for Todd is some kind of superpower, and lands with her body spread over Todd. Protecting him. Absorbing Zinkowski's fall. Making sure that Zinkowski's fingertips do not connect with Todd. That they find her instead.

Michaela shimmers and glows orange. That lasts only for an instant, and then all three of them disappear in a sudden and explosive burst of orange cheese.

Smith and I instinctively fall back, pulling our shirts

up to cover our mouths and noses from the noxious smell.

I wish I was making that up. I wish I was making all of this up.

Zinkowski is the first to arise from the orange haze. A low keening noise comes from him as he staggers around before finally collapsing in the farthest corner of the room, curled into himself as if he cannot stand to see what he's done.

Todd pops up next. He looks confused. We watch as he pats at his own body, as if making sure he's still all there. Then he seems to take in the cheese coating him and everything around him. He bends down to pick up one of the many Cheetos scattered across the floor. "M-M-M-Michaela?" Dropping it, he flees, not seeming to care about the Cheetos smashed beneath his feet or the trail of crumbs he leaves in his wake.

"Did that just happen?" Smith asks, sounding as shaken as I feel.

Before I can answer, my uncles come charging into the room. Uncle Dune drags an incredibly good-looking guy behind him in an inescapable headlock. I realize after a moment that this must be Blobert, er, Robert Blouson.

"Damn it!" Jet curses loudly when he sees the slowly settling cheese cloud at the center of the room. Then when he sees me, another "Damn it," this at an even greater volume than the first one.

"Don't move," he barks at me. Then my uncles as one turn toward Zinkowski.

Of course, I move. "No," I say, jerking forward but not getting far as Smith refuses to budge. "He took out Michaela. Stay away from him! You'll get Cheetos'd!"

They ignore me, except for Uncle Dune who gives me a mildly reproving look. "We already got him once, before this joker"—Uncle Dune indicates Robert, who winces—"got him all agitated and running off again. So don't worry. Okay, Lennie? We got this."

And they do. Somehow they manage to coax Zinkowski back to his feet and sort of nudge him—without ever touching him—out the door.

"Stay here," Uncle Rod commands right before the door shuts behind them.

"I need to sit down," I announce at the same instant that my legs give way beneath me. Luckily, Smith isn't quite as weak-kneed and manages to grab me with his free hand and gently lower us to the softly carpeted ground.

"Yes," I say, finally answering Smith's unanswered question. "That did just happen."

Smith nods, as if I've settled something important, and then nudges my shoulder with his. "You okay?"

"I guess," I say, and am surprised to hear how shaky

and breathless I sound. "All right, maybe I'm not okay," I admit. "It's the shock. And when my uncles came in. I was so afraid that they'd end up like . . ."

I can't say it, not without breaking down into hysterical sobbing. Beside me, Smith closes his eyes and exhales deeply, like he's trying to hold back tears of his own.

"Michaela. Dead. I mean, she is dead, right?" Smith says after a protracted silence.

Something snaps inside me. I want to pound things and howl and scream with the unfairness of it all. Instead, I lash out at Todd Wilkins. "Yes, she's dead. I don't think there's any coming back from that." I gesture to the orange cloud slowly settling. "She's dead because of that idiot. Wee Willie Winkie. When she wouldn't give him the time of day, he couldn't get enough of her. Then when it flipped, he couldn't run far enough away."

Smith tips his head back to stare up at the ceiling. It is, like everything else, a burnished shade of gold. "Yeah, well, she was out of his league and he knew it. He was scared shitless. I mean, if he was smarter maybe he would've enjoyed it while it lasted, but I can't really blame him for running instead."

I glare at Smith, unable to believe his nerve. Out of his league. Scared shitless. Enjoy it while it lasts.

"I get it, Smith," I finally respond, barely able to control my shaking voice. *"I'm* out of your league. Whatever happened this afternoon was just you slumming it while you're stuck with me. Right? But you got a few things wrong. I'm not scared of you and I'm not trying to enjoy it while it lasts. I know there's nothing between us"—I lift our two linked hands—"except this.

"And don't think you're shattering any of my illusions here." I hold my stupid dead phone up between us. "I've had your number for a while now." And then I play his message while repeating his horrible words verbatim. I even get his mixture of hurt and angry and so fucking deeply sad exactly dead on.

"It's Smith. I just wanted to call and say, to call you and tell you, that you should know, in case you don't already . . . It shoulda been you, Cash. Not Dyl, but you. She didn't deserve to go that way. She—" I let myself take the pause where he sounds close to tears. I could get an Academy Award for this performance. I finish it the same way he did. "Fuck."

"I was drunk!" Grabbing the phone from my hand, Smith throws it across the room as if this will get rid of the message. "Stupid, blasted, out of my mind drunk."

"So what?" I sneer. "That's an excuse? Are you gonna tell me next that you don't even remember calling me?"

He shakes his head and sighs. Several long moments

pass before he finally answers me in a much lower voice than before. "No, I remember. I just thought . . . I didn't think you'd care. Stupid, I know. But . . . after Dyl . . . I'd see you around and you looked like you were made out of stone. Like none of it could even touch you. You became friends with Larry and I saw you laughing about something at lunch one day."

"What?" I interject, still loud and angry. "So I'm not allowed to have friends? Or I'm not allowed to laugh?"

"Both. Neither. I don't know. It, it—it pissed me off. Okay? I'm mean, it's not okay. I get that. But then I was really drunk and I was mad and I was gonna say something to you the next day about how I didn't mean it and stuff, but then I saw you and I thought you'd probably already forgotten it." He sighs, glances toward me and then back up to the ceiling once more. "I didn't know you'd save the message. Or remember it like that. You always seem like you don't give a shit."

I snort. "That's funny coming from you, the original Mister Cool."

"Well, maybe we have that in common. But that's about the only thing." Smith suddenly takes his focus away from above and back down to me. He spins, turning his whole body so that we are directly facing each other and neither of us can look away. "You wanna talk about slumming it?

About who between the two of us has the power? Think for two seconds before you open your mouth, Lennie. You brought my sister back from the dead. You made Zinkowski into a really messed-up monster and gave another kid wings. You literally grant wishes. *I'm* the one who's scared. Of you. I'm scared as hell. But I'm also . . ."

Somewhere in the house someone howls, *"Michae-laaaaaaa!"* Smith ignores this, his laserlike focus never wavering from me.

"I'm also enjoying it while it lasts. The way I see it, you're stuck with me, not the other way around."

I think my mouth falls open.

While I sit stupefied, Smith faces forward again and goes back to studying Michaela's ceiling as if he didn't just say something monumental and so heavy that it felt like my whole world tilted sideways. Suddenly, I am looking at things from a whole new angle.

I'd been thinking of the whole wish-granting thing as a colossal mistake and the world's biggest screw-up. And yeah, it's still that. But it's also fierce and powerful. No. *I* am fierce and powerful.

That thought reverberates through my head like a new math concept I can't quite grasp. Yet.

I look at Smith with new eyes too. He said he was afraid. Of me.

But unlike Todd Wilkins, he isn't running away. Okay, yes, he doesn't really have a choice there. Except when we were here earlier this morning, he could've left me behind. And since then he's done his best to protect me.

"Smith." I say his name and as I do my own skin begins to burn with a red-hot blush. Unable to meet his eyes, I look down at our interconnected hands. "I'm scared too. About everything." I don't say more than that. I can't. It's a freaking miracle I was able to get those words out with my mouth, which is suddenly Sahara desert levels of dry. But I hope he understands that when I say "everything," I don't just mean the wishing stuff plus him. I mean him, too. Or maybe especially him.

Being near him. Kissing him. And most of all, hearing that he might feel the same way. That last one scares me most of all. Because like lame old Todd, I'm realizing it's one thing to watch someone from a distance and daydream about them and think *what if*, but it's a whole 'nother thing to have them in front of you making your heart beat so hard it might explode out of your chest.

The former is safe, the way I always like to be. The second is bungee jumping with a cord made out of moonbeams and promises. It's falling without knowing if you'll bounce back up.

And I'm falling. I'm falling hard.

AS AWFUL AS
IT CAN BE

We bury a cardboard shoebox filled with Cheetos in the backyard.

I am fairly certain Michaela would not have approved.

Actually, I know it for a fact. One of Michaela's heartbroken minions informed me in a whispered aside as I led the informal funeral procession through the house that this was not the protocol. Prior to Michaela, three other people had reached an unfortunate end at Zinkowski's hands, and after each . . . er, death, Michaela had ordered a moment of silence over their remains. Then she'd gathered them up into a Tupperware container and hid it in the attic to be used as emergency rations.

So, no, she would not be happy to have her decision overruled just because she's no longer around to enforce it.

No doubt she would've been equally critical of the

shallow hole hurriedly dug in the rose garden.

And of the battered old shoebox we'd chosen to hold her remains.

But most of all, I can imagine her scorn if she had witnessed the awkward shuffling of feet after she'd been lowered into the ground as we all wondered what to do or say next.

Perhaps she would have liked the moment when Todd appeared, tearing at his own clothes in grief, before throwing himself upon her grave and watering it with an abundance of hot salty tears.

Probably, though, she would've told him to knock it off before he killed all the roses.

None of us do that. Instead, everyone disperses and scatters, quickly taking refuge inside the house until only Smith, my uncles, and I are standing there watching Todd noisily sob and beg Michaela's forgiveness.

"Poor bugger," Uncle Dune says in a low voice. "Love wishes never end well."

Jet and Rod nod in sage agreement.

"Okay, so how can we fix this?" I ask, feeling more than a little impatient with my uncles, who have been maddeningly silent.

When they returned to Michaela's bedroom where Smith and I had obediently waited for them, they barely acknowledged our presence. And when I asked what happened with Zinkowski, they only said, "He's okay. Tucked away where he won't hurt anyone." And when I asked what we should do next, meaning "let's get some new wishes going," they told me it was time to bury Michaela. Still, I'd pushed back, demanding to know what happens next. For that I got a sharp reprimand from Uncle Rod. "A girl's dead, Lennie." He paused and I could hear him editing out, "because of you."

I could have explained that doing something was my way of paying my respects to Michaela. But instead I followed their orders to, "Find something to put her in," and so dug through Michaela's gigantic closet looking for a box to hold her remains.

Now, though, I am done with waiting. It's past eight o'clock, which means that we have a good amount of time to grant some wishes before the sun rises again. "Michaela told me what you said about me granting wishes to fix this."

My uncles are already shaking their heads. "We told her a few carefully chosen wishes might make everyone a little more comfortable. But trying to wish your way out of this . . ." Uncle Jet pauses to give another shake of his head, this one almost mournful. "More wishes would only make this worse."

"But you told me, Michaela—" I start to protest, but Uncle Jet cuts me off.

"It's complicated," he booms, which, duh. Luckily he elaborates. "Trying to undo a specific wish almost never works. When a wish is granted, the natural order of things is changed permanently. Say you broke a vase into a bunch of tiny pieces and then glued it back together. It wouldn't be the same as it had been."

"It would look like shit," I say.

Uncle Jet frowns. "Okay, forget the vase. What's one of the wishes you granted last night?"

I exhale in a rush. "You've seen most of them."

"How 'bout his wish?" Uncle Rod chimes in. "That boy holding her hand."

"All right," Uncle Jet says. "That's a good one to start with. So if you wished that he didn't want to hold your hand, at first it would be fine."

"At first?" Smith and I ask at the same time.

"Yeah. At first it would seem like the second wish canceled out the first one. But in reality, there would be two wishes battling it out inside of the boy, and he would eventually find himself fighting against two contrary impulses."

I don't want to ask. I don't want to know.

Smith, though, isn't interested in being kept in the

dark. "And then?" he demands.

"Best case scenario . . ." Uncle Jet sighs deeply. "Madness. A complete break from reality, resulting in an inability to function within the world. Worst case—"

Not wanting to hear, I break in, "Losing your mind is the best case scenario? Seriously?" I can't help but think of the way Smith had fought for control over his own hand. It was easy to see how it tore him apart to give in to the wish. But to give up control over his own mind . . . "Most people would rather be dead."

"Yeah, well, *that's* the worst case scenario."

Silence descends. I cannot look at Smith. Then again, I don't really need to. I can feel the despair coming off him in waves.

Uncle Jet clears his throat. Loudly. "There's one other option," he says at last. Reluctantly, like he'd rather not mention it.

"What?" Smith and I demand as a tiny spark of hope flashes in an ocean of black ashes.

"Tell 'em, Dune," Uncle Jet says. "You're the one that knows the most about it."

It's rare for Uncle Jet to cede the floor to anyone, but when he does it's usually to Uncle Rod. Uncle Dune's more the silent listening type, but now he steps forward, clears his throat, and proceeds to blow our minds.

"It's a time machine of sorts," he says. "Or basically a wish that takes you back to an earlier point in time, before the wishes you wish to un-wish were wished."

"Okay, Dr. Seuss," I say, while trying to wrap my mind around this. "Then can we just reset the clock to Friday afternoon?"

Uncle Dune shakes his head. "Too close to the event, it's unlikely you would be able to perceive what had already occurred in time to choose a different path."

And I'm lost again. "What now?"

"Wishes cannot be undone. Nothing in life can ever really be undone. Even with this method. There's a shadow, a feeling that lingers of events that already occurred. The idea is to put you back in time far enough to sense this and change course, but not so far back that you simply shake it off, or worse, settle into the groove of what's already happened."

Groaning, I stare up into the sky, as if it might provide some answers. Sadly, it does not, but the movement must at least get the blood in my brain flowing, because an idea occurs to me. "What if I wish to go back *and* have a note in my pocket saying, 'Hey moron, ask your uncles about the whole wishing thing.'"

I can tell from Uncle Dune's expression that he thinks this is the dumbest thing he has ever heard. "Would you take this note seriously? Or would you dismiss it as a weird joke?"

Oh. "I wouldn't believe it," I admit with a sigh. "I'd think it was nuts. I had no idea about the wishing. I had no idea about anything."

"Yep, that's not good," Uncle Dune says, which sorta seems like an understatement.

We are all silent for a moment, mulling this all over, when Smith pipes up. "How do you know all this anyway?"

To my surprise, Uncle Dune goes bright red. "Dated a girl a long time ago. She knew things. Things that had happened and could happen. Almost married her, but she turned me down. Said she was gonna die young and didn't want to break my heart. Broke it anyway, though."

Uncle Dune looks so sad, I can't believe I'd never heard of this lost love of his. But at the same time I can, since he almost never talks about himself. It's especially surprising, because I've always known Uncle Rod as the ladies' man and Uncle Jet's had the same girlfriend he's been stringing along saying they might make things permanent for almost two decades now. But Uncle Dune has never shown any interest in the opposite sex. I've always seen him as somewhat monklike. Now that I think of it, him nursing a broken heart makes a hell of a lot more sense.

"All right," Uncle Jet says, taking control once more. "Enough chitchat. I vote Lennie heads home and—"

"No!" I burst out. "You're not getting rid of me! I don't care if all our options suck, I'm wishing for something—anything—to try and make some of this better."

"Then go home and do it!" Uncle Jet bellows back at me, loud enough to blow my hair back.

Normally, I'd back down. Going against Uncle Jet is like trying to stand upright during a hurricane. But normal's gone and may never be back again. Besides which, I'm pissed, too.

"Stop trying to get rid of me! I'm sorry I'm not Michaela. I'm sorry I fuck everything up. I'll stay out of your way. Okay? I'll stay so far away you won't even know I'm here."

Uncle Jet sucks in another lungful of air and just as I'm ready for him to shout it back out at me, he deflates instead. "Lennie," he says, suddenly uncharacteristically quiet, "I don't wanna get rid of you. It's only that I can't stand the idea of something happening to you." I look at him then and notice how tired he looks. No, not simply tired. Beaten. Exhausted. Worn out. "None of us can," Uncle Jet adds, and Uncle Rod and Uncle Dune nod in affirmation.

"Oh," I say, wondering when my uncles started giving a shit about me and then wondering if maybe they have all along . . . in their own kind of rough way. It occurs to me that they might not know how I feel either, and even though it goes against everything I've been raised to believe, I confess, "Well, I'm worried about you guys too."

If I was expecting my uncles to get all misty eyed, I should have thought again. Instead, they look offended. Like, majorly insulted. "We can handle ourselves, Lennie," Uncle Rod informs me, while puffing his chest out.

Realizing there's no way I'm gonna win this fight, I give in. "Okay, fine. I'll go home. But if I think of a way to wish us all outta this, I'm gonna do it."

I wouldn't blame them for forbidding me to do so, for coming up with all kinds of threats. It's not like I've done one damn thing that's shown even the tiniest shred of good judgment.

Uncle Dune's oversized hands raise up and I prepare myself to be forcibly locked away somewhere, probably near poor Zinkowski, where neither of us can do any more damage. But instead he grabs hold of Uncle Jet and pulls him away. "You gotta do what you gotta do, Lennie," he says, which sounds like a condemnation, until he adds, "And we trust you to figure out what the best move is."

Uncle Rod leans in and hands me his little plastic sports bottle with a few fingers of shine sloshing around the bottom. He's always carried it on him, for as long as

I've known him. I guess so he could grant wishes anytime, anywhere. "You might as well have this now, in case you gotta wish your way outta anything."

It's as close to "I'm proud of you" as I'll ever get. Hell, it's better than I'm proud of you, 'cause that's for something you've already done, but this, this is them having confidence that they'll have reason to be proud of me at some point down the road. It's enough to make me want to forget Uncle Dune's idea about turning back time, because in that version of my life I might never have this moment.

I shove the bottle into the front pocket of my hoodie. "Thanks," I say in a shaky voice. "I'm gonna . . ." I stop, realizing I have no idea what I'm gonna do.

I take a step away from them, and then another. There's a feeling of finality to this moment, and instead of immediately running from it, I do something crazy.

"I love you guys," I say. Before I can see whether they look dumbfounded, disgusted, or something else, I spin away so fast Smith stumbles behind me, and take off for Smith's Cherokee.

GOOD NEWS
AND BAD NEWS

As we come around the side of the house, we run into Dyl and W2 and . . . the odd hairy man they're talking with. As if sensing my gaze, the hairy man turns and waves at me in a friendly way, and that's when I recognize him as the guy I met at the bar last night. Rabbit. The one who "takes care of" things for my father.

"Hello, hello!" he says, coming at me with an arm outstretched and ready for a hearty handshake. After pumping my hand up and down a few times, he finally releases me and folds his hands on top of his rounded little stomach. "What luck to run into you! I was just asking these two where you might be."

"Yeah, this Rabbit guy is gonna take us to your daddio," W2 interrupts. "*And* let us do a group selfie with him if at all possible." He looks around to the rest of us.

"That would be sick, right?"

"No way," I say, having no problem with bursting W2's bubble. "I've got enough shit to handle right now, I'm not adding him to the mix."

Rabbit smiles in this strained way. "Well, yes, that's the thing. You see, your father has become aware of your, erm, problems and thinks he may be able to offer some help."

"And if I say no, you're gonna drag me there anyway, right? You're not the first of my father's friends to hunt me down today, you know."

"I do know, and I apologize for such tactics. Dragging you," Rabbit shudders. "And bringing you to your father, against your will. No. I would never do such a thing. Lennie, you may recall I put you in a cab the other day. Had he known, Cash would've preferred that I'd detained you."

"Why didn't you?"

"Well, Cash never gave specific orders on what to do if you were to show up at the bar soaking wet and . . . Ahem. Excuse the presumption, but drunk as a skunk as well. So I used my own judgment and decided that kidnapping you hardly seemed an auspicious way to kick-start a father-daughter reunion."

"Right," Smith says, bleeding skepticism. "Tell that to the two psychos who broke into Lennie's house a few hours ago."

"Stay away from us," I add, as Smith and I start to make a detour around Rabbit, all the while making sure to stay out of snatching range—just in case.

"Of course, I respect your wishes . . . er, bad choice of words—that is to say, your desires, and I would leave it at that," Rabbit calls after us in his gratingly ingratiating way. "But the thing is, your father has a way to break wishes. One hundred percent guaranteed to work as long as the original wish granter is present and recalls more or less the wording of the original wish."

"More or less?" I ask, intrigued despite myself. My footsteps stall even as Smith attempts to keep tugging me along. "I was totally wasted, or you know, drunk as a skunk, when I granted all those wishes. What if I can't remember exactly how the wish went?"

Rabbit shrugs. "You'll have to ask your father for the exact details. I'm afraid that I'm merely the messenger."

I glance over at Smith, wanting to know what he thinks and if I'm totally crazy for even considering this. "It's something," he says, which is pretty much what I'd been thinking, but then he adds, "Or a bunch of bullshit so your father can get his hands on you."

"And give you a great big hug," Rabbit interjects.

Smith and I ignore him.

"I still think it's a total badass move," W2 chimes in.

We ignore him too.

For better or worse, Smith and I are connected, and this is our decision to make.

"Okay," Smith says, leaning in close and shutting everyone else out. "If this Rabbit guy hadn't shown up, what was your next move?"

"Um . . ." I chew on my lip, waiting for something to come to me. Nothing does. "Go back to my house and try to think of an idea?"

Smith says nothing in response. He doesn't need to. We have no options except for this one really shitty one. If Larry wasn't injured, if Michaela wasn't Cheetos'd, if none of those horrible wishes had been granted in the first place . . . But they had. I'd done something stupid and maybe that meant I needed to do something even more stupid to correct it.

As if reading my mind, Smith says, "I'll be right there beside you."

"Okay," I say, turning to Rabbit. "Is he at the bar?"

"You'll come, then?" Rabbit claps his hands gleefully when I nod. "Excellent, excellent. Cash will be thrilled. You don't even know."

"We're coming too," Dyl announces, jerking her thumb to indicate W2 beside her.

I expect Rabbit to object, but he just grins. "Wonderful!

The more the merrier, is what I always say!"

As if that settles everything, Rabbit scampers off, promising to meet us at the bar, while the rest of us climb into the Jeep. The bar is on the outskirts of town, but we still get there sooner than I'd like.

The idea of having to face my father makes me more than a little sick, and the only thing that keeps me from turning and running is my connection to Smith. He's the anchor holding me here, but more than that, his hand fused with mine seems to lend me some of his strength. And right now, I need it.

I look over my shoulder at Dyl. She sits with her arms wrapped around herself, staring through the back window, watching an empty corner of the parking lot.

How could I have forgotten for even an instant? No matter how wrapped up I am in this train wreck of a day, how has it not even crossed my mind that this is where Dyl was last seen and where her remains were found weeks later. In that suitcase, in the trunk of a car, in this parking lot. Perhaps it was left in that very same parking spot she has her gaze locked on.

Rabbit knocks on my window, making us all jump. "Why are you all just sitting around? Come on inside!"

Now that we're here, looking at the dingy building, which is oddly empty and quiet for ten o'clock on a

Saturday night, we all hesitate.

"Came this far," W2 says at last, swinging his door open and trotting behind Rabbit into the bar.

And for some reason, we all decide to follow the lead of the biggest idiot in the group, perhaps even the biggest idiot in the world.

The interior of the bar is dark and musty. Despite the sprinkling of cars in the parking lot, there isn't a single person inside. The parking lot lights filter through windows thick with grime, and the tables are covered in a sticky layer of residue. If I hadn't been here last night and seen how packed the place was, I would swear from the broken-down and neglected ambiance that it had been shut down and left to slowly rot away years ago.

Behind the bar, Rabbit fills four cups with a sprayer thingy. "Who's thirsty?" he calls when he's finished.

Again W2 eagerly leads the way and the rest of us reluctantly follow. The glasses, in keeping with the rest of the décor, are greasy to the touch and something that looks like a roach floats at the top of mine. Without taking a sip, I quickly set it back down again.

"Look, Rabbit," I start, "I don't have a lot of time—"

Rabbit claps his hands together. "Of course, I understand completely. We'll just let your friends stay here and enjoy their refreshments, while we go seek out your father." Turning toward Smith, Rabbit gives him a strange little bow. "Young man, if you would hand the young lady over to me, I assure you I will take excellent care of her."

Smith smirks. "I bet you would." He holds up our linked hands. "But right now where Lennie goes, I go. We're stuck. See?"

"Oh." The friendly smile that had been on Rabbit's face since he found us fades away. "Oh, I do see. That's not . . . Oh, dear." His little eyes dart between us nervously. "And I suppose that's the result of a wish?"

"Yeah," Smith answers.

"I wonder if you might be able to share with me the exact wording of that wish?"

"It was sick!" W2 jumps in. "I wasn't there, but everyone was talking about it. It was a total burn. No offense, Lennie, but Smith totally slammed you. He was all, 'I wish I could see you in hell, bitch.' See what I'm saying? Buuurrrrnnn. And then she was all like, 'Um, well, uh, you can hold my hand all the way there.' I . . ." W2 shakes his head. "Sorry, Lennie, but that's a super lame comeback. You know?"

"W2," Smith says while giving W2 a physical shove out of the conversation. But apparently the conversation is already over, as Rabbit is taking several little hopping steps backward.

"I just remembered. The storage room. A delivery from earlier today. I need to get it put away. It's a mess. A messy mess. Wouldn't want you to think we run a slovenly establishment, Lennie. Let me see to that, after which we'll um, well, hmm . . . Okay?" By the time the last words exit his mouth, he's halfway across the room, and upon finishing he turns and scurries away until he disappears behind a swinging door.

"That dude is a freak," W2 announces as soon as Rabbit's out of sight. I expect him to rag on Rabbit's appearance or his generally weird deportment, but W2 surprises me by not really surprising me at all. "As if we're gonna drink ginger ale like a bunch of first graders when we're at the most legendary bar in the state—hell, maybe even in the whole country." W2 clambers over the bar and grabs a bottle. After dumping our glasses of pop, he refills them to the rim with vodka.

I push mine away. "No thanks."

W2 shrugs. "More for me." Bringing my glass to his lips, he drinks half of it down in a few thirsty gulps.

Dylan makes this disgusted sort of noise and I prepare myself to applaud as she finally rips him a new one, but instead she grabs her own glass and drains it. Then she grabs my glass from W2 and finishes that too. She turns to Smith with that dangerous sparkle in her eyes. "Your turn."

I don't expect him to hesitate. I've spent enough years around Smith to know that he drinks like a fish who likes to spend a lot of his time drunk. And I especially don't expect him to shake his head and say, "Not feeling it."

Dyl continues to stare at him in that I-might-explode-at-any-moment kind of way. If it were me on the receiving end, I'd be nervously trying to talk her down, but Smith just shoots a nearly identical expression right back at her. They're having some sort of twin showdown, and despite being only inches away I can't say with any certainty what it's about or even who's winning.

W2, realizing that no one is paying attention to him, lets out a loud belch and chucks a piece of ice at Smith. "Dude, you worried Lennie'll pull more of her voodoo shit on you if you take a drink?"

"Hey, that reminds me." Dyl breaks the showdown between her and Smith to focus on me. "I wanna make a wish. Sounds like everyone got one except me." She leans closer, breathing in my face, and instead of getting a big whiff of alcohol fumes, I smell something else instead. Something worse. Death. Decay. Rot.

"Dyl," Smith says, that one word a warning.

She reacts like it's a curse, spinning away from me and back toward Smith. "Tell me again what you wished for, Smith. 'Cause I'm confused. I thought you wished to bring me back, but now W2's story seems to say otherwise."

His jaw tightens. "You heard him. He wasn't even there. And neither were you."

"No." She laughs and the sound is so bitter and angry. "I was busy being dead."

"Guys, stop this." I try to step in, to defuse things a bit. Neither of them even looks my way.

"I remember," Dyl says, and with those words the fire dies. She trembles, closes her eyes, bites her lip. I can see the struggle. A blind man two miles away could see it. She loses this fight too, as a single tear slides down her cheek.

Everyone cries, of course. Except that Dyl doesn't. Or she doesn't anymore. It's part of some oath she made after her dad died in Afghanistan. She said she gave him all her tears and would never shed another for anyone or anything. Seeing as how she promised that when she was twelve I don't think anyone in their right mind would expect her to stick to it for the rest of her life. But Dyl's never been in her right mind. And as soon as that tear escapes, she hisses as if it burns her cheek. As if she's betrayed her dead dad and herself.

My hand that's attached to Smith is locked down at my side, as stiff and unmoving as the rest of him. Clearly, no comforting hugs are coming from him anytime soon. It occurs to me that he doesn't know how to deal with this sad and broken version of Dylan. Their dynamic is to keep each other tough by constantly throwing shit at each other. That's why he was goading her just now. Or why he never did something so simple as kiss and hug her when she woke up. An angry Dyl he knows how to handle. But this version of his sister has left him shaken.

Since Smith is useless and W2 is . . . well, since W2 is W2, I take a half step forward and reach out with my free arm. I'm not really a touchy-feely person and I obviously didn't grow up in a hug-and-kiss type of family either. But even a robot can see that Dyl needs some sort of response other than shuffling feet and nervous titters (the latter from W2, of course).

I get my arm halfway around her back when Dyl jerks away. "Don't," she says in a choked voice. And then she runs out the door.

"What's her deal?" W2 asks.

"Go after her." Smith points at W2, so there is no mistake. "Make sure she's okay. And don't let her go too far."

W2 sighs and gulps down another drink before climbing back over the bar. "You owe me, man," he says before jogging with a slight side-shuffling sway to the door.

As W2 exits, Rabbit returns. And he looks terrible.

Earlier he'd seemed a little jumpy, but now his darting eyes and full-on trembles are paired with a case of the sweats so bad that his shirt is soaked through in several places. He looks fully freaked out.

Since I have a suspicion that he was just talking with my father, this worries me more than a little bit.

"Okay." He claps his hands together as he hurries over to us. "I have good news and bad news. The bad news is that I'm afraid only Lennie will be allowed on the tour. The good news is that I'm going to help get you two kids separated. How does that sound?"

"We already tried to pull apart. It's impossible," I say, and Smith nods in confirmation.

Rabbit's pasted-on smile only gets bigger, though. "Nothing is impossible if approached in the right way. It may be painful, but not impossible." Turning, he waves his hand at the lineup of liquor bottles behind the bar. "And with that in mind, you'll need some anesthesia, my friends. Pick your poison."

"No thanks," Smith snaps.

I glance over and can't miss the pigheaded expression that tells me arguing will be useless. He looks toward the exit, and I know he's worried about Dyl and regretting this wish and five thousand other things, but going into "go ahead, make my day" mode is not really helping things right now. I attempt to communicate all this to him with a pithy, "Don't be stupid."

Despite my compelling counterargument, Smith remains unswayed. He slaps our linked hands on the bar top. "Let's just get this over with."

Rabbit's mouth spreads in a big toothy smile that doesn't fit in with the rest of his face, which remains tight with fear. "Wonderful!" For the third freaking time he claps his hands, a tic that's quickly becoming unbearable. "Now, if you two don't mind . . ." Reaching beneath the bar, he comes back up with a pair of handcuffs.

"You always keep handcuffs around?" I ask nervously.

"Mmm." Rabbit smiles in a way that I think is meant to be reassuring. It's not. "The bartender here was a boy scout, I believe. He likes to be prepared for anything," he explains as he snaps the cuffs around each of our wrists.

Smith smirks. "That hardly seems necessary." I look over at him, marveling at his ability to pretend he's ice-cold when in reality he must be scared shitless.

"I'm not done yet," Rabbit replies as he shows us an oversized metal staple, at least an inch thick. Placing it between the three metal links that act as a bridge between our handcuffs, he then produces a mallet and hammers the staple into the bar top, effectively pinning our coupled hands in place.

But apparently that's still not enough, because he then circles around the bar until he's standing directly behind us. Producing a second pair of handcuffs, he snaps it around my free wrist and attaches it to the metal backrest of my bar stool. After repeating the same procedure on Smith, he returns to his place behind the bar.

"Is this really necessary?" I ask, realizing we are now literally chained up inside my father's bar and that W2 and Dyl won't be able to save us this time with a tennis ball machine and hair spray flamethrower.

Rabbit wipes the sweat from his brow and then gives me a sad smile. "Don't worry, you'll be released the moment the separation is complete."

"I'll bet," Smith says, sounding belligerent and looking bored. If my hands weren't locked down, I'd punch him.

After tugging at our handcuffs a few times to make sure they're secure, Rabbit looks up at Smith. "Last call. Sure you don't want that drink?"

Smith rolls his eyes. "All I want is to get this over with and have my hand and my life back. Let's get on with it."

A lump fills my throat and tears suddenly threaten. Smith and I are still connected, but I can already feel him pulling away. Funny how lonely it feels, how in such a short time I've come to count on him being here beside me.

"Okay, then. You ready, Lennie?" Rabbit places both of his hands over mine while his red and watery eyes stare at me in this disconcerting way. "I'm really sorry."

Trying to be cool like Smith, I shrug. "It's fine, Rabbit. Just do what you gotta do."

"Such a sweet girl," he says, while pulling a lighter from his pocket.

With one more muttered apology, Rabbit clicks the lighter, producing a flickering flame that he brings toward me until it's licking at the thin skin stretched over my knuckles.

I stare in disbelief, and then, as the pain hits, I begin to scream.

FEEL
THE PAIN

I blubber and scream and cry, but it doesn't stop.

A mixture of tears and snot streams down my face. It still doesn't end.

I writhe in pain, trying to escape my own skin, certain I can't take any more. Yet somehow I do.

Clenching my eyes closed against the sight of my bubbling and blistering skin, I try to focus on something—anything—else.

There's Rabbit's trembling hand, holding the burning lighter.

Not that. Don't look at that.

Beside me Smith thrashes, looking even more crazed than me. I actually check to make sure that Rabbit isn't burning him too, but no, only my half of our conjoined hands is being used for kindling. Still Smith screams, his voice ragged and raw, threatening Rabbit, promising he's gonna kill him if he doesn't stop. And then when it becomes clear that Rabbit isn't going to stop, Smith reverts to repeating, his voice growing higher pitched and nearly frothing with each iteration, "You're dead. You're dead. You're fucking dead."

I've never heard him so unhinged and out of control. All his earlier cool isn't just gone, it's like it never existed at all. I'd almost think he's in more pain than me, except that's impossible. The terrible agony guts me and I swallow, trying to keep from spewing out the churning bile in my stomach. I am still in the midst of this battle when the hurt surges upward, filling my head with a bright white light. Smith's curses grow distant. I am floating away. Consciousness is fleeting, but I have one last thought. *This is hell. I am in hell.*

A horrible sound, guttural and pained, brings me back down to earth. My eyes flicker open.

"Lennie, forgive me." Rabbit sprays a stream of cold water over my blackened hand, which is no longer connected with Smith's.

It comes together then. I held his hand all the way to hell and when I reached it . . . he released me.

Beside me Smith's limp hand is still held by his handcuff. I follow the line of his arm. He's slumped over, unconscious, falling off the bar stool and only held there by his handcuffed wrists.

"Uncuff him," I snap at Rabbit.

He stares at me and then stammers, "But, but your b-b-burn."

"Get the cuffs off!" I roar, hardly even recognizing myself.

Without another word, Rabbit scurries around the bar. Despite my objections, he frees me first. I grab Smith, holding his body, so that when his hands are released he doesn't fall to the ground. With my cooked nerve endings still screaming for relief it's impossible to hold his weight, and I end up quickly lowering him to the filthy floor.

"Smith." I give him a little shake. "C'mon, Smith, wake up."

He groans and his eyelashes flutter, but he doesn't come to.

"What did you do to him?" I stand and advance toward Rabbit. "Were you trying to kill him? Me? Is this all on my father's orders? Was it even true about him being able to undo wishes?"

Rabbit hops backward. I lunge forward, suddenly not caring about answers anymore. Suddenly wanting nothing more than to slam my unburned fist into his face. Sensing my intentions, he pivots and scurries away. I am on his heels when he darts into the ladies' room. Slamming my whole body against the door, I follow him in.

Even though his hands are above his head in surrender, I can't stop. I keep coming at him. One step after another until he's backed into a corner.

"Okay," Rabbit squeaks. "It was your father's idea. He doesn't want you tied up with the boy." Tears fill Rabbit's eyes and pour down his cheeks. "And yes, it's true about your father being able to undo wishes. I would never have lied to you about that."

"Oh, yeah, you're a stand-up guy." I throw my own hands up in exasperation. "I need to check on Smith. Make sure you didn't kill him." Spinning around, I march out of the bathroom and back to where I left Smith. Except Smith is gone.

A movement catches my eye and I turn in time to see the glow of the parking lot lights come from outside as one of the big security guys walks out with Smith flung over his shoulder.

"Smith," I scream after him at the same time that Rabbit trots toward me yelling my name. Ignoring him, I head for the exit, but Rabbit heads me off. He flattens himself against the door.

"Lennie, stop. Look, please, can't we sit and talk? When you keep moving around like this, I can't stop myself from chasing you. It's my nature, I guess. The need to hunt, pursue, track my prey. That's why everybody calls me Rabbit, you know." He flashes me a nervous smile.

I shake my head, trying to make sense of this convoluted logic. "That doesn't make sense. Rabbits don't hunt—they run away."

"Don't they?" Rabbit shrugs. "Maybe not. Or maybe we know different kinds of bunnies."

"Whatever." I want to wrap my fingers around his throat and squeeze, but with my flambéed hand out of commission, I settle for grabbing his shirt and giving it a good shake. "Just let me out of here."

Rabbit doesn't budge. "If it helps, your friend is fine. The shock of the separation seemed to be a bit much for him. And, um, well, since you are no longer in hell, I assume the need to hold your hand will return. For those reasons he was taken outside for his and your own health."

"Our health? You set me on fire! And Smith was passed out on the floor. How does it help to drag him somewhere else?"

"He wasn't dragged, he was carried. Gently. Well, maybe not gently." Rabbit grimaces slightly, as if considering this. "But he's alive! And you want him to stay that way, right?"

I swallow. This guy just held a lighter to my hand. My father told him to, or maybe he's insane, but either way he's right—Smith is better off as far away from here as possible. And while the same is no doubt true for me as well, I've gone through this much to hear what my father has to offer, so I might as well see it the rest of the way through.

Screwing up every last bit of courage, I make myself take one and then another step away from the door. "Okay, take me to Cash."

"Let's get you bandaged up first." Rabbit smiles as if we're friends again, as he shadows my retreat deeper into the bar.

I come to a stop, planting my feet. "I don't trust you."

"And why would you? But you'll soon see that I never meant you any harm and now I only want to fix what I've broken." Placing a hand on my back, he gently steers me through the bar to the swinging kitchen doors. Boxes fill the space, stacked all the way up to the ceiling. I eye them curiously, but don't say a word.

"This way," Rabbit says, pulling open the door to the walk-in freezer.

"Really?"

He nods in a way that is meant to be reassuring. I am not reassured. But I've come this far, so I walk inside. The door closes behind us with a soft thunk.

"What now?" I ask, feeling slightly reassured that the air inside isn't cold.

"Have a seat." Rabbit gestures to one of the boxes on the floor. With a shrug, I sit. "Can I see your hand?" Rabbit pulls a tube of something from his pocket. "I've got burn cream and bandages here."

Following the same nothing left to lose fatalism that has brought me this far, I hold my hand out. Rabbit takes it gently into his own surprisingly soft hands. I can't stand to watch as he treats the ugly burn on my hand, but by the time he finishes wrapping the bandage and gently places my hand back on my own knee, the terrible throbbing pain is already starting to fade.

"Now," Rabbit says, taking a seat on the box beside me. "I would like to explain myself before we go see your father. He won't like it, so I'd appreciate it if you didn't share this conversation with him."

"If he won't like it, why do it?"

"I feel like I owe you an explanation." Rabbit presses his hands together in a prayerful gesture. "If you'll allow me."

Even though I've had enough of Rabbit's company, I am still not super eager for my upcoming father-daughter reunion. A little procrastination with the side benefit of giving me extra info can only work out in my favor. But that doesn't mean I'm gonna make things easy for Rabbit. "Fine. Don't think this evens us out, though. You'd have to spill an oil tanker's worth of explanation for me to be okay with this." I hold up my bandaged hand and Rabbit winces.

"Of course, you've been hurt. I understand that." Rabbit pauses and then reaches into his mouth and extracts his teeth. The whole mouthful of them are fake and now rest on his palm. With the teeth missing his face shrinks and his lips nearly disappear. "Your father's the one who gave me these teeth. He took the ones I was born with. Pulled them from my mouth one by one, all the while telling me I was lucky he wasn't sawing off my fingers instead."

I can't help but shudder. "Why do you keep working for him?"

Rabbit laughs. "Your father and me, we're friends."

"Friends? That's not what I call a friend."

"Well, like I said before, different bunnies, you know? He didn't mean nothing by it—he just needed something from me. In fact, the same something you need."

"And what's that?" I ask.

"Information. You're trying to put a puzzle together without all the pieces. You don't know much about your father, do you? Well, besides the stuff that made the papers, right?"

I'm about to argue—to be difficult—when instead,

almost against my will, I nod. It's strange, but before I can worry about it, Rabbit starts talking again.

"Yes, that's what I figured. You can't explain what you don't understand, and no one's ever understood your father."

"But you do?"

"Understand him?" Rabbit laughs. "Nah. But I do know his secrets, and that's something."

This conversation and Rabbit's detour-heavy way of explaining things is giving me a headache, so I try to push him toward the point. "Like the secret about how he once tried to kill me?"

"That is a juicy one, isn't it?" Rabbit agrees. "Your father only married your mother because of her wish-granting abilities, but he gravely overestimated her powers, and as you can imagine, the marriage suffered because of it. But then, he found the loophole. When a wish granter willingly—that's the important part—passes his or her ability on to another wish granter, it gives the second wish granter unparalleled powers. The theory for why this happens is controversial, but most believe that it's not only the wish-granting talent being passed along, but the giver's actual life force."

"But my mom is still alive."

"Well, certainly. Many people live long lives with no will to do so at all."

I put my head in my hands, feeling battered. I wish I could pretend it was bullshit, but after what Benji told me earlier, it all makes perfect sense.

Rabbit pats my shoulder gently. "Not that you asked, but my advice is get out of town while you can. Got any money? Savings?"

I open my mouth, intending to tell Rabbit there's no chance I'm gonna run. Instead, I hear myself say, "My uncles have six thousand four hundred thirty-three dollars and thirteen cents hidden in an old pizza box." This is the second time since I've been in Rabbit's presence that I've said more than I intended to, and it doesn't feel like a coincidence. "What the . . . You made me tell!"

"Compelled you to, actually. That's why they call me Rabbit, because I'm rascally." This last bit he does with a full-on Elmer Fudd inflection, replacing the Rs with Ws. I ignore his latest attempt at misdirection. I need to know exactly what I'm dealing with.

"Who the hell are you?"

"Well, if you really want to know . . ." Rabbit stands and puffs out his chest. "I am the last of the once great and now almost forgotten Snitches."

He is so obviously proud that I almost feel bad poking a hole in it. Almost.

"Never heard of 'em."

Rabbit isn't so easily deflated. If anything, he stands even straighter. "Of course you haven't. You've already made it abundantly clear that you know nothing. No offense."

"None taken," I reply drily. "I wish I knew even less about all this shit."

"Ignorance didn't really work out all that well for you either, Lennie. So please allow me to educate you."

"Actually, you don't—" I try to stop him before he launches into what will doubtless be another longwinded story, but Rabbit waves away my protest.

"No need to thank me." He clears his throat and then, clasping his hands behind his back, begins to speak. "Wherever there was power, there were Snitches. They lived in kings' courts and were tasked with knowing the secrets of their enemies and whispering them in royal ears. It was a good life, until one cocky fool blabbed to the wrong people and ended the Romanov dynasty. When a whole family is slaughtered and it gets out that the Snitch who was supposed to be working for them had been telling tales to the enemy . . . well, you could say there was suddenly a lack of trust there. Without the protection of the powerful, the Snitches faded away pretty quickly."

This last part is said quietly, and Rabbit's tiny eyes look almost watery as they meet my own. "They all died," he says now. "Except for me. The one who betrayed his whole race was the one who survived."

He bows his head and for a moment disappears into his sweater completely. I know that I should get back to the topic of my messed-up life, but can't resist asking, "It was you? But why'd you do it?"

Rabbit's head snaps back up, and he takes two steps— more like hops—forward, then leans down so close that his sour breath fans my face. "Why? Long ago, Snitches were trusted advisors, sitting at power's side, but decades passed and somehow we were sitting at their feet, like trained dogs. Our information kept them strong against their enemies, and we gave it away to them for nothing more than a soft place to sleep at night. And one day that wasn't enough for me. I wanted more."

I shrink back. It isn't his horrible breath pushing me away, but rather his words. Those last three ring in my ears, reminding me of my own rationale for crashing Michaela's party.

My yearning for more blew up in my face. And now I'm so scared of making things worse, I may never again stretch for anything beyond my reach.

"And now you're my father's trained dog," I say to Rabbit, feeling cruel and not wanting him to guess at the hollow ache his speech opened up inside of me.

If my words bother Rabbit, he doesn't show it. "I wouldn't be so sure about that. You don't pull the teeth of a trained dog. No, sir. You take the teeth of a dog you're afraid might still bite." There's an odd sort of logic to this, and I can't deny that Rabbit doesn't seem fearful right now. If anything, he exhibits an almost defiant spark.

I, on the other hand, am more scared than ever. "I never should have come here," I say, feeling so out of my depth that it's all I can do not to sink totally into despair. "I thought maybe 'cause I'm his daughter . . ." I don't bother to fill in the stupid reunion fantasies for Rabbit, since he's probably snitching them directly outta my head anyway. "What was I thinking? He hates everyone."

"Hate?" Rabbit strokes his beard for a moment as if considering the question. "You know, people say hate is a strong word. But it's not, not really. I've seen lots of people hate and it always looks the same. Now, love, on the other hand, oooh boy, that's another story. If somebody loves you, or you love somebody, you never know how it's gonna come out."

I look up at Rabbit. "So you're saying he loves me and that might be even worse?"

"Or better." Rabbit shrugs. "It's hard to say. One thing I know for certain—we gotta get a move on. Cash is gonna wonder what's been holding us up."

"You're right about that." The reply doesn't come from Rabbit, but rather from a voice thick with scorn. I whirl around, unable to believe anyone could sneak up on us in this small enclosed space.

But my father is not just anyone and, of course, that's exactly who's standing directly behind me.

RATHER
BE DEAD

"So, you do recognize me," my father says, his voice changing to something warmer with even a hint of a chuckle. "You see that, Rabbit? Told ya my little girl would recognize her daddy."

He's right. I recognized him immediately from the fuzzy old pictures I've studied over the years. I've always wondered how it was that he could appear so shockingly normal. Dark hair. Friendly smile. Good enough looking, but not so handsome you'd look twice. I always figured that was how he was able to keep from getting caught, by being the type of person who blends in.

After more than a decade of being on the run, I'd imagined him turning pale and withdrawn, reduced to a mere shadow of his former self. But my theory was all wrong. In reality, Leonard Cash is magnetic and fully alive. His presence seems to fill the freezer, and then overflow it. I wouldn't be surprised if the door flew off its hinges.

He leans closer to me. "Hey, you made of Swiss cheese? You too scared to even say hello?"

If there had been any doubt, it vanishes with these words. That phrase, in his distinctive gravelly voice, opens a door, and a pile of old memories fall out.

I was six. It was my birthday. Good old Butter Bear, my stuffed animal/backpack hybrid, was slung on my back, his steadying, reassuring weight a nice counter-balance to Daddy, who I never felt quite solid around. Daddy took me to the toy store and let me ride one of the bikes up and down the aisles. I didn't want to leave, but he told me we would come back and buy it and bring it home after he ran a few more errands. The bike had pink streamers and a horn so loud that when I honked it I couldn't hear the store manager yelling about how the bikes were for display only.

The first errand was ice cream. I got a chocolate cone with rainbow sprinkles. I held it in one hand, the chocolate dripping down my wrist, while Daddy held tight to my other as we walked to the bank next door. Then there was a gun in Daddy's hand, and people screaming and bleeding and dying and Daddy asking me if I was made of Swiss cheese.

It was the same question he asked when I cried after skinning my knees or because one of my uncles' dogs had bitten me. All those other times I'd been able to stop crying and tell him no. No, I wasn't made of Swiss cheese. This time, though, I puked up chocolate ice cream and Daddy swore and told a nice-looking lady to clean it up or he'd put a hole in her fat ass. After we'd gotten away and were speeding down the road with sirens wailing in the distance, Daddy told me he'd been tempted to leave me behind. That a getaway was tough enough without having a kid made of Swiss cheese along for the ride. "You gotta buck up if you wanna stick with me," he'd said. And I'd tried. I'd tried to hide how I was so full of holes I could practically feel the wind whistling through 'em.

But in the end, he left me behind anyway.

Now, feeling the weight of his eyes on me, I don't merely remember how hard I'd always tried to please him, but I actually feel it again. I can feel myself being drawn toward him, wanting to laugh with him and impress him and have him say more things to me in that chummy way.

I push these feelings away, and instead focus on the years of practice I've had in hating Leonard Cash. "I save my hellos for people I'm happy to see."

The teasing laughter on my father's face is replaced by a disapproving frown, and I have to force my spine straight so that I don't shrink away from it. "You have one hell of a chip on your shoulder. I gotta warn you, Lennie, it's not the most attractive quality. And you also might wanna remember it's not the best way to act toward someone who's here because you need help."

It's a mild scolding, and yet I find myself squirming. Fighting the urge to say something that'll make him smile again. I put my chin up instead. "I didn't ask for your help. Rabbit showed up offering it. And I only took him up on it because I'm . . ." *Drowning in shit creek.* No. I fish for words that will make me sound less desperate and come up with, "I'm exploring my options."

"Right. Good one." Cash laughs and I'm amazed by how quick and constantly shifting his moods are, making it impossible to predict his reaction to anything. "And here I thought you were in way over your head and I would have to throw you a life preserver. But if you're only exploring options." He pauses to laugh again, not bothering to hide that he finds me ridiculous. "Well then come down to my office and I'll be happy to give you another option to consider." As he speaks, a small section of the wall behind him slides down into the floor, revealing a passageway.

At least now I know how he magically appeared. It's somewhat reassuring that no actual magic was involved.

After a moment of hesitation and a last glance at

Rabbit, who has been unnaturally still, I follow my father. The passage curves before leading to a steep staircase, stretching down so far that I wouldn't be surprised to learn my father's renting rooms from the devil himself.

The reality, when I finally reach it, is a bit disappointing. It's nothing more than a basement that's been converted into an office. File cabinets line the walls. A large desk sits at the center. Another table holds a coffeemaker with the last quarter of a pot still sitting on the burner. The whole scene is laughably ironic: my FBI's Most Wanted killer dad works in a boring old office. I'm tempted to pull out my phone and take a picture so I can caption it "Crime Doesn't Pay."

"Sit," my father commands as he settles into the chair behind his desk. Obediently, I perch on the edge of the folding aluminum chair opposite him. Even though he just sat down, he's up again a moment later, grabbing two bottles of water from a mini fridge underneath the coffeepot table. He holds one out to me, and since my throat is a little raw from all the screaming today, I gratefully take it.

That gratitude doesn't last long, as my father lifts his eyebrows and asks, "Where are your manners? What do you say, Lennie?" Like I'm in kindergarten and he's a real dad who's been around providing a good example instead of disappearing into his life of crime.

"Screw you," I respond, and then take a giant swig of water.

"Such a spitfire. My little Lennie girl all grown up. We're cut from the same cloth, kiddo." He says this in a bemused yet gently chiding way, like some dad in a cheesy sitcom. Except it's not cheesy at all, because I can remember him calling me his little Lennie girl years and years ago. Even though I was too little to remember too much about him, the bits I've retained are incredibly vivid, as if the force of his personality ensured that he was permanently burned into my young mind.

"You know, Lennie, I always thought that when we were finally able to be together again, we'd click, as if no time had passed at all. But I see now it might take a little more time for us. That's okay, though. We'll figure it out. The important thing is that you're becoming who you were always meant to be." He wags his finger at me. "I gotta admit, I've been worried these last few years that I'd overestimated my little Lennie girl."

"I am not your little Lennie girl," I snarl through chattering teeth, trying not to let him know how much he is affecting me.

He ignores me. "Although, I did know you well enough to guess that when you started granting wishes it would be with a bang. It's about time you realized you were meant for bigger things than your uncles."

His words hit me like a knife of betrayal. My father is right. This all started because I'd looked at my uncles' lives and found them to be small and not at all what I wanted for myself. The idea of my life being like theirs made me feel depressed. I didn't just let them down, I turned on them. And now, even worse, I'd left my uncles behind at Michaela's to come here and sit with my father and ask him to solve all my problems.

I push my chair back with a loud screech. "If you think this was some grand plan, that I wanted all of this to happen, then you're crazy. I didn't even know I could grant wishes until today. And now all I want is to undo them and be normal and boring and safe and small and to never have anything exciting happen to me for the rest of my gray little lifetime."

Okay, that's a bit of an exaggeration. Still, I imagine I'll need at least a good decade of boring to recover from this weekend.

"Sit down!" Showing a flash of temper, Cash bangs both hands against his desk. "It's past time you lived up to your potential. You are meant for great things and I am done idly standing by while you waste your life away."

"You think I'm wasting my life away?! You're a felon.

In hiding. Beneath a crappy bar in an even crappier office. Gee whiz, Dad, I hope I grow up to be just like you." This last bit oozes sarcasm, but Cash doesn't even seem to notice.

"Yes, you should want to be like me." He leans across the desk, his eyes glittering dangerously. "You've been brainwashed like everyone else to believe that life is about accumulating things. Car. House. Fancy shoes. Diplomas. Important job titles. What you should really want is something that lasts. Something you can't hold in your hand, but stays deeper inside yourself, where it can never be taken away. That's when you're onto something. That's when you begin to live not as a mere man, but as something bigger and more powerful than any president or captain of industry could ever aspire to."

Despite the crazy shit coming from his mouth, I find myself wanting to nod in agreement, simply from the force of his belief. When he's done I have to take several more gulps of water. Wiping my mouth with the back of my sleeve gives me the needed time to collect myself. To remember that no matter how alluring the beat, this is a man whose tune I don't ever want to march to again.

I force my rigid backbone into a slouch and smirk. Only then am I able to reply, "The thing deeper inside of you. It's self-esteem, right? Better than gold and no one can take it away? They actually taught us that in second grade."

Not only does my father have the captivating personality of a snake charmer, but he is also apparently impervious to snark.

He falls back into his chair, at ease except for his burning gaze that never wavers from mine. "Do you think it's a coincidence I married your mother, a woman who comes from a long line of well-concealed wish granters? Or that I keep Rabbit, the Snitch who can't hold his tongue, close by my side? And those are only two of the many oddities I've collected over the years. I have hunted and found ways to bind the powerful, the magical, the extra-human, and the inhuman, to me. And it's lucky for you I have, because that is how I came across this."

He produces what looks like a homemade birthday candle made from lumpy gray wax with an extra-long wick. "I heard you granted some wishes that you now regret."

Understatement of the year. But I just shrug. "I guess."

"Take this," he commands, and after a moment of hesitation, I do. "Now, repeat aloud one of the wishes you granted."

Again, I am uncertain, but can't see what harm it will

do. "To Larry's and everyone else's moms staying chill no matter what. May—" I stop with a little gasp of alarm as the wick of the candle bursts into flame.

"Don't drop it!" Cash cautions as I lurch to my feet and nearly fling it away. "It won't work if it's broken."

Slowly I sit back down, staring at the odd candle and the little flame dancing at its tip. "Now what?" I ask, no longer skeptical.

"Put it out."

I purse my lips and blow. The flame resists. Almost like it's fighting back. I blow harder, even add a little spit to it. Finally, the flame flickers and dies. A second later the candle crumbles to dust.

"Whoa," I say. I brush the bits of it from my legs and then look up at Cash. "Did it work, then?"

He nods, looking more than a little smug.

And he should, because suddenly I am willing to do whatever he wants to get more of those candles. "Can I have more? I need at least . . ." I do a quick mental calculation. Turlington, Zinkowski, Cat Girl, Stace's sister, Todd, Michaela . . . No. Not Michaela. "I need a lot."

"As many as you need," Cash says, in this reassuring way that has me almost melting into my chair with relief. "Unfortunately, I don't have any more here. You see, a friend of mine makes these himself. We can find him at my beach house. You'll love it there. The views are just—"

"Hold up," I cut in, unable to ignore the sinking feeling telling me of course it can't be that easy. "This friend who makes the candles. Is he really a friend? Or is he more like a prisoner?"

Something ugly crosses Cash's face. "You've been talking to Benji and Jules." He shakes his head. "I did so much for them—"

I interrupt again. "Like getting rid of Benji's pesky extra eye? Depth perception. Who needs it, right?"

"I wanted their help in finding my daughter! Is that so terrible? Perhaps I went too far, in my desperate need. But I missed you, Lennie. It's a terrible thing to lose a child."

He's so convincing. His face is suddenly haggard. And yet . . . I don't quite believe it. "You missed me?" I ask. "Or you missed getting me to grant your wishes?"

"My little Lennie girl." He shakes his head at me, sadly, like he can't believe how I can be so confused. "You already gave me my one wish a long time ago, so that well's been dry for some time now."

I blink at him. "I . . . What? When?"

Cash frowns, looking hurt by my confusion. "It was a powerful moment between us, Lennie. That you've forgotten it . . ." He shakes his head. "Never mind. I won't hold it against you."

"Gee, thanks." I realize he's not gonna fill me in on whatever wish I gave him, so I cut to the chase. "If I granted your wish already, what exactly do you want from me?"

"Damn it." He stands and crosses until he's standing right in front of me. Then he kneels before me on one knee. "I want what any father wants. To know you. To be there for you. To help you reach your full potential."

My throat goes tight. This is what I've wanted to hear for what seems like my whole life. And sure, this is probably bullshit, but he's doing all he can to sell it and damn if I'm not ready to buy. I fight it, though. "If that's true, then where have you been? Ten years and I haven't ever gotten a crummy birthday card or even a stinkin' phone call."

He reaches for my hand, the burnt and bandaged one—still tender and aching from his orders. Or that's what Rabbit told me, but maybe he's the liar here because Cash takes my hand so gently, as if he could never stand to see me get hurt. "Do you think I would have let even a day go by without seeing you if the choice was mine to make? They hid you from me. The same way they've hidden themselves all these years. There was no way for me to have a moment like this until you sought me out of your own accord."

"They hid me with a wish," I say. "A wish to keep me safe from you."

"Safety," Cash scoffs. "If they cared about that, they'd have kept you far from the moonshine. But they needed a successor, I suppose. So they selfishly decided to use you for their own means."

I stare at Cash, shocked by his twisted interpretation of the uncs. I am ready to defend them when Cash releases my hand and stands, brushing himself off while adding, "I can't say for certain as to the exact wording of their wish, but I assume it was something along the lines of keeping your true identity and abilities hidden. That's how your friend was so easily mistaken for you."

I'd been nodding along, happy to finally get some answers and wondering beneath that if my father was not the villain he'd been made out to be all these years. But that last bit stops me cold.

"My friend?" I ask.

"Yes, the one who got herself chopped up." Cash walks over to one of the filing cabinets, opens a drawer, pulls out a sandwich bag, and tosses it to me. I catch it reflexively. After a short glance, I immediately throw it away with a frightened yelp.

"Those are fingers."

"That's right," Cash casually confirms. "A man by the name of Rollo Grange sent them to me along with a note saying if I wanted to see my daughter alive again, he wanted a meeting and money and . . . Well, I don't really know what else. I stopped reading it."

I gape at him. "You stopped reading?"

"I don't deal with people like that," he says with a shrug. "Giving in to blackmail is a sign of weakness."

I stand, pick up the stupid folding chair, and fling it at the line of filing cabinets to my left. It hits them with a satisfying *clang* and then bangs to the floor just as loudly. Only after it settles am I able to turn and face my father once more. "How did you know those weren't *my* fingers? Or did you even know? Did you even care?"

He sighs, looking harassed. "I had a hunch it wasn't you. But either way, my hands were tied."

"They weren't tied!" The words explode out of me. "That was my best friend. *Her* hands were probably tied. Until he cut them off! He chopped her into pieces! You could have stopped that, but instead you let it happen without . . ."

"Lifting a finger?" Cash asks with a slight smirk.

"You think that's funny? How he . . ." My voice fails and tears blur my vision. I impatiently brush them away. "How could you?"

"Hey," he snaps back at me, the friendly dad act finally fraying at the edges. "I caught him, okay? Not in time to save your friend, but I got the guy and made him pay a hundred times over. If you coulda heard his screams and the way he begged for mercy, maybe you'd give your old man a break."

"Never." I reach down and pick up the bag with Dyl's chopped-off fingers. "You are out of your mind if you think I'll have anything to do with you after hearing that. I thought maybe they'd made you out to be worse than you are, but they didn't. If anything they made you sound too nice."

At last the curtain rises and Leonard Cash, the real Leonard Cash, takes the stage. Oh, he is every bit as magnetic as the man I've been chatting with. The same burning energy fills him to overflowing. His eyes glitter and glow in that same mesmerizing way. But there's no charm.

This is the man who would order Rabbit to hold a lighter to his daughter's knuckles. The man who'd receive a girl's fingers in the mail and simply file them away for later. The man who left me in that Chuck E. Cheese's all those years ago.

I remember now with sudden clarity that I'd gotten in that ball pit to hide from him. And I'd stayed buried for so long because I'd been convinced that he would find me. How had I ever forgotten that?

"You need me, little Lennie girl," he says, and this time there is pure poison in that nickname. "You need me because you've gotten yourself into a mess only I can get you out of."

"Not you," I spit back at him, feeling reckless. "You're nothing. Powerless. Only good at catching people with abilities way beyond your own."

I immediately regret my words when Cash's hand finds my throat. "The moment you started granting wishes—not safe little wishes, but big, messy, life-changing ones—you might as well have hung up a billboard announcing yourself and your services. That wish of your uncles' can't hide you anymore. Now think, how many people out there might see a wish-granting girl and ask themselves how such a person might be of use to them."

I should be smart and stay quiet if I want to continue breathing, but I open my big mouth anyway. "I know at least one."

Cash only grins in response, but there is none of his earlier warmth in it. "Yes, well, I know at least twenty, and the only reason they aren't already ripping you apart and fighting over the pieces is because I put the word out that you belong to me. But what would happen if I changed my mind and said it was open season on my little Lennie girl? What if I decided that you weren't gonna be of any use to me after all?" His hand tightens slowly, and I draw in a final strangled breath before my windpipe is completely restricted. I claw at him, desperate for air, while he eyes me coldly. "Lennie, trust me on this, you'd rather be dead than let them other people catch up with you."

Spots appear. I try to blink them away, but they multiply. And then darkness and then . . . he releases me. I gasp and choke while he strolls back to his desk chair as if nothing's happened.

He smiles and again the coldness in it is enough to make me shiver. "I'll give you time to think about coming with me."

"I don't need time." I take a step toward him, but stumble. The room whirls around me. It must be from the oxygen loss. Squinting to focus on Cash, I finish my thought. "You're right, I'd rather be dead than have anything to do with you."

"Don't be hasty," Cash counters. "Sleep on it and maybe you'll feel differently when you wake up."

"When I wake up? But I'm not even—" A gigantic yawn interrupts me. And just like that, my eyelids start to droop. For a moment I think Cash's power of suggestion is so great that he can even make me feel sleepy, but then I trip over my water bottle and realize . . .

"You drugged . . ." I trail off, my lips too heavy to finish forming the words.

"It was good seeing you again, Lennie," Cash says as I

collapse to the floor. "We'll have to do this again soon."

No, I think. *No. No. No.* I fight to keep my eyes open, but it is a losing battle. They fall hard and heavy, like a dungeon door clanging closed, and an instant later, I am asleep.

DOWN
AND OUT

I wake up stiff and cold and still half dreaming.

In that dream world, I am six years old and my father is yelling at me.

"Say it," he demands. "'May all your wishes come true, or at least just this one.'"

I tremble, scared and confused. The awful man looks like my father, but this mean face is not the one I'm used to seeing. Still, I try to say the words the way he wants. They come out wrong, mixed up and half forgotten while snot runs into my mouth.

He brings his hand up and I wince. Instead of hitting me, he slowly brings the hand back down. Smiles. Says he lost his temper. He's sorry. I deserve a treat.

We go to Chuck E. Cheese's. Sitting outside in the parking lot, he reminds me of all the delights to be found inside. I nod eagerly, my hand on the doorknob. "Wait," he says. "Not yet." Then he brings out the jar of moon-shine and tells me we need to do the toast first. I start to tremble once more, not wanting to mess up again. Daddy tells me to focus, his voice hard and unbending. Somehow I do.

"To being invisible—" That big word trips me up a bit, but I somehow get it out and then continue on, "except for when you want to be seen. May all your wishes come true, or at least just this one."

Daddy takes a swig from the jar and passes it to me. But I don't want to drink the moonshine. I push it away and the jar falls and gushes out all over the floor mats. Daddy grabs the jar and smashes it into my face. "Drink it, damn you!" He grips my shoulder with one hand while the other pinches my nose. The lid of the jar grinds against my wiggling front tooth and, afraid that I'll swallow it and won't get a visit from the tooth fairy, I finally open my mouth and let him pour the moonshine down my throat.

I am still gagging and coughing when he drags me inside the Chuck E. Cheese's, his mood changed once more, telling me how much fun we'll have. I hide in the ball pit and he is looking for me when they come. Calling my name. Demanding I come out. I am the reason he does not run away until it is almost too late. "I'm not leaving without you," he says again and again. But in the end he does. Still I keep hiding. I stay in that pit for so long I fall asleep and begin to believe it was all just a bad dream.

I'm awake. Not in a ball pit. But in my father's office. I have not managed to escape him after all. Perhaps I never will.

I push up onto my elbow and then pause to rub out the kink in my neck. My eyes are sticky and it is a relief to open them and find darkness. I swallow a few times, trying to unglue my tongue from inside my cottony mouth.

"Lennie." Dyl's hand finds mine and gives it a squeeze. "We're gonna get you out of here."

"Hurry," urges a second voice that I recognize as Rabbit's. "I don't know how long he'll stay away. Even now he may know we're here."

"Can you stand?" Dyl asks, as her arm slides around my back. Even with that help I barely get my legs beneath me, and before I can straighten them the room begins to spin.

"Can't," I explain as I collapse. "Gimme a minute," I quickly add, not wanting them to give up on me.

Rabbit squeals his alarm.

"A minute won't make a difference." I can hear the annoyance in Dyl's voice. "If you're so worried, go upstairs to keep watch."

"But if she can't make it up—" Rabbit protests.

Dyl cuts him off. "We'll manage."

Silence. Then Rabbit sighs. "Call if you need me." His dragging footsteps make a soft *shush*ing sound as they fade away.

"How long was I out?" I ask.

"Not long. Maybe two hours? We gave you a shot of adrenaline or something like that. I dunno. Rabbit said it would help."

I groan. "What'd I miss? Anything good?"

Beside me I can feel Dyl shrug. "Just Rabbit freaking out about how we need to hurry and get you out of here."

"Sooo . . . this is the rescue?"

Dyl laughs her crazy laugh that always sounds on the edge of hysteria, although for once there's actually a reason for it. "I guess. I mean, if you wanna be rescued. Personally, I don't think cutting out of high school a year early for a Rio vacay sounds all that bad."

"It's not a vacation if you aren't allowed to leave."

Dyl makes this impatient noise and I can imagine her expression of disgust. I've seen it many times. She could never believe that I saw being my father's child as anything but a wonderful bonus. "You're being a little hard on him, Len. He wants the best for you."

"Did he tell you that?" I struggle my way back into a sitting position, not wanting to have this argument lying down. When she was alive, Dyl always made me wonder if I was being too harsh. She would bring up my deepest kiddie fantasies that my dad was the only one who'd ever truly loved me. Now with those illusions truly shattered, I am no longer content to end this argument by agreeing to disagree. Cash is a bad guy. There's no other side to the story. But Dyl is off and running before I can say any of this.

"Actually, he did tell me that. We chatted for a bit upstairs. He was nice, Lennie. He told me he wanted to make up for lost time with you and he wanted you to be happy. And . . ." Dyl hesitates before leaning closer to me so she can speak quietly. "He said I can come too. He thought it would make it easier for you and he said—"

The rotting smell I'd noticed earlier is even stronger, and I almost gag. I shift, so her breath isn't directly in my face, and then cut off this stream of bullshit. "He's using you to get to me, Dyl. It's so obvious. You're being played." I almost add "again," as I think of the internet guy who lured her away and chopped her to pieces.

Maybe Dyl is remembering this too, because her voice is raw when she answers me. "It's not always about you, Lennie. He said I'm special because of what happened to me. Coming back from the dead, he said, can sometimes give you certain powers."

"That's even worse, Dyl! He collects freaks. Uses them. You wanna be like Rabbit?" A mixture of anger and disgust fueling me, I push myself to my feet. "Let's get out of here."

Dyl grabs hold of my arm, her grip surprisingly tight as her fingers bite into my skin. "I need this Lennie. I can't go back to the way things were. I don't feel right. I feel groggy and achy and confused and worst of all . . ." She stops and I can actually hear her swallow. "I hurt and I want to make other people hurt too."

This stops me. As she knew it would. I cover Dyl's hand with my own. "Don't tell me you wish I hadn't brought you back. 'Cause I would do it again. I'm sorry it sucks, but I'm glad you're alive."

"Lennie . . ." Dyl sighs and I can feel her soften. "I'm glad you made that wish. I mean, thank you, or whatever. Guess I shoulda said that earlier. The thing is, I wish I'd never been dead at all."

Something in me lifts. "That's it, Dyl! That can be your wish! I can grant it right now."

I wait for Dyl to start jumping up and down beside me, but she turns to stone instead.

"What?" I demand, starting to feel impatient with her and annoyed with being unable to see her face. "You don't want that? You just said you feel weird and achy and stuff.

Is that how you want to feel?"

"That might go away," Dyl answers, her voice low and sullen. "I just woke up today; maybe it'll get better."

I'm still confused. "Are you afraid the wish won't work? Or that it'll undo the other wish? I know I've messed a lot of this wishing stuff up, so if you don't trust me—"

"Shut up, Lennie," Dyl interrupts. "It's not that. I . . ." She pauses. Sighs. And when she speaks again her voice is barely a whisper. "If I wasn't dead, then I'm not special anymore. Leonard might not even want me to come then and—"

Now it's my turn to interrupt. "Leonard?! You're calling him Leonard now? That's super. And it's because of him that you would rather be in pain and stuff. Well, that's stupid."

"Thanks. Thanks a lot." Dyl's sarcastic voice is the worst. It's her with all the warmth removed. "I'm stupid, then. Now can we get this rescue over with?" She tugs at my arm, but I resist, pulling away. I don't want to end things with her this way. Ever since she woke up, I've felt like we haven't been able to find our old groove, like our friendship had been buried along with Dyl and I needed a special wish to resurrect that as well.

"When you died, Dyl, it was the worst thing that had ever happened to me. It hurt so bad and I just thought: it should have been me. You have no idea how many times I wished that it had been me instead of you."

I don't know what I expect in response to this, but after baring my soul, I am at least hoping to avoid hearing that hard, sarcastic voice again.

"You're such an idiot," Dyl replies at last, her tone softer than her words. "If it had been you, the cavalry would've charged in to save you. Your dad. Your uncles. Even your nutso mom. They wouldn't have let you go down like that."

I reach toward Dyl to give her a shake. "This is the problem. You think my life is so great. So cool. But you can't see that my father is crazy and only wants to use me. My mom wouldn't notice if I went missing. And my uncles, c'mon, they aren't people you can count on in a crisis. I mean yeah, they're at Michaela's now, but their first instinct was to get totally wasted. Maybe you can't see it clearly, but I can. I'm nothing special and not one of them would think I was worth the effort of saving."

"You see it clearly? Really?" Dyl laughs. "You grant wishes, Lennie. That's pretty fucking special. And your uncles were beside themselves at Michaela's house. They want to fix this. They want to fix this *for you*. Your mom too. You like to make excuses and feel sorry for yourself. Oh, nobody's nice to poor Lennie 'cause her dad's a killer. But that was never it, Lennie. You keep yourself sealed off from everyone else and you are so frickin' afraid to live that you go running every time something the slightest bit exciting might happen to you."

"Shut up!" I yell, not wanting to hear anything else she has to say. "I went to Michaela's stupid party because of you. To live 'cause you couldn't anymore. Look how that worked out. And I could be running away right now, but I'm not. I'm trying to figure out how to fix things before more people end up dead."

"And let's say you do that. What happens next?"

It's a question I haven't taken time to consider. But now, I realize the answer is easy. "I'll do what my uncles have always done. Have somebody make a wish to keep me hidden and after that only grant small wishes that nobody'll ever notice."

Dyl makes this low noise in her throat. Like disapproval. Or worse. Pity. All she says, though, is, "That's really what you want?"

I swallow past the lump in my throat. "I don't know what I want, except to be far far far away from my father." I turn and start up the steps. "Speaking of which, we're wasting time. Cash could come back at any minute."

"He said he wanted to help you, Lennie," Dyl protests as I start taking shaky steps forward.

"Himself," I correct. "He wants to help himself."

"What if you're wrong? What if he's the only way to clean up your mess?"

"I'll take my chances," I shoot back without hesitation, and I keep moving forward. Dylan fell for Cash's act, and she fell hard. I could tell her about him having her missing fingers on file, but I'm honestly not sure that would be enough to pull her out of his spell. She's convinced herself that he's the answer to every problem that ever was.

A light shines under the door at the top of stairs, lending a tiny bit of illumination so that when Dyl comes up beside me, I can just make out how distorted her whole face looks. The skin is stretched tight across her cheekbones and her eyes seem strangely oversized as she stares at me.

"I know you think I'm stupid for going with Cash, the same way you thought I was an idiot to run off with someone I'd met online. It wasn't like I didn't know it could go badly. I knew that was possible and I didn't care. I took my chances. And you know what? For a few days . . . For a few days, it was amazing. He looked like his picture and he talked the same way we had online and it was totally worth it . . . until it wasn't." Dyl laughs that crazy laugh, except now it is more manic sounding than ever, reminding me that for her this didn't end several months ago. For her it probably feels like yesterday.

"Dyl . . ." I reach toward her, full of sympathy.

She slaps my hand away, not angry but impatient, as if I'm not getting the point of her whole story. "I took my chances. I took my chances once and I'll do it again. And you should too."

I shake my head. "I'm not like you."

She smiles, tentatively. "You could try to be."

Again, I shake my head, since it seems kinder than saying that I'm pretty sure I don't want to be like her. Maybe once I did. I'd definitely admired her boldness . . . except now it looks more like recklessness and not giving a shit what happens to anyone except herself.

Maybe Dyl senses my hidden thoughts, 'cause she mimics my head shake and says, "You know Teena always said we had one of those friendships that wouldn't last after high school. The two of us would go in opposite directions and never meet again."

"Yeah, and you always said Teena was full of shit."

Dyl shrugs. "Mostly full of shit. She said one or two things I took note of."

I look at Dyl. Past the crazy eyes and the burning determination to do whatever the hell it is she's gonna do. I know she's telling me our friendship is at that breaking point Teena talked about, but that's not only up to her and I don't want it to end this way.

So I force a grin. "I thought the only time you took note of Teena was when she said, 'Girls, size matters. And I'm talking about a man's manhood, if you know what I mean. Unless he's very good at going downtown, in which case you make allowances.'"

And Dyl laughs, her too-wide eyes relaxing with it. "Like I said. One or two things worth listening to."

I laugh with her. Then I swing the door open, wanting to end on that note without any more harsh words being exchanged. Rabbit greets us with a relieved smile. "Hurry, hurry," he whispers, ushering us through the dark bar.

I glance over my shoulder at Dyl. She gives me a reassuring smile, like everything's okay between us now. I'm not reassured. Still, I smile and nod back, willing to pretend too.

When we reach the front door, Rabbit cracks it open. He sticks his head out before quickly drawing it back inside. "Lennie, you go first. We'll be right behind you."

"Are you coming with us?" I ask.

He nods. "Can't stick around here after helping you escape. Your father will have me taken care of, if you know what I mean."

I give him a weak smile in response. "Yeah, I know what you mean."

"Now go." Rabbit gives me a little push. I glance back

at Dyl once more. She's not looking at me, but down at her hands, or more specifically, at her missing fingers. I watch as she grimaces and then balls her hands into fists.

Impulsively, I reach out and give her a quick hug. It's a little weird since Dyl and I are more the type of friends to punch each other in the arm. Still, it needs to be done. And as my arms wrap around her I realize that I should have overcome the weirdness of it and done this the moment she first woke up.

"Is it wrong I'm glad you're here?" I ask as I pull away.

Dyl gives me a twisted smile, like even that pains her, but all she says is, "Of course it is, you freak."

"Touching," Rabbit says. "Really. But can we go now?"

In answer I shove the door open. Smith's Cherokee idles only a few steps away and I run toward it, fling the back door open, and throw myself inside. "Augh!" I scream as I bump into Benji. I lean way forward to see around his bulk and sure enough, Jules is tucked next to him, still giving me the evil eye. "What the hell are you doing here?" I demand.

"Change of heart," Benji says, at the exact same moment a shrill cry rings out.

I twist around in time to see my father stab a knife into Rabbit's gut. Everything seems to freeze for a minute or two, but it's really just my brain that's slowing down as it tries to make sense of the long silver blade, so terrible and smooth, sliding into flesh.

Eyes red and watering, Rabbit stares down at the knife piercing his abdomen, then back up to my father. "You said you'd stick a knife in my heart if I ever betrayed you."

"Yes, I know," Cash answers in his casual, only vaguely menacing voice. "Sometimes it takes me a few times before I get it in the right place. Here, let me try again." His hand reaches for the knife . . .

"No!" I leap from the car.

"This is grown-up business, Lennie." My father's glance flicks my way and then back to Rabbit, dismissing me.

"I'll wish you to the bottom of the ocean," I announce in a trembling voice. "I'll wish that you drown slowly but never die. I'll wish that the fish slowly nibble away at your skin. I'll—"

Cash breaks in. "That's quite enough." He pivots slowly, so that he's facing me. "I must admit, you paint a compelling picture. The question is, who would ask you to grant that wish?"

An angry, guttural growl comes curling up over my left shoulder. I know without looking that it's Jules. "Me too," Benji adds, to slightly less dramatic effect.

"Try us," I challenge, without hesitation. That knife did more than wound Rabbit, it also cut free any last bit of tender feeling I'd had toward my father. And without that small trace of sentimental emotion, I am able to tell him with absolute honesty, "I'd gladly see you dead."

"I believe you would." He smiles then. "This must be what parental pride feels like."

"Rabbit, get in the car," I say, never taking my eyes off Cash. When Rabbit only continues to tremble, I nearly lose it. "Get in the damn car! Now!"

Finally, he side-shuffles toward the Jeep. Once he's within my reach, I grab hold of him and help him into the backseat. Benji helpfully hauls Jules onto his lap to make more room for the rest of us.

"Dyl," I call once Rabbit is seated. Scanning the area, I find her huddled near the front door. "C'mon."

Cash laughs. "She's staying with me. And before you start making threats again, please understand that this is her choice."

"No," I shake my head in full-on denial, although I already know it's true. I think I knew even when I hugged her a few minutes ago. "Dyl?"

She advances a few steps, but then stops next to Cash. "I'm sorry, Lennie." Her eyes lock with mine as Cash's arm slides around her shoulders and he pulls her close to his side. I'd expect her to look smug—she got me good—but all I see is grim determination.

Or maybe she's only mirroring what's on my face, because instead of pleading with my best friend to change her mind, I simply nod and say, "See ya on the other side, Dyl." Then I reach out to swing the door closed while yelling, "Let's get out of here! GO!"

"Are you sure?" This query comes from W2, who is in the driver's seat.

"Dyl wants to stay. We don't. Let's go already!"

I expect Smith to object, but he doesn't make a sound from where he's huddled in the passenger seat. W2 doesn't need any further encouragement. He slams his foot on the gas pedal and we shoot forward and away.

Leaving Dyl and Cash and so many dead hopes behind.

DYING

"I'm sorry about your friend," Benji says softly. "Even when you know it's not really her, it's still hard."

"What do you mean?" I demand.

"I thought you understood," he says. "When people are brought back from the dead, they're different. Inside. It's almost like . . ."

He trails off, looking squeamish, like he doesn't want to be the one to break it to me. But I already know. "She's rotten inside," I say.

"Yeah," he admits, before adding, "sorry."

I wave his apology away. Too exhausted to be any more upset than I already am. "And you're here because you've decided I'm a good guy and want to help. Right?"

Jules reaches across and gives me a thumbs-up at the same time Benji says, "Pretty much."

"Well, welcome aboard, I guess." I lean forward,

wanting to make sure Smith is okay. I flick on the over-head dome light to see him better and then wish I hadn't. His skin is pasty white with an overlay of sweaty shine. The hand that I'd held is clutched to his chest and the rest of his body curls in toward it.

"Smith," I say, reaching out to him.

W2 slaps my hand away. "He doesn't want you touching him. Those were his orders. He wants you kept away."

"Oh," I say, snatching my hand back. It's not a betrayal. I know that. And yet . . .

I take a deep breath and hold it for a few seconds before releasing it slowly. I'd been ready to ask if he was okay, but now, up close, it's so obvious that he's not. I swallow those words and reach for new ones. "We had to leave Dyl behind. I mean, she wanted to stay behind. With Cash. My father. She thinks . . . I don't know what she thinks, and I'm sorry, Smith, I tried to tell her—"

"Fine." He cuts me off with one word, dismissing both me and Dyl.

"But," I protest automatically, unable to believe that Smith would let Dyl go so easily. Or maybe I only want an excuse to talk to him. To be near him.

Smith turns toward me but not the way I wanted. Not like me. Even now, in obvious, terrible pain, I still need him more than he needs me. He snarls, lips curled back and teeth flashing, "Enough. Get back. I don't want you near me. I don't want you."

With that he twists away again, curling into himself, and I fall back into my seat, blinking back tears. I barely notice when I bump up against Rabbit, but then he groans and I quickly jump away, horrified that I let myself forget for even an instant that I was sharing the backseat with someone who had just been stabbed.

"Sorry. Are you . . ." For the second time, I stop before I can ask if he's okay. No one in this vehicle is okay. Rabbit least of all. The knife juts from his midsection and now a steady stream of blood pours from it and pools on the seat around him. I make myself focus on Rabbit's pain instead of my own. "Is there anything I can do? Should I pull it out? No, wait, I shouldn't, right? You'll bleed out faster."

Rabbit waves a hand at me, as if shooing away my silly medical questions. "Cash always carries through on his threats." Rabbit's voice is low and tight with pain. "Although I guess that makes them more like promises, huh?"

It's clear that speaking is using up more energy than he has. Still, I can't help but ask, "Why, then? Why did you help me get away? And tell me all that stuff?"

Rabbit's head lolls back and his eyes flutter closed.

"You. Know. Why." Rabbit strains to drag each word from his mouth.

And I do know. "You wanted more."

"Heh," Rabbit wheezes. "You thought that was inspirational, didja? Well, let me set the record straight. More hardly ever works out for anyone."

"Great," I tell him, more disgusted with myself than him for having taken his words to heart. "I'll put that on your tombstone."

"You can do that, or . . ." I wait while Rabbit takes his time. "Or you can help change my mind."

"Sorry," I say, remembering what I'd just admitted to Dyl and myself about being ready to settle for that quiet future. "You got the wrong person."

Rabbit doesn't respond, and his heavy breathing becomes quieter.

"Rabbit? Rabbit?" I ask, afraid that he is gone, that he might have faded away that quickly. Relief floods me when he speaks once more.

"Won't be much longer now."

"Don't say that. We're on our way to the hospital, right, W2?"

"Uh . . . sure," W2 answers after a long moment of hesitation. A second later the tires squeal and we all lurch sideways as the Cherokee makes a sudden U-turn. "Hospital coming right up," W2 proclaims triumphantly.

"No." Rabbit grabs at my arm. "No hospital. A place like that isn't good for someone like me."

"Actually, a place where they fix people who have been stabbed is the perfect place for you," I correct him as gently as possible.

"Lennie," he replies, his voice even fainter than before. "Have to tell you . . . you're a lot like your mother. Remind me of her."

"Bat-shit crazy, you mean?"

Rabbit shakes his head. "Brave. Selfless." He pauses. "Maybe a little bat-shit crazy."

"You mean 'cause she saved me?" I ask.

"Saw it when I met her years ago. Took it right out of her own head." Rabbit squeezes my hand with surprising strength. "She willingly granted Cash's first wish. She made him charming. Irresistibly so."

"Oh, yeah," I say. "He's a charmer, all right. You should have seen the way you were blushing when he stuck that knife in you."

"Lennie, shut up." Rabbit groans, and I immediately feel bad for making dumb remarks when he's struggling to tell me something obviously important.

"Sorry," I mutter.

"After that wish he wanted more. He charmed others into making wishes on his behalf and your mother would grant them. If she didn't, he threatened you. Your safety. He'd never wanted a child. Seems you were a mistake."

"Of course I was." I groan and then remembering my vow of silence, slap a hand over my mouth. "Sorry," I mumble again from between my fingers.

Rabbit sighs, whether from pain or annoyance, I can't say. "His wishes got bigger and more outrageous, but she didn't dare stop. One time, she said no and he nearly killed you before she gave in. Maybe that's when she finally saw the way to outsmart Cash. She gave her powers to you, willingly, without anyone forcing her hand. You could barely speak at that age, much less get all the words out needed for wish granting. Cash nearly killed her when he found out. That's around the time I first met her. I'd never seen someone being tortured take it with such calm, even at times boredom. Eventually, he let her go, convinced himself this was the way he'd wanted it to go. That you and your greater power was all part of his grand plan from the beginning."

And finally I have no words to say in response. So I sit quietly, holding Rabbit's hand until—after what seems like a ridiculously long amount of time, but is more like ten minutes—we reach the hospital.

"Benji and Jules, can you take Rabbit in? I gotta get to Michaela's before sunrise."

"Me and Jules?" Benji asks. "You know he's how Cash found so many of us."

"Well, get him better so he can beg your forgiveness. C'mon. You owe me this."

Jules makes a low grunting noise.

"All right," Benji says.

"Thank you," I say. I turn back toward Rabbit. "I need a favor from you too. Don't die." A faint smile crosses his face. "I mean if you die, then you won't be able to spill all my secrets to someone else."

At this, Rabbit's eyes fully open and connect with mine. "Lennie, your secrets—" he says, and then pauses to take a pained breath. "Your secrets are shit." And he grins at me with his big, toothless smile and I can't help but laugh.

I am still smiling when W2 opens the door and says, "C'mon, hairy dude, let's get you outta here."

Benji takes over then, carefully lifting Rabbit, while Jules runs into the hospital and comes back out a moment later pushing a wheelchair. As we get him into the chair, a siren howls in the distance. It becomes louder and louder until an ambulance screeches to a stop in front of us.

"Damn," W2 says. "They think they're hot shit."

"Whatever, it's a good distraction. Benji and Jules can slip in behind them, while we get away." I slide out of the car. "If they ask what happened—"

"Tell 'em to suck it," W2 advises before proceeding to helpfully demonstrate the best way to do this with what is quickly becoming his signature move: a crotch grab followed by a hip shake that makes his balls ring.

"Perfect," I say, somewhat amazed that I'm not being sarcastic. Well, mostly not. It's weird being allies with W2.

As W2 slides behind the wheel again, I watch Benji and Jules slowly make their way past all the activity centered around the ambulance. The way it's parked, I can see the stretcher coming out and how the poor kid on it is convulsing like he's being electrocuted. It's hard to see with all the shaking, but he looks a lot like Larry.

Larry. Convulsing.

And his mother beside him. Hysterical. Screaming, "Someone please help my son. It musta been drugs. I just dragged him out of this crazy party. Oh God, oh please, someone help my poor baby!"

Something in my brain goes *klunk*.

Oh, shit. Oh, hell. Oh, no.

I ungranted his wish. And his mother came for him. Larry must have been so happy. So relieved. Until she said, "It's time to go home." He's such a damn momma's boy, I wonder if he even tried to argue with her. Or if he lamely did as he was told, knowing it would kill him.

"It's Larry," I cry. I don't even know who I'm talking to since Smith has not made the smallest move or noise since I got into the Cherokee and W2 is obliviously singing along with the radio.

Without making a conscious decision to do so, I am moving toward the activity and then into the middle of it, shoving away the doctor or nurse or whoever or whatever this useless person is sticking things into Larry, trying to get him to live when the farther they take him from Michaela's, the more he is dying.

Dying.

People are screaming at me, but I ignore them. I think I hear my name on Larry's mother's lips. Cursing me, no doubt. Probably thinking how she had my number from the very first time she met me. God, I hate proving her right.

Grabbing hold of the stretcher, I shove it back toward the ambulance. Someone grabs onto me from behind and distantly I hear someone else calling for security.

A part of me sorta remembers this is not part of the plan. But that thought doesn't make it to my limbs, which are swinging and kicking wildly, striking anyone who tries to get between me and Larry. I scream his name, promising that it will be okay. That I will fix this.

Then I am on the stretcher, my body thrown over his, yelling at the people trying to pull me off that they are killing him and he needs to go back. Arms wrap around me, lifting me off and away. I screech, hysterical. Spitting. Cursing. Completely mad.

Suddenly, inexplicably, I'm released. I fall back onto Larry.

Around us everything is eerily silent.

"Lennie, get down." This calm, certain voice takes a moment to find its way to my totally out-of-my-mind brain. Eventually it connects and I realize with a mixture of shock and relief that Smith is standing beside me.

Smith.

With a gun in his hand.

Pointed at the hospital people.

And W2 at his side, grinning like a maniac, muttering something under his breath that sounds like, "Oh, man, this is so badass."

A film of sweat covers Smith's face, but he stands tall and solid beside me. "Lennie, push Larry back into the ambulance and then get behind the wheel."

I don't want to drive an ambulance. To be honest, I sorta suck at driving. But we are way past the point of rea-sonable objections, so I slide off Larry, push the stretcher back into the ambulance, and finally run around to the front and climb inside. The keys are still in the ignition.

"Okay," I yell to Smith.

A second later several shots ring out and the ambulance trembles as the back doors clang shut. An instant later Smith yells, "Go!"

I punch the gas, realize I didn't put the damn thing in drive, and, without taking my foot from the pedal, shift gears. The ambulance shoots forward. My door, which I'd forgotten to close, bangs against a pillar and then slams shut. In my side mirror, I see W2, now holding the gun and growing smaller as we drive away, leaving him behind to hold all those people back. If it was anyone other than W2, I'd be concerned. But that boy's got balls of steel. He'll be just fine.

Realizing the lights are still blinking, I search for the off button, but then decide that since I have no plans on stopping this ambulance until we reach Michaela's I might as well leave them on. In fact, we might as well get some sound going too so everyone knows to get the hell out of our way. After a few false tries, I locate the switch and the siren begins to howl.

It takes everything in me not to join in.

FLATLINE

As I make the turn onto Michaela's street, I have almost no idea how I even got here. I mean, turn brake steer. Those were the mechanics. My hands and feet were doing those things and I guess a bit of my brain must have been involved, but most of it was in the back of the ambulance with Larry, telling him to please just hold on a little bit longer.

I have no actual plan for what I'll do once we reach Michaela's house, other than drive up onto her lawn. And when, upon turning the corner, I see that half of her street is blocked off by cars and a huge group of people are clumped around the driveway entrance . . . well, I'm stumped.

I screech to a halt at the edge of the action. It's an insane scene. People everywhere. I see my uncles at the edge of the action talking to a confused-looking cop. Dazed, I open my door and step outside. My only choice is to somehow carry Larry through this, against the tide of what I realize now are aggravated and angry parents forcibly dragging their kids home.

A scream rings out as a father steps across the edge of the property line with his daughter slung over his shoulder. "Help!" he yells in my direction, and I realize that he thinks this ambulance is here for him.

"No! Take her back!" I holler, while making big shooing gestures with my hands.

Confused, the man stops. Then the cop and my uncles are at the man's side, reversing his steps.

I cling to the side of the ambulance, not sure if my legs will support me. Leaning against it for support, I press on until I'm at the back doors. I open one of them, climb in, and then quickly close it again behind me.

"Smith, we gotta—" One look at Smith's face and my words stop. There is no gotta. No need for the plan that I don't have anyway. No nothing.

"He stopped breathing almost ten minutes ago," he says softly.

"No," I counter, still unable to look at Larry, to confirm what I already know is true. Tears roll down my cheeks unchecked. "No." I say it once more, not a denial, but a protest. This is not the way this was supposed to go. But then again, that's been true for over twenty-four hours now.

I slide to the floor. Smith is seated only a foot away from me, but he makes no move to come closer.

I hold a hand out to him. Inviting him to take it. *Needing* him to take it.

He shakes his head. Scoots a little farther away. And then says the most devastating thing he could after announcing Larry's death. "I'm sorry, Lennie. For everything. I just want you to know . . . I'm really sorry."

Not one, but two apologies. Sincere ones too. He says it the way you would to a dying friend, trying to get it out while you still have a chance.

"No," I say again. I have turned into a petulant toddler. I turn away from Smith and crawl forward until I am at the foot of Larry's stretcher. His face looks tired. Stretched out with pain and . . .

I turn away, unable to see anymore. Why couldn't he at least have looked peaceful? Like he'd gone on to a better place? Why did he have to look exactly like he must have felt—alone and wishing his mom was there? I took him away from her. Trying to do the right thing and once again getting it all wrong.

"Lennie," Smith says, his voice reaching toward me, a mixture of caress and condolence, but his body distinctly distant.

"Smith." I hold my hand out again. "Please hold my

hand. I really need someone to hold my hand. I need you to hold my hand. I need—"

His arms wrap around me, pressing my own arms to my sides, keeping our palms apart. I would protest, but his lips are on mine and even though it is in bad taste to kiss next to the body of your recently deceased friend, I don't care. Or I don't care enough to stop.

It's not a sexy kiss.

It is the kind of kiss I'd never imagined or only imagined as something that forty-year-olds in the dark corner of a seedy bar might exchange. It's a little salty from tears and snot. To be honest, it's sorta desperate and sad.

In an odd way that's what makes it nice. Or what I need right now, anyway. And what Smith needs too, I think, as some of that snot and desperation and sadness is his as well.

But then it changes—or I change. I no longer think of the kiss as something that belongs with awful worn-out old people. Instead, it belongs to two people who have been through something together and have come out on the other end transformed in ways they don't understand yet. It's a kiss that works much like pricking fingertips and declaring a blood bond. It's a kiss and an oath all in one.

Or maybe I'm reading too much into it. Maybe that's what I need to believe right now. Maybe my brain is simply spewing crazy shit as a distraction from everything else.

I never get a chance to find out, because the doors fly open and a cop pulls us apart. Before I can even blink Smith's arms are cuffed behind his back and the cop tosses him across the ambulance with brutal force. Smith's head snaps back and connects with the edge of Larry's stretcher. I watch in horror as his eyes roll back into his head and he slumps to the floor.

"Smith!" I scream his name as the cop drags me away.

Outside, my uncles are still fighting to keep the parents from unintentionally killing their kids, but I barely register them, too preoccupied with keeping my eyes on Smith until finally the cop shoves me into the backseat of his car.

The door slams and I slide away from it only to bump into another person. I glance over and am too worn out to be shocked or even surprised, really. Truth be told, I recognized that terrible smell of decay first. A dull feeling of unease would be the best description of my state of mind as I find myself going from one dead friend to another.

"Hey, Lennie. Funny meeting you here," Dyl says with a little smile.

I am too numb to say with any certainty what expression I give her in return, but I am fairly certain it is not a smile.

END OF
THE ROAD

The cop slides into the driver's seat, flings off his hat, and turns to face me. At first I think something is wrong with the plastic divider between us when his facial features start to change. The eyes change colors, his nose grows shorter, and finally his lips thin and curl up into a smile. He goes from being someone I've never seen before to my very own father. This is his wish in action. The ability to hide in plain sight.

"You again," I say.

He smiles. "Didn't think I was done with you already, didja?"

I shake my head. "Only hoped."

"Hmmm," Cash says in response, which seems pretty mellow until he adds, "You need to reconsider your attitude or I'm gonna go back and gut the guy you were playing kissy face with the same way I did Rabbit."

And that wakes me up. I slap my hands against the Plexiglas divider. "Don't you touch him! Don't you even go near him!" Cash merely watches me with cold eyes. I get the feeling he's a little miffed with the way I got the upper hand during our last showdown over Rabbit. And I'm pretty sure that threatening him again will only backfire.

I appeal to Dyl instead. "He's talking about Smith. You know that, right?"

She swallows in response, but doesn't look surprised. "You just have to grant his wish, Lennie." Her voice is low and her gaze doesn't hold mine for longer than two seconds before she looks down at her hands.

"I already granted his wish a long time ago." Sickened, I turn back to Cash. "Remember that?"

"You're granting her wish," he says, jerking his head in Dyl's direction. "She's got herself a jar of shine all ready to go and everything."

I see the jar then, tucked against her far side. My instinct is to grab it and smash it. Except I can't do that. I can't risk Smith like that. Then I remember Uncle Rod's plastic sports bottle full of shine tucked into the pocket of my hoodie. And it feels like an opportunity.

A chance.

An incredibly slim one, but a chance just the same.

"What's the wish, then?" I ask, keeping my voice

neutral, not wanting to give anything away.

Dyl says nothing. She almost seems to be shrinking before my eyes.

"Dylan," Cash nudges with steel in his voice.

"I wish Lennie was bound to Cash forever and could grant him an endless number of wishes." She mumbles it so quick and low that I have to lean in to catch it all. And when I do, it almost takes my breath away. Suddenly I am so mad at Dylan for putting us both here, and that goes all the way back to her dying. Truth be told, I've never really forgiven her for that.

I grab hold of her chin and jerk her face toward mine. "You should wish to have your spine back," I sneer.

At that a bit of the old Dyl flashes in her eyes. "What I want is my old life back, but that's not gonna happen, is it?"

"And what about my life? That wish turns me into his prisoner, his slave. What kind of life is that?"

Tears well up in Dyl's eyes, but they don't move me a bit. I shove her away so hard that she bounces against the door.

"I wished you back to life, Dyl." I don't add that it was the worst wish I granted. My biggest and worst mistake out of an endless list of them. The words are there, and it would be so easy to twist the knife in deeper. The thing is, it's not true. I would bring Dyl back again. And again and again. I can't imagine not making the same choice. The same terrible wish. That's what Uncle Dune was talking about, I guess. If I went back in time, I would redo it all the same bad way and end up right back here. It would be better to wish myself unborn or—

Dyl interrupts my train of thought. "You shoulda wished that I'd never died in the first place. Did you ever think of that, Lennie? Maybe you coulda made a wish that didn't end with me being a freaking zombie!" She is screaming the words at me by the end, but I barely hear them.

"Or maybe I could have wished that it was me instead of you that died," I say, the words coming out of my mouth slowly. "Maybe that's what you should wish for now. Wish that I hadn't been so stupidly scared of everything all the time and that I'd gone to meet that guy like you wanted me to."

"I can't wish for that."

"But you want to."

Dyl doesn't reply, but our eyes meet and the answer is there. She would happily sacrifice me in her place. Because she blames me for her death. For everything. She thinks it should have been me instead of her. In that way, it's not her condemning me, but righting things back to the way they should have been. That guy wanted me. Me to get to Cash. Dyl just got caught in the middle.

"Yeah," she says at last, admitting it.

"Sun's coming up any minute now," Cash says, finally breaking into the showdown between me and Dyl. "You don't make that wish, your friend won't see it."

"Okay," I say in a hoarse voice, holding my hands up to show that I'm giving in. "Let me get a drink of water first." A sense of inevitability fills me as I reach into my hoodie and pull out the water bottle. I take a small swig. I try to hold back the coughing fit of the liquor hitting the back of my throat, but I hack a few times anyway. "Wrong pipe," I explain. Then I hold the bottle out to Dyl. "A little water to wet your mouth before the shine?"

She eyes me suspiciously, but takes the bottle and takes a long swallow. She gasps and chokes worse than I did and in the front seat, Cash has figured out what's going on because he curses and pounds the barrier between us before flinging open his door.

I am already grabbing the bottle of shine back from Dyl while the words pour from my mouth. I can't wish to die, though. Or I can't wish to only die. If I'm gonna reboot everything, I at least want to give myself time to live before I die. So I wildly build on Dyl's wish, figuring that I'm at least keeping the spirit of it intact.

"To me being a person who wants more and takes chances. Good and bad chances and everything in between, like going with that terrible guy instead of Dyl and—" My door swings open. Cash reaches in. I finish in a rush, "May all your wishes come true, or at least just this one."

The bottle touches my lips. Cash grabs hold of my arm. He jerks me out of the car. Too late, though. The shine is on my tongue and then burning all the way down once more.

His hands hold me in a bruising grip and he's shaking me the same way he did such a long time ago, when I was little and gave him his wish.

But not this time. I smile. Barely feeling the pain.

"Not made of Swiss cheese." I push the words out between my rattling teeth while behind Cash, the sky lightens.

My eyes remain fixed on that distant ribbon of color where the sky meets the earth, watching. Waiting. It doesn't take long.

The noise and lights and Cash all recede as the sun finally creeps over the horizon and swallows everything—including me.

GONE TO
THE DEVIL

SIX MONTHS EARLIER

"I gave you my name for a reason, Lennie. It might not be worth much now, but someday, someday real soon, I'm gonna make it so Cash is a name nobody ever forgets. I'm serious, Lennie. People are gonna remember us."

When I was a little kid, I didn't get tucked into bed with a story or a song. Instead, I listened to the ravings of my father. The nightly routine ended on my sixth birthday. That was the day he made the nightly news for the first time and they rechristened Leonard Cash the Bad Daddy Bandit.

Over the next two months, Daddy and I crisscrossed the country on a hold-'em-up, shoot-'em-down crime spree. With me in tow, he took down six banks and three toy stores, killing two people who got in the way. He was finally pinned down at a Chuck E. Cheese's, but managed to escape by taking the guy dressed in the mouse costume as a hostage. They found me hours later, burrowed deep in the ball pit, still waiting for Daddy's all-clear whistle.

The only place I've seen him since then is on the FBI's Ten Most Wanted webpage.

That all happened eleven years ago, but it's not the sort of story people forget. Maybe if I'd become a super-smart honor-student nerd or a chipper rah-rah leadership council type, they'd dwell on it a little less often. But I'm not either of those things, and most people think it's just a matter of time before my daddy comes back for me and the two of us pick up where we left off at Chuck E. Cheese's oh so many years ago.

To a stranger, I might look like a typical sullen, angry teenager, but everyone in town knows I'm the furthest thing from typical.

I'm Lennie Cash.

And my famous name is a big part of why, at this exact moment, instead of dividing my time in English class between clock-watching and trying to figure out exactly how those two crazy kids, Romeo and Juliet, managed to mess things up so badly, I'm hanging out with a total nutcase who just forcibly removed two of my fingers.

I can't help but ask myself, how the hell did I get

here? And then I remember.

Dyl.

My best friend, Dylan, really wanted me to meet up with this weirdo guy named Rollo she'd met online, and even though I knew it was the worst idea ever, I did it anyway. That's what friends are for. Right?

Ha.

Despite what my uncles might say (during one of their many lectures on "exercising caution," Uncle Jed told me that if I can't tell if I'm being brave or just stupid, I should go ahead and assume it's the latter), it was a calculated risk. Also. I met Rollo in a brightly lit Denny's and we hung out for about an hour, during which time I never gave him a chance to slip anything into my drink. Then, having fulfilled my friend obligation, I left thinking I'd never see him again.

And that's pretty much how it played out.

Except.

He followed me home and grabbed me the next morning while I was walking to school.

Who saw that one coming, huh?

Turns out, though, that Rollo isn't superinterested in me—I'm simply a way to get to my notorious father.

Despite being kidnapped and hidden away in a dark

room that smells like cat pee, I was still sorta thinking he was a mostly harmless lunatic . . . until he chopped off two of my fingers.

At least Rollo was kind enough to give me a few fortifying swigs of my uncles' moonshine afterward.

Good of him, right? I took the opportunity to propose a little toast, wishing him to hell. "To Rollo in hell. May all my wishes come true, or at least just this one."

He didn't like that. Not one little bit. He'd like it even less if he knew the wishes I grant have a way of coming true.

It's sort of a family secret. My uncles broke the news to me a few years ago. After the first wave of disbelief passed, it made a whole lot of sense. Then I was all, "Holy shit, this is gonna be awesome! Oh, the wishes I will make." My uncles let me dance around for maybe ten minutes before bursting that bubble and giving me the "With great power comes many possibilities for royally fucking up" speech. I guess I didn't look crushed enough, though, 'cause then they were like, "BOOM. History."

And they told me all this stuff about my dad and mom and, well, I won't go into details, but the whole thing's seriously messed up. I was pretty bummed out after that, so they let me grant one wish, just to get a taste for it. Uncle Dune did the wishing—it was sorta repayment for being the one who drew the short straw and did all the actual explaining. I was excited to grant my first wish, but also a little freaked out. Still, I had to know how this whole thing worked. Would it tingle? Would it hurt? Would I like it?

Dune wished that my father could never hurt anyone again. I could see he got a little choked up too. Him and my mom were the two youngest kids, and I guess had been pretty close before Cash showed up and ruined everything and turned my mom into a chain-smoking half person.

Anyway, that brings me back to good old Rollo. He got over me wishing him to hell and we kept drinking and then got to talking, and the tension between us eased a bit as the moonshine loosened our tongues.

Now Rollo tells me how he'd bought the moonshine from my uncles a few weeks back and we discuss how weird my uncles' little toast is. After some nudging, he admits how he'd wished for courage to do the things he'd only dreamed of. Turns out his mom had been killed during one of Cash's robberies years back and it messed him up a bit. Seems that without that motherly influence, he became the sort of person who dreamed of kidnapping girls and chopping their fingers off. And once my uncles granted his wish, well, suddenly he was no longer afraid of making those dreams come true.

Funny the way we all connect, huh?

More time passes after that revelation and we get pretty chummy by this point, and also blind drunk. Rollo's also feeling pretty bad about cutting my fingers off and I feel sorta bad for wishing him to hell.

So as we come down to the last swig in the jar, I tell him to make a wish.

Okay, I probably shouldn't have, but at this point I felt like he'd had one too many bad breaks. Also, I'd already wished him to hell and there's no undoing a wish. My uncles say that trying to make a second wish to fix a bad first one is like trying to undo a knot by tying another one. It's never gonna work out. And wishing someone to hell, well, that's pretty serious and I can't help but think that maybe I went a little too far.

But again, he had just cut two of my fingers off, so extenuating circumstances, you know?

Anyway, Rollo wishes that he could remember his mom better. She'd died when he was pretty young and he can't remember the sound of her voice or the way she looked when not frozen in a photograph.

It's a nice wish. We both agree that maybe this is the one he should've used when he went to visit my uncles. Certainly seems like lots of things might've turned out differently if he'd done that.

He didn't, though.

Too bad about that.

The night drains away faster than the shine, and knowing the sun will be rising soon, I wonder if I should give poor Rollo some type of warning about what's coming his way.

Then the door crashes open and my uncles come charging in like the fucking cavalry. Honestly, a part of me had been wondering what the heck was taking them so long. They practically raised me, and I've always known they've got my back . . . in their own unique way. So while I'm happy and a little bit relieved to see them, I also can't help but think they have the worst timing ever.

Because moments after they barrel in, I find out that besides the wicked knife Rollo used to chop off my fingers, he also has a loaded gun. He swings it toward my uncles, wildly, and then, probably realizing he'd never hit all three of them before they reached him, he turns the gun on me.

Most times in movies they hold the gun to a person's head, but Rollo presses his against my heart.

"You pull that trigger and I'll wish you to hell, boy," Uncle Jet growls at him in a voice I've never heard before. I can actually see the shivers it sends down Rollo's spine, while at the same time, despite having a gun trained on it, my heart swells.

"She already did that," Rollo says, jerking his head toward me.

Uncle Jet glances toward the windows covered with newspaper and then back to us. "Well then you don't got much longer."

Rollo swallows. "What's that supposed to mean?"

A smile spreads across Uncle Jet's face. "It means that in our family, wishes really do come true. All three of us can grant them. And she can too."

"That's not true," Rollo whines. "If it were true, you'd never tell me all that."

"I'm telling you 'cause once that sun rises, there won't be much left of you. That's when the wishes get granted, you see? Now if you don't want to be sent into the devil's fires, I suggest you let Lennie go right quick, after which I'd be happy to grant you a wish that'll make the afterlife a little more pleasant for ya."

Rollo's gaze shifts from my uncles and then back to me. The gun pressed to my chest begins to tremble.

I'm almost certain he doesn't mean to pull the trigger. That he's simply drunk and panicked and in a stressful situation that causes his finger to contract at an incredibly inopportune time.

But it hurts like hell just the same.

I'm lucky in one way, though. The pain, while intense,

is short-lived. Vividly and excruciatingly, I feel the bullet rip straight through my heart like an express train racing toward the end of the line, until finally—mercifully— everything goes dark.

SHINE ON

I should be dead. That's what everyone says. The doctors say it so often, I can't help but think they're a little miffed I'm still alive.

Not just alive. After a few months chilling in a coma, I woke up, and—besides feeling a little stiff from lying around for so long—I feel fine.

They tell me I've been a mystery case from the beginning.

Apparently, that bullet of Rollo's getting fired at such close range should've torn my heart to shreds.

I should've been killed instantly.

Or if by some odd chance it merely nicked my heart, I should've bled out before I reached the hospital. That's what they call dead on arrival.

But my heart wasn't shredded. I didn't die instantly

or bleed out. There was no DOA. Instead, by the time we reached the hospital (my uncles tell me they broke at least a dozen different traffic laws), the hole in my chest had already stopped gushing blood. And when they did an ultrasound they couldn't find any damage to my heart at all. The entrance wounds on my chest and back (both of them already starting to close up on their own by this time) indicated that the bullet would've passed directly through my heart. Except somehow it hadn't.

It's almost like I was bulletproof.

Actually, that's exactly what it was.

The morning I left the house on my way to school, never once realizing I was moments away from being kidnapped, I stopped to say good-bye to my mom. Ever since my uncles told me everything she had done to keep me safe from my father, well, it's changed our relationship. On my side at least. She's still a distant basket case. But I know that somewhere deep down inside of her she must still love me. How else can I explain what happened on that morning? Instead of ignoring me and blowing smoke in my face, Mom shoved her Niagara Falls souvenir mug into my hands.

Usually that mug was her ashtray, but on that day it was filled to the brim with moonshine. Kinda grayish-looking shine. I don't think Mom had done too great of a job cleaning the mug out. But anyway, she said, "Grant my wish."

And I said, "Grant what wish?"

We went back and forth like that at least six times, before I was like, "Mom, stop!"

She took a moment to light a cigarette from the butt of her last one before finally nudging our conversation forward. "You get a chance to make a wish, Lennie. You ask to be bulletproof."

"Oooo-kay. Good talk, Mom. I gotta get to school." I handed her back the mug, but she refused to take it.

"Grant my wish."

"Mom," I said, sorta sighing and then feeling guilty for being annoyed. So I explained. "The uncs don't want me granting any more wishes. I've already done one, and you know they don't want me anywhere near to that third-wish threshold for at least another two years. So, I'm sorry, but I'm not gonna do it."

I sorta patted her then, trying to comfort her. She pushed me away. "Bulletproof. You. That's my wish."

I probably should've walked away then, but the thing is, I'd been getting antsy with my uncles "don't make any more wishes" rule for a while now. And let's face it, when I get antsy, things can get a little hairy. Also, it probably wouldn't hurt for me to be bulletproof, what with the whole antsiness leading to hairiness problem.

"Okay, Mom, but I really think you should wish to stop smoking."

In response she grabbed the mug and glugged down half the moonshine.

"All right then," I said. "To having a bulletproof daughter. May all your wishes come true, or at least just this one."

As soon as I made the wish, I wished that I hadn't. Of course, now I'm glad that I did, but at the time, not realizing a bullet was in my near future, I felt bad about disobeying my uncles' rules. I sort of justified it by promising myself I wouldn't make that third wish (the one that would transfer all of their wish-granting abilities over to the next generation, otherwise known as me) anytime soon. And if for some reason I did end up needing that third wish sooner than expected, well, I figured I'd break the news right after presenting each of my uncles with an extra-big bucket of KFC to soften the blow.

Obviously, that plan didn't end up working out, so when I woke up from my coma, I was a little worried they were gonna be upset. And I didn't even have a fried chicken distraction.

Imagine my relief, then, when I realized they were mostly critical of the wish because I hadn't followed their rule of specificity. Broad wishes like being bulletproof left too many things open to interpretation by whatever being or greater power out there makes wishes come true. Also, they thought it might have been smarter if I'd been knife-proof along with bulletproof. That way I might still have had all my fingers.

I couldn't really argue with that last point.

So I felt better about granting my third wish, but I was still worried about what my uncles would do for money, since they used the shine/wish granting as their livelihood, and I'd essentially put them out of business. They laughed about that, and then confessed that the swear jar that had always sat in the kitchen was wish-powered. Instead of them putting a dollar inside every time someone swore, one magically appeared. Now I also finally understood why none of them had ever told me to watch my language.

So with my uncles taken care of, I started asking questions about what happened after I exhaled my last shuddering, pain-filled breath. It's kind of crazy, but I really wanted to know how things ended for poor old Rollo.

Turns out, not so well.

From what I've been told, the sun rose and Rollo started screaming, crying, and begging for forgiveness. He wasn't talking to my uncles, but instead to his sainted dead mother, as if she were standing right in front of him and eyeing him with the sort of parental disappointment that could drive a certain sort of person insane. Rollo was that certain type of person. You could even say this was his own personal hell. My wish and his had come together in the most devastating way possible.

Three days after he shot me, the poor bastard hung himself in his jail cell.

I try not to think about that. Luckily, I have a permanent distraction who's been by my side holding my hand from the minute I woke up from my coma.

Dyl's wan little face was the first one I saw after opening my eyes.

She looked awful. Pale and skinny and drowning in contrition, she looked like she'd been living underground for the last six months.

"Lennie!" she'd cried, with actual real tears falling, when she saw my eyes were open and looking her way.

"Not gonna say I told you so," I replied in my raspy voice.

Dyl gave me a little bit of water to wet my throat, and then as if my waking had lifted some sort of spell from her too, grinned. "Technically, you just did."

"Respect the hospital bed," I replied, using the controls to get myself into a more upright position.

Dyl fluffed my pillows. "Respect."

I waited a beat, letting her sit down again, before reminding her, "You owe me a blind date. Don't think I forgot."

And Dyl laughed. "Is that why you've been lying here for the last six months? You've been wracking your brains for the worst possible person to make me go out with?"

"Six months?" I'd asked. Then Dyl called in my uncles and all the doctors and everyone explained about Rollo and the coma and everything else. But a few hours later we continued our blind date conversation and I told Dyl exactly who I had in mind for her.

"My bio lab partner, Larry."

"The one who's in love with you?" Dyl asked. "He's been here, like, a hundred times." She pointed to a pile of various stuffed animals holding hearts between their little paws.

"Those are terrible. But trust me, he's a really good guy. And I don't know, I think you'd hit it off."

Dyl looked down at her hands and didn't say anything for a long moment. Finally, she mumbled, "You're right. We would." That horribly guilty look back on her face, her gaze met mine again. "We've made out in the hospital stairwell, like, three times. He keeps wanting to bring me home to meet his mother."

And then it was my turn to laugh, "I guess your date won't be so blind after all."

For the record, their date went really well.

Now Dyl is making noise about a double date. And I'm like, "Hello, I'm still in the hospital while the doctors poke at me and try to figure out what kind of freak I am. Also, I need a date for myself to make it a double and not a horrible third-wheel situation."

Of course, Dyl has to mention Smith. "He's not dating anyone right now. Hasn't since you—"

"Oh, no no no." I shut that down real quick.

Smith is Dylan's twin brother. He's cool and hot at the same time. We've been flirting since forever, but have never taken it any further than that.

Well, except for this one time.

It was one of those impulse things. I was at their house, hanging with Dyl, and I happened to walk by the bathroom while he was gargling mouthwash and . . . I don't know. Spit and rinse had never been a big turn-on of mine before, but at that moment . . . it felt almost déjà-vu-ish. Like I'd been there before and I knew Smith. Like, really knew him, down to the bottom of his soul.

So I threw myself at him and we kissed. Which sounds pretty tame, except it wasn't. It was crazy. Our lips met and that déjà vu feeling nearly swallowed me. Then Smith's hands went into my hair and I freaked out. Pulled away, babbled something. He was freaked too. I could tell. He kept looking down at his right hand and clenching it like it hurt him or something. We nearly sprinted in opposite directions and have kept our distance since then.

So no. No Smith and me. No me and Smith. It's not gonna happen. Even if a part of me wishes that it would.

Besides which, I have bigger things to think about than double dates. Tomorrow I finally get out of the hospital and then it's on to senior year and after that—the rest of my life.

I'm feeling pretty good about that, though. Something about being bulletproof makes me optimistic about the future. My uncles can see me turning over the possibilities in my head. They know it's not in me to lay low the way they have. I'm gonna do things my own way, and it's probably gonna get messy. Or as Uncle Jet put it a few minutes ago, "If you're not careful, by the time you're twenty you'll be so full of bullet holes, people'll think you're made of Swiss cheese."

I told him he was acting like an old lady and he stormed out. Then Uncle Dune and Uncle Rod went after him, leaving me alone for the rest of the night. Which is how I like it. Having them hovering at my bedside like little old ladies makes me nervous. It feels good to fall asleep with no one watching me, worrying I'll slip back into another coma.

You can never get rid of them for long, though, and the next morning I wake up with someone once again holding my hand. I try to jerk it away, but Dyl is holding tight this morning. Peeling my eyes open, I turn to ask her how the third date with Larry went. Instead, my mouth falls open and I blink stupidly.

It's Smith. His hair is mussed and his expression uncertain, but only for an instant and then that confident smile slides into place.

"Smith," I say. The word nearly gets caught in my throat. "What are you doing here?"

"Lennie," he answers, that smile not wavering. "Everyone was asking about you at Kayla's party last night."

It takes a minute for me to remember what he's talking about. Then I do. Michaela's Labor Day party is an annual event for all the people who matter at our school. Smith is on this list. I am not. That doesn't mean I haven't been to the party. On the contrary, I make it a point of going every year, just as Michaela makes a point of humiliating party crashers. Except she's never been able to catch me. I'm actually a bit notorious for being the only person to crash her party and get away unscathed three times running.

"Everyone knows I'm in the hospital," I say now. "You know, that whole being in a coma thing?"

Smith shrugs. "I guess people figured that wouldn't stop you. Or maybe they were hoping against hope to see you there." His eyes meet and hold mine in this significant way that seems to be saying *he* specifically was hoping. But then he looks away, and I wonder if I imagined it. "Anyway, you didn't miss anything. Not even the challenge of crashing. I don't know if you heard, but after you were shot, Michaela had some sort of weird 'come to Jesus' moment or something. She started this whole anti-bullying thing, and apologized to everyone she'd ever hurt, and to top it all off, started dating Wee Willie Winkie."

"Yeah, Dyl told me about some of that. She also said Michaela brings the pain to anyone who dares call Todd Wee Willie Winkie."

"True," Smith admits with a laugh. "But I like to live dangerously."

I laugh too and then Smith entertains me with a story of how Zinkowski and Turlington were the bright spot of an otherwise boring party. Apparently, they showed up totally baked and starting doing this Jedi mind trick thing. According to Smith, it was pretty cool at first. They sat facing each other and would then say the same thing at the exact same time like, "Cheetos touch" or "wisdom of the ages, man." They swore it wasn't rehearsed, but after a while everyone lost interest and started drifting away. Turlington and Zinkowski didn't even seem to notice.

It's a pretty funny story, but when he's done, I can't help but ask the question that's been on my mind this whole time. "So what are you doing here, Smith? Why aren't you passed out on Michaela's floor like everyone else?"

Smith shakes his head. "No one is passed out on Michaela's floor. A little after midnight, she turned off the music, turned up the lights, and began dumping all the liquor down the sink. Then she went room by room telling people to get out. I asked her what the deal was, and she just said she had this nervous feeling that if they didn't leave now, she might be stuck with them forever. It was crazy, but I also sorta think she had a point. You know?"

"Yeah," I agree, without quite knowing why. Then, refusing to let him off the hook, I ask again, "Why are you here, Smith?"

It comes out a little too cool, almost like I'm trying to get rid of him. But apparently Smith isn't bothered 'cause he leans in closer and rests his head beside mine on my pillow. "Would you believe I woke up this morning and could think of nothing I wanted to do more than hold your hand?"

He holds up our interconnected hands. Making me see how right it looks and feels to have his palm pressed against mine. Our eyes meet over the tips of our matched fingers.

"Some new kind of kink?" I ask, my voice low and raspy like it was when I first woke up from my coma. Funny, 'cause this feels like another kind of waking up.

"Maybe," Smith replies.

This is the part where I should jerk my hand out of Smith's and put a lot more space between us before blushing and babbling about how we're just friends and it doesn't mean anything and of course he doesn't like me, or not like that, anyway.

But that feels like something another version of myself would do.

A lamer, play-it-safe Lennie, who can't see that sometimes you gotta take risks.

A Lennie who's afraid to admit she wants so much more.

A Lennie who thinks "be careful what you wish for" means never wishing for anything at all.

Yikes, right? Thank God I'm not that girl.

Grabbing hold of Smith's shirt, I pull him closer, until it's more than only our hands pressed together. "I'm gonna make all your wishes come true," I say, grinning at him. "And mine too."

And then—without the aid of any shine—that's exactly what I do.